KATE'S WEDDING

KATE'S WEDDING

CHRISSIE MANBY

LARGE PRINT

Oxford

First published in Great Britain 2011
by
Hodder & Stoughton

Published in Large Print 2012 by ISIS Publishing Ltd.,
7 Centremead, Osney Mead, Oxford OX2 0ES
by arrangement with
Hodder & Stoughton
An Hachette UK Company

British Library Cataloguing in Publication Data
Manby, Chris.
    Kate's wedding.
    1. Weddings - - Fiction.
    2. Chick lit.
    3. Large type books.
    I. Title
    823.9'2–dc23

ISBN 978–0–7531–8980–1 (hb)
ISBN 978–0–7531–8981–8 (pb)

Printed and bound in Great Britain by
T. J. International Ltd., Padstow, Cornwall

To Josephine Annabel Christine Hazel

Prologue

29 July 1981, Littlehampton, Sussex

To the two little girls waking up in their caravan that morning, 29 July was going to be a bit like Christmas. All the usual rules were to be suspended on the day when Lady Diana Spencer married her prince. Even though they were holidaying in a caravan at a Caravan Club rally held on a sports field, the young sisters were going to be allowed to dress up. The bridesmaids' dresses they had worn for the wedding of their mother's younger brother had been brought all the way from Birmingham for this very special second outing.

Kate, who was, at nine, the elder by two years, was first to get out of bed.

"I've made a royal wedding breakfast," her father, John, called from the awning. He had draped a Union flag over the little fold-up table. There was bunting hanging from the guy ropes that held the brown and orange awning in place.

"Red strawberries, white cream and blue —"

"Pancakes!" Kate squealed. "The pancakes are blue!"

"Food colouring," her father explained. "I don't suppose even Prince Charles is eating such a patriotic breakfast today."

Tess, just seven, refused to eat anything that wasn't its *proper* colour. The girls' mother, Elaine, was dispatched to make some toast.

The whole campsite was beginning to wake up now. After weeks of speculation about the weather, the sun was shining like a smile. Everyone had a greeting for their neighbours as they went about their business. After breakfast, Kate accompanied her father to empty the chemical toilet. The festive mood prevailed even by the cesspit, where several other fathers admired John's Union Jack shorts.

Around the camp leader's caravan, preparations for the celebrations ahead were well under way. There was to be a huge buffet lunch in lieu of the street parties people were missing back home. Every caravan had received its instructions: each person should bring their own chair, a plate, a knife and fork, and a teacup; Kate's parents had chipped in for their family's allocation of barbecue food.

Dressed in her bridesmaid's finery, Kate turned cartwheels in the middle of the field while she waited for something to happen. Tess tried to follow suit, but she could just about do a forward roll. Meanwhile, John and Elaine carried chairs and beer and wine bottles to the trestle tables by the camp leader's caravan. In return for three bottles of cider, a colour television with a remote control had been borrowed from a house that backed onto the campsite.

The morning dragged. Kate turned more cartwheels. Someone's radio played "songs for a princess". Every tune had something royal in its lyrics or music. Until at

2

last, at last, the montage of scenes from the lives of the Prince of Wales and his future wife was replaced by live footage. The royal wedding had begun.

Just before eleven twenty, Kate and Tess joined their parents in the circle that had formed round the borrowed television. Kate climbed onto her father's lap. The sun was shining so brightly they could hardly see the screen. Kate struggled to the front of the circle and the shade of the camp leader's awning to get a better view.

Up and down the country, millions of loyal citizens watched Lady Diana Spencer glide up the aisle of St Paul's on her father's arm, to the sound of the "Trumpet Voluntary". In her dress, with its yards of taffeta, Diana was the embodiment of every little girl's dream. She was celebrated that afternoon with toasts of champagne, of cider and of dandelion and burdock. On the campsite at Littlehampton, there was dancing until dawn.

Kate Williamson fell asleep beneath a trestle table. Her father scooped her into his arms to carry her back to the caravan. Halfway across the field, she stirred into wakefulness.

"One day," she told her father, "I'm going to marry a prince."

CHAPTER
ONE

20 October 2010, Paris

It was much too cold and wet to be standing in a queue to go up the Eiffel Tower, but Ian was insistent. How could you go to Paris without seeing the Eiffel Tower? Especially as, Ian reminded Kate, he had never been to Paris before. That was a sore point. Ian had been so proud of organising this surprise mini-break in the City of Light. He was gutted when Kate told him that not only had she been to Paris before, she had actually stayed in the very hotel where he had booked a junior suite.

Kate stopped short of telling him that on her last visit — just two years before — she and Dan had stayed in the hotel's *honeymoon* suite. Not that there was ever any chance of a honeymoon with Dan, as he had somehow managed to be involved in complicated divorce proceedings for the entire four years Kate was with him, despite having officially separated from his wife two years before Kate arrived on the scene.

So Ian had sulked all the way from St Pancras to Gare du Nord. He seemed set to keep sulking all day. At the Hôtel Renoir, Kate prayed that the receptionist would not recognise her, as she had recognised Dan

4

two years earlier. How awful that had been. Putting two and two together to make five, the receptionist had greeted Kate by Dan's ex-wife's name.

"We have put you in your favourite room, Mrs Harper," the girl said.

That was how Kate and Dan came to be in the honeymoon suite. She told him it was one thing to be taken to the hotel where he and his ex had tried to save their marriage — on several occasions, as it turned out — but it was something else to have to sleep in the same bloody room. Dan was forced into a hasty upgrade.

Despite that inauspicious start, Kate had liked the Hôtel Renoir and for that reason she persuaded Ian that there was no need for them to find a different hotel for their mini-break.

"This trip is already a hundred per cent better than the last time I was here because I am with *you*," she assured him. "Everything is different." That much was absolutely true.

Neither did she mind doing the tourist sights since Dan, of course, had been to Paris dozens of times with his Francophile wife and so refused to spend even a minute of Kate's birthday weekend queuing to see the *Mona Lisa*. Kate wanted to see the *Mona Lisa*. She also wanted to see the Venus de Milo. She wanted to go to the Musée d'Orsay and see the Impressionists at the Orangerie and have her picture taken beneath the Arc de Triomphe. The Eiffel Tower, however, had never been high on Kate's to-do list. Given her slight fear of heights, she had no particular desire to spend an hour getting to the top of the thing to spend five minutes looking at the ground. Especially on a wet, grey day like this. What would they be able to see, anyway? They should go to Saint-Germain instead, she suggested. Find a little bar and get quietly hammered on pastis.

"No," said Ian, digging in his heels. "I've always wanted to go up the Eiffel Tower."

And so they went up the Eiffel Tower, squashed into the lift with a group of American tourists who were commiserating with one of their number over a handbag snatched. At the top, Ian pulled Kate away from the crowd. At least, as far away from the crowd as was possible in one of the world's most visited monuments. There was no hope of being entirely alone.

"Shame about the weather," Ian muttered.

"Hmm." Kate looked out over the city towards the fairytale white domes of the Sacré-Coeur, barely visible through the mist. She was remembering standing in front of that cathedral, hearing Dan say that even now his divorce was through he wasn't sure that he was, you know, ready to "move on" and make their relationship permanent, when Ian interrupted her reverie with the question she should have known to expect.

"Sorry?" Kate didn't quite catch what he'd said.

"Will you marry me?" he asked again. He looked so scared. He was actually shaking, though maybe that was only through the effort of *half* sinking to one knee. Ian didn't want to put his knee down properly because the floor was wet and his trousers were new. Kate asked if he was joking.

6

"No," he said, "of course I'm not joking. Kate Williamson, will you marry me?"

Two of the American matrons from the lift were watching.

"Oh God," said Kate, so intensely aware of her audience that she caught the cat's-bottom tightening of lips her blasphemy elicited. "I mean, yes," she said, and it was as though she'd said it as much to appease the American matrons as to please Ian. She hadn't had time to consider whether it pleased her. This was all so sudden.

"Oh, Kate." Ian pulled her into a bear hug. "My Kate, my Kate, my Kate."

Kate dropped her camera. One of the matrons picked it up and obligingly took a series of snaps.

"You'll want to remember this moment for ever," she told Kate as she handed the camera back. "We are so pleased for you. You two young people take care of each other now."

"I am going to take care of this woman until the day I die," Ian responded proudly. He hugged Kate close again, rendering her unsteady on her feet.

"You've made our vacation," the matron assured him. "To see a proposal in the most romantic place on earth!"

Ian was looking at the photos on the camera already.

"There we are," he said. "That's us. That's you and me getting engaged."

The Kate in the photographs looked ambushed, staring over Ian's shoulder with wide and frightened eyes.

"Were you surprised?" Ian asked her, beginning the reminiscing before the moment was even complete.

"Well, yes," said Kate. "I suppose I was."

"Are you happy?"

"Of course I am."

She felt breathless and tearful. Exactly as she'd felt the time she almost died stepping out in front of a bus while exhausted from an all-nighter at the office. She could almost hear the squeal of the brakes. Was she frightened? Relieved?

They joined the queue shuffling back towards the lift.

"I haven't got a ring yet, because I didn't want to get something you didn't like. I'm sorry," he said.

"Don't be sorry," said Kate. "We can choose something in London."

You're not properly engaged until you've got the ring, said a little voice at the back of Kate's head. *There's still time to change your mind.*

No, Kate told the voice firmly. This is exactly what I've always wanted. This is the best moment of my life so far. She looked at Ian's handsome profile as he pushed ahead through the crowd. She hadn't been lying when she told Ian that everything about this, her second romantic weekend in Paris, was better than the first. She loved her kind and generous boyfriend. He made her feel so much better than any of the muppets she'd dated before him. She knew that when he promised he would always look after her, Ian actually meant it. He was steadfast and trustworthy. He was a proper, grown-up man who would never give her cause

8

to worry or distrust him. She knew that he had made his proposal out of the very purest love, and there was nothing she wanted more than to spend the rest of her life as Mrs Ian Turner. Yes, Kate told the little voice. This is brilliant. Oh my God, I'm getting married!

"Let's not go back down to earth just yet." Kate caught her new fiancé by the arm. "I want to savour this moment for a little bit longer."

Kate easily persuaded Ian back to the viewing platform, where she threw her arms round his neck and kissed him so passionately that she raised a cheer from a coach party of pensioners from Frankfurt.

CHAPTER
TWO

20 October 2010, Cliveden, Berkshire

Unlike Kate Williamson, Diana Ashcroft was absolutely expecting her proposal. In fact, it was she who had suggested the ideal date, 20 October 2010.

"Twenty ten, twenty ten," she spelled it out. "That way, we'll never forget it."

Diana's boyfriend, Ben, nodded mutely while Diana issued instructions. Since her birthday was on 21 October, she continued, it made sense for Ben to take the Wednesday, Thursday *and* Friday off work for a mini-break at Cliveden. Diana had always wanted to go to Cliveden. Either there or Belvoir Castle. It had to be somewhere classy. Somewhere special.

Somewhere expensive, thought Ben.

Going during the week would make their hotel stay slightly more economical, Diana added thoughtfully. And she would love him for ever if he granted this one wish and made their engagement a real *event*. She gave Ben the coy smile that she knew he couldn't resist.

Ben duly booked the hotel and started shopping for the ring. At least that wouldn't be too difficult. Diana and her mother, Susie, had already been into Goldsmiths at the West Quay Shopping Centre and spent an hour narrowing the contenders down to two, so that Ben could pick his favourite.

"Of course, you get the final say," Diana promised.

However, as he was standing in the shop, taking in the prices in stunned dismay, Diana texted to tell him that she really, *really* preferred the princess-cut invisible centre and diamond-set band from the new Excitement collection, which was the more expensive ring by several hundred pounds. Ben was altogether less excited than panicked as he handed over his credit card to be swiped to the tune of £3,499.99.

"You're supposed to spend a month's wages on the ring," Diana told him when he returned to their house looking pale, "so you should probably get me some earrings as well."

With the engagement ring, the matching earrings and the mini-break at Cliveden, Ben figured that he had spent all his disposable income for the year in one fell swoop. But how could he put a price on Diana's happiness? he reminded himself. And her forgiveness. This engagement, which had come upon him rather more quickly than he expected, was the sign of commitment Diana had demanded after discovering he had cheated on her with a girl from work.

"It's the only way I can ever trust you again," she told him.

After the tears and the terrifying screaming matches that had followed his being busted, Ben was happy to agree to just about anything. Like most men, Ben would sooner have faced a machine gun than a crying girl. Forget waterboarding, water*works* were the ultimate torture.

Ben told himself that he would have proposed to Diana at some point anyway. Diana was the love of his life. The fling with Lucy, the girl from work, was a huge mistake. They had flirted for months, while working on the same project, by text and email, and in late-night "meetings" at the pub. The build-up in sexual tension was incredible, but anyone might have predicted that as soon as the tension was released in an untidy bedroom in Lucy's damp flat, the scales would fall from Ben's eyes.

Even as he lay in Lucy's bed right afterwards, he started to compare her unfavourably with Diana, his girlfriend of seven years. Lucy's sheets needed changing for a start. Ben shuddered at the thought that he might not be the first guy to have slept on this set. The walls of her bedroom were depressingly bare but for an Australian flag held up by drawing pins. She had nothing in her fridge but a carton of sour milk, which Ben only discovered was sour when he took an unfortunate swig from it. Lucy's bathroom was filthy. The pink plastic backing strip of a panty liner curled obscenely on the floor beneath the toilet bowl. She was far from being a domestic goddess.

When, a couple of days later, Diana found a saucy text from Lucy on Ben's mobile and all hell broke loose as a result, it was that grubby bathroom in particular that loomed large in Ben's remembrance. Diana kept their starter home immaculate and spotlessly clean. Sheets were changed twice a week. The walls were tastefully adorned with prints from John Lewis. The fridge was always full. Comfort and cleanliness. Was he willing to trade that for Lucy's sexual athleticism? He knew the acrobatics wouldn't last. They never did. Diana had been like that in bed once. Years down the line, Ben knew better than to make a move when Diana was wearing her tooth-whitening trays or a face mask.

So, faced with the choice between dirty sex in a dirty house and hardly any sex at all in a relative palace, Ben confounded popular beliefs about men by going for practical celibacy among the John Lewis cushions. And so the engagement was brokered and the moment itself was stage-managed. A bottle of champagne upon arrival. The ring handed over in the elegance of Cliveden's terrace dining room to polite applause from the other guests. The first shag in six months in a deluxe suite with separate dressing area.

"I am so happy," Diana said as she stretched her arm out from beneath the sheets to admire her brand-new diamonds.

"Me too," said Ben. "Me too."

He stroked a finger down Diana's arm. She would make a beautiful bride. Every man would envy him. Unknown to Ben, Diana was thinking exactly the same thing.

CHAPTER
THREE

21 October 2010, Bride on Time, Washam,
a small town on the south coast

Whatever the statistics suggested about the decline of marriage, Bride on Time seemed to be bucking the trend. Even this latest recession had left Melanie Harris's bridal-gown business untouched. Perhaps romance wasn't dead after all. Perhaps people were actually flocking to the safety of marriage in these difficult times. Or perhaps it was that Bride on Time had benefited from the collapse of its nearest rival store when the couple that ran it divorced after the husband came out. Such a shock. A man who knew his silk from his chiffon running off with another guy? Whatever the reason, the appointments book at Bride on Time was always full.

Still, people driving past the unassuming aluminium-framed doorway, which led to a converted flat above a 24/7 mini-market, would never have guessed that Bride on Time was tricked out like the inside of a jewellery box, with swags of satin pinned to the ceiling and a pink velvet chaise longue in every corner, or that in an average week nearly thirty brides would be dressed for their big day by Melanie and her team. Newly engaged women (and, memorably, one slim-hipped man) looked good in everything) came to Bride on T from miles around. Melanie had clients from Southampton, Portsmouth and Petersfield. Several girls had made the trip down from London. She was even making a dress for an expat bride based in Palma, who flew in for a fitting once a month. Such was Bride on Time's reputation for perfection.

In 2010, Melanie's little shop was almost thirty years old. She'd started the place just a year after her own wedding, sinking the money she and her husband had saved for a mortgage deposit into the first season's stock. Melanie had worked as a seamstress since leaving school. She knew that bridal fashion was big business and luckily Keith believed her. There were some lean years to begin with, when the newlyweds lived on dented tins from the supermarket downstairs, but it wasn't long before Bride on Time was VAT registered and employed two full- and seven part-time staff. Heidi and Sarah, the current full-time staff, were both excellent seamstresses. Heidi had worked for Vivienne Westwood before quitting to come back to Southampton to look after her ageing mother. Sarah, likewise, could make a catwalk model out of any checkout girl with a bit of clever stitching.

But Melanie's husband and friends credited Melanie herself with making the shop such a stellar success. Melanie had a way with people. It was as though she could tune in to their most secret desires. She knew within moments of meeting a bride which dress the girl would walk out with. She knew how to tactfully

bride who wanted a Disney-themed
grown women dressed as Minnie Mouse
ds that the pictures might not stand the
She also knew how to calm the nerves of
the bride who wasn't flat-out delighted to find herself
wedding-dress shopping. There were more of those than
you would imagine. Sometimes it was just the stress of
planning the big day. Plenty of girls dreaded being the
centre of attention. Sometimes it was something more.
Melanie had often played agony aunt as she laced up
bodices in the chiffon-tented changing rooms.

"What was *your* wedding dress like?" her customers
often asked her.

No word described it better than "meringue", but
that was the height of fashion in 1981, she told them,
including leg-of-mutton sleeves and a skirt so
voluminous it almost obliged the bride to walk sideways
on her way down the aisle. Melanie's own enormous
dress was made of a heavy silk taffeta that creased like
buggery. It had driven her mother insane in the hours
immediately before the wedding, which fell on the same
day as the marriage of Prince Charles and Lady Di.

29 July 1981

"These bloody creases won't come out!"

Melanie's mother, Cynthia, had her stand in front of
the ironing board so that she could at least try to press
out the worst of the wrinkles in the train. The result was
a small brown burn that had to be covered with a silk

flower. But not even a burn on her wedding dress could ruin Melanie's wedding day. She was marrying Keith Harris, the man she had met for the first time at a youth club when they were both just thirteen years old. He was her best friend in the world, the only lover she would ever have or need. Some girls might have found the prospect of only ever knowing one man slightly daunting, but at twenty-one, Melanie was ready to promise him the rest of her life.

Cynthia felt a little calmer about the creases in her daughter's dress after the bridal party broke off their preparations to watch the arrival of Lady Diana Spencer at St Paul's Cathedral. The royal bride stepped out of her carriage in a veritable cloud of crumpled taffeta and antique lace.

"Look at that dress. It's like a bloody dishrag," Cynthia pronounced. "Those puffball sleeves are bigger than her head!"

"But she's radiant," said Melanie's maternal grandmother, Ann. "No one's looking at the dress. Just look at her smile. She's so much in love, that girl. Like our Melanie is. Anyway, scrunched-up taffeta is obviously all the rage."

Melanie's mother conceded that Grandma was right.

Meanwhile, Melanie beamed as she took in the similarities between her dress and what she could see of the future princess's dress on the tiny television screen. Same sort of fabric. Same shape. It was a pity Melanie hadn't thought of having more detailing round the collar, and of course Melanie's train was never going to be that extravagant — twenty-five feet! The aisle at the village church just wasn't that long — but all in all Melanie felt that she and Diana had been on the same wavelength and that added another layer to Melanie's happiness. How lucky they both were to be marrying the men of their dreams on this beautiful day. Possibly, Melanie decided, she was even luckier than Lady Di, since she was marrying Keith, the most handsome man in her town, while Diana was marrying a man nearly thirteen years her senior with ears like a toby jug. Melanie wouldn't have traded Keith for *that* particular prince.

"The car's here," Melanie's sister, Michelle, shouted up the stairs.

Melanie took a few deep breaths as her mother, her grandmother and two of her bridesmaids gathered up the taffeta skirt and train, and helped her down the narrow stairs towards the start of her new life as Mrs Keith Harris, with all its attendant Orville jokes.

CHAPTER
FOUR

23 October 2010

Washam

Kate had often walked past the unassuming entrance to Bride on Time while staying at her parents' new house in a little town on the coast near Southampton. The place had always fascinated her. The red prom dress in the window display (Melanie Harris had seen an opportunity in the imported trend for high-school proms) looked unflattering, uncomfortable and highly inflammable. Who on earth was going to buy that, and who was going to be encouraged to buy a wedding dress by the monstrosities that flanked the red frock? They were perfect early-*Neighbours*-era Kylie. In fact, it was quite possible that they had been lurking around in the stockroom since the 1980s. None of the dresses benefited from being seen through a film of yellow cellophane, designed to stop the fabric from discolouring in the sun.

Kate couldn't imagine how the business survived, stuck above a mini-mart with such an uninspiring window display. Perhaps it was a cover for a brothel, she suggested to her father, John, as they walked by together one afternoon. John said he thought his daughter might be right. He liked to imagine all sorts of goings-on in the small town where he and Kate's mother had chosen to spend their retirement for its proximity to Kate's sister and their grandchild. Kate's parents had a nickname for every familiar passerby.

"There goes Keith Richards on his way to the bottle bank," Kate's mum, Elaine, commented as a man who hadn't changed his look since 1973 shuffled by the kitchen window.

"I see Joan Collins is being measured for some new guttering," said John as a van pulled up outside a house owned by a glamorous widow.

"Do you think that's a wig?" Elaine asked Kate as Joan Collins opened the door to her visitors. "Your father thinks that's her real hair. I keep telling him it's a wig."

Kate humoured her parents both. Commenting on the neighbours kept them off the subject of her own life, at least.

That said, one of the many things Kate would always be grateful to her parents for was the care they took not to interfere in their grown daughters' private lives. Kate had many friends who claimed they had been endlessly pressured by their parents to get married and start producing grandchildren. By contrast, Kate's own parents had never been anything but supportive of Kate's right to live her life exactly as she chose. Married, single, straight, gay, left, right . . . they didn't mind at all. They never once mentioned how nice it would be to have Kate settled down. Except for one incident when Kate had just turned thirty and her father came in from the garden with a toad.

"Kiss it," he said. "It may be your last chance."

Kate hadn't brought a boyfriend home in seven years when she introduced Ian to her mum and dad. She would have liked for them to get to know Dan, but Dan seemed to think that agreeing to meet her parents would be tantamount to agreeing to a wedding and so he never did meet them, though he was always polite enough to ask how they were.

Ian was different. He insisted that he be allowed to meet Kate's family surprisingly early on, perhaps only three months after they first met.

"Are you sure?" Kate asked.

"Of course I'm sure. I want to know everything about you," he said. "I especially want to know where you came from."

So Kate drove him down to the south coast for Sunday lunch. He did all the right things. He brought flowers, praised the food and offered to help wash up. He complimented Kate's sister, Tess, on her new boots. He found common ground with Kate's brother-in-law, Mike, on the subject of a disastrous cricket season. He was suitably enthusiastic when Kate's five-year-old niece, Lily, insisted on demonstrating the song she would be singing in the school play. He didn't even seem to mind that Lily started from the beginning every time she made a mistake. Which was often. He just kept on smiling through.

Later in the afternoon, the entire family went for a walk down by the seafront. Ian strode ahead with Mike

21

and John, carrying Lily on his shoulders. Kate lagged behind with her mother and sister.

"Lily likes him," Tess observed.

"I like him," said Elaine. "He's a very nice young man."

"Young?" Kate laughed. "He's forty-five."

"And he's never been married, you say?"

"Never."

"That's good," said Elaine, before adding in a stage whisper, "None of that *complication*."

Though Elaine refrained from saying it out loud, Kate knew she was thinking about Dan and his never-ending divorce proceedings.

"Your father seems to like him too," Elaine continued.

"I know he must be special," said Tess, "because you haven't brought anyone home since that bloke with the BMW. What was his name? Nice car, shame about the —"

"God, that was ages ago. Let's not talk about him," said Kate. Her entire body shivered as she remembered Sebastian, the BMW driver, who had asked her to whip him while he cavorted in a pair of her stockings. Kate knew Tess already thought her private life was a bit of a joke. Tess didn't know the half of it. There were many good reasons why Kate hadn't brought someone home in so long.

Anyway, Ian definitely passed muster that afternoon. From that day forward Elaine always asked after him whenever she phoned for a chat. Ian was a big fan of West Ham FC, so John made an effort to know how the team was doing and asked Kate to pass on her congratulations if a match had gone well. Never before had Kate's parents been so keen to know about a boyfriend. Tess, too, always wanted to know what Ian was up to and what was his opinion on this, that or other aspect of her sister's life. They could not have made it more obvious that they approved of Ian Turner. That was how Kate knew her family would be pleased with their news.

It was difficult to keep quiet about the engagement until they were able to tell their parents. After the initial shock of the proposal, Kate's feelings on the subject had quickly settled into the proper euphoria. The rest of the mini-break in Paris was just wonderful. For the first time in her life Kate found herself actually going *into* a jewellery shop with a man. Dan had always tugged her past jewellers' windows at high speed, as though the unobtainable glitter might send her insane. Now Ian was insisting that they visit every jeweller on the Place Vendôme — Boucheron, Chaumet, Bulgari. In Boucheron, Kate tried on a yellow diamond as big as an almond. When the sales assistant announced the price, which was roughly equivalent to the cost of a brand-new Porsche, Kate kept her nerve and continued to admire the stone, while Ian told the assistant that the ring was "too big for anyone but a transvestite".

Afterwards, back out on the street, Kate and Ian laughed so hard they thought their sides would burst. They tried on a considerably more modest solitaire in Tiffany at Galeries Lafayette, but ultimately decided to get a less expensive copy made in Hatton Garden when they got home.

When they weren't shopping for a fantasy engagement ring, they stopped on street corners all over Paris to share kisses. They held hands over dinner, breakfast and lunch. They twirled round the Tuileries like a couple half their age.

On the Eurostar back to London, Kate felt a sense of calm underlying the excitement of what was to come. She looked at Ian dozing beside her. That snore of his was now hers for life, but she didn't mind about that. Ian really wanted her, and she wanted him too. More than anything. They would look after each other. Together they would build a wonderful life. At last Kate had found her for-ever love.

Back in London, the guy in the dry-cleaner's asked Kate if she was sure she hadn't flown to Poland for a quick nip and tuck, rather than to Paris for a mini-break.

"You look radiant," he said.

Kate's mother agreed with the dry-cleaner's pronouncement when she saw Kate climb out of Ian's car the following Saturday. When the news had been shared, Elaine clapped her hands together and said, "I knew it! I knew it the moment I saw you get out of the car. You look transformed."

And Kate really did feel transformed. All her adult life she had told herself that it didn't bother her whether she got married or not, but the truth was, she had been blindsided by joy. And there was something about her parents' reaction that gave the lie to the notion that they too had been entirely happy with her prolonged bout of spinsterhood. The only word for her parents that afternoon was "ecstatic". Their unabashed happiness made Kate feel happier still.

When Tess arrived, an hour or so later, she squealed her own delight at her big sister's announcement. Mike shook Ian's hand and assured him, in dark tones, "The fun starts here."

Lily, just turned six, seemed a little confused by all the congratulations and the kissing.

"You're going to have an uncle Ian," Tess told her.

"I thought you said I could have a Dream Pony stable set," Lily responded.

After much prompting, Lily eventually wished her Auntie Kate "Congratulations" and gave her new Uncle Ian a reluctant kiss on the cheek. Then she insisted on all the lights in her grandparents' living room being turned off so that she could put on "a show" in the newly engaged couple's honour.

"This is such good news, Kate." Tess wouldn't stop squeezing her hand all afternoon and evening. "Especially, you know, especially right now." Tess looked deep into her eyes.

At last Kate caught her meaning. In all the excitement about the engagement, Kate had forgotten that her mother had been in hospital that week, as an outpatient, for some tests following an abnormal mammogram. Nothing serious, they'd hoped, but Kate had completely forgotten to ask the outcome. She followed her mother out to the kitchen to help her make another round of tea.

"How was the hospital visit?" Kate asked.

"Let's not talk about that now," said Elaine. "It was boring. Today is about your engagement." Elaine cupped Kate's face in her hands. "My little girl is getting married!"

"I'm not a little girl. I'm thirty-nine."

"You'll always be my little girl. I can't tell you how much it means to me and your dad that you've got someone to take care of you now. It's such a relief."

Elaine's eyes glittered. She didn't need to say anything else. Kate knew that the hospital visit had confirmed that something wasn't quite right. Though they continued to celebrate for the rest of the evening, the happy engagement bubble had already burst.

CHAPTER
FIVE

Having been given much more notice than Kate Williamson's parents, Susie Ashcroft was able to make sure that her only daughter's engagement was celebrated in real style. Of course, Susie had keys to her daughter and future son-in-law's house, so while they were still at Cliveden, basking in the post-engagement glow (and running up a credit-card bill that would take Ben months to clear), Susie and Nicole, Diana's best friend since primary school, let themselves in to set up a party.

They invited forty other close friends and relations to help share the joy. Everyone mucked in, hanging brightly coloured "Congratulations" banners all over Diana's tastefully neutral decoration scheme. Nicole inflated fifty gold and silver balloons. The effort nearly killed her. Susie cut the crusts off 200 smoked-salmon sandwiches. An enormous cake was brought in from the very best local bakery. When the bride-to-be texted to say that she and Ben had just turned off the motorway, Susie ushered the engagement-party guests into hiding in the darkened living room.

"Surprise!" they shouted as Ben shuffled in first.

Ben, who had been looking forward to a restorative hour on his Xbox for the entire drive back to Southampton, gamely put on a show of delight. Diana, however, was genuinely delighted. A surprise party was the best thing in the world, as far as she was concerned. What was the point of bagging her man if everybody didn't know about it? She flashed her new engagement ring and regaled the entire gathering with a description of their suite at the hotel.

"It had a separate dressing area. That makes such a difference. I told Ben we should knock through from the box room and have a separate dressing room here."

Then she wowed her friends with the news that one of last year's *X Factor* contestants had been staying at Cliveden at the same time.

"He's much smaller in real life," she said, "and his girlfriend looked like a right old skank. But then didn't I always say he was gay? She's probably his PA, helping him scotch the gay rumours. They didn't look very together in a real way."

No one seemed to notice, or care, that Diana hadn't described the proposal itself. Not when there was *X Factor* gossip to be had.

The clingfilm came off the sandwiches and champagne corks were popped. The champagne came courtesy of Diana's father, who was unfortunately unable to attend that evening's celebrations. He was still at work. He had his own business fitting kitchens and often carried on over the weekends.

"Trust him," said Diana. "He's always working."

"He'll need to work twice as hard now," said Nicole, "to pay for your wedding. Have you thought about your venue yet?"

"Cliveden would be amazing," said Diana.

It was possibly for the best that Diana's father wasn't there. His doctor had recently told him to avoid putting too much stress on his heart.

Diana and Ben's engagement party was still in full swing at midnight. Ben grinned his way through it all, though he wanted nothing more than a few moments to himself. He managed just twenty minutes on his own in the master bedroom's en suite before Diana came knocking on the door, demanding to touch up her makeup. She seemed very happy. She pressed a kiss on Ben's cheek as they passed in the bathroom doorway. She might have been less affectionate had she known who he'd been texting in those few brief minutes of alone time.

Ben had been texting Lucy, the girl from work. She had sent him several messages over the past couple of days, asking if he was OK. Ben hadn't told her that he was taking three days off work to get engaged and thus she had assumed that he must be absent because he was unwell. Nobody had told her otherwise.

Oh God. Every time another sweetly concerned text came through, Ben's heart sank a little deeper. He knew he had to tell Lucy the truth before he got back to the office. She didn't deserve the humiliation of finding out at the same time as everyone else. If he texted her now, on Saturday night, then by Monday morning she might have got used to the idea. There was no way he would be able to keep the engagement quiet for any longer. Diana's best friend, Nicole, had a cousin who worked in the HR department. Ben wouldn't have been at all surprised if she had already made the announcement for him on the company intranet. So he knew he had to man up and let Lucy down. And, boy, would she feel let down.

Though Ben had promised Diana that Lucy knew the status quo, the truth was that Lucy still had every reason to think that Ben had actually left Diana. With Diana raging at home, Ben hadn't been able to face the thought of getting earache in the office as well, so he'd told Lucy that he and Diana were coming to the end of their seven-year relationship. It was just a matter of making the final break, which would naturally be difficult after such a long time. They had a joint mortgage. A big mortgage. That would take some unravelling. But unravelling it was, or so Lucy thought. It was on that basis that she had gone to bed with him. As yet, Lucy didn't even know that Diana had found out about their night of passion, so while Ben was busy patching up his relationship, Lucy was biding her time, assuming that Ben was just waiting for the right moment to make his exit. Ben was going to have to write one hell of a text. In the end, he wrote, **Got some bad news, D and me back 2gether. Got engaged. Am sorry.**

He didn't know whether to be relieved or terrified when Lucy failed to text her response.

"Come on, you." Diana emerged from the bathroom, looking immaculate as ever, and took her future

30

husband by the hand. "Mum has brought a cake. We've got to cut it together."

"Shouldn't we wait until we're cutting our wedding cake?" asked Ben.

"You're such a spoilsport." Diana pouted. "Don't ruin my evening. Besides, the sooner we wrap this party up, the sooner we can go to bed."

Diana fluffed up her long, glossy hair and smiled seductively.

Ben followed her downstairs like a puppy.

CHAPTER
SIX

29 October 2010

Kate's instinct that all was not well with her mother was right. Though her parents had refused to talk about it on the day they celebrated Kate's engagement to Ian, the very next time Kate phoned, Elaine admitted that the hospital visit had brought bad news.

"The second mammogram again showed what they thought might be calcifications, but it might be DCIS."

"What's that?"

"Ductal carcinoma in situ, a beginner's cancer, if you like."

Kate felt the C-word like a blow.

"They want to do a biopsy. It's the only way to know for sure."

"How soon can they do it?" Kate asked.

"End of the week. But I don't want to go into it now," said Elaine. "Cheer me up. Talk about the wedding."

Carrying on an excited conversation about wedding plans after that revelation was anything but easy. Still Kate tried. She told her mother that she and Ian had decided they wanted to get married as quickly as possible. Kate was about to go on gardening leave for two months as she moved from one law firm to another. Ideally, they would get married before Kate started her new job in February. Maybe as soon as late January if they could get everything sorted out in time. There was no point waiting any longer at their age, and a winter wedding could be so romantic. They liked the idea of the register office in Marylebone, followed by a lunch. Just a few people. Definitely not more than forty. Did her parents think enough water had passed under the bridge to invite both her godmothers, who had fallen out ten years before? Elaine didn't seem entirely engaged with the conversation, but every time Kate attempted to steer her back to the biopsy, Elaine asked about wedding cakes, invitations and party favours instead.

"Mum," said Kate, "we're not having party favours, whatever they are. We're planning a simple wedding."

Kate had a long-awaited day off work later that week. She abandoned her plan to spend the day getting the boiler serviced and doing some early Christmas shopping and instead travelled back down to the south coast to accompany her mother to hospital for the biopsy.

Kate sat in the waiting room with her father.

"Katie-Jane," he said, reverting to the pet name he hadn't used in years, "I can't tell you how worried we are. If we didn't have your engagement to celebrate, your mother and I might have reached for the arsenic."

"Dad," Kate pleaded, "it could be nothing. Wait for the results." But she could imagine what he said was true. Her parents, who had married at the tender age of twenty, had spent less than seven nights apart in their whole almost five-decade-long marriage. Even through her darkest dating disasters, Kate had been sustained by the idea of a marriage like the one her parents had built together. They proved it was possible to find for-ever love. Nothing was too difficult for them to get through together. Except this, perhaps, if it turned out to be breast cancer. That day, privately and separately, each told Kate how much they feared for the other in the face of such a foe.

The mood remained sombre even when they were back at home and their neighbour "Keith Richards" tripped over their low garden fence as he staggered by en route to the bottle bank.

"Poor man," said Elaine. "He's got no one to look after him."

Elaine made a grab for her husband's hand and squeezed until his fingers went white.

Kate knew that her mother was imagining a day when John might be the one tottering towards the bottle bank with no comfort but a bottle of whisky.

The arrival of Kate's sister for lunch was a huge relief.

"Why didn't you tell me what was going on?" Kate hissed when their parents were safely in the kitchen.

"No one wanted to rain on your parade, stupid. You've waited long enough to bag your Mr Right."

"I can't believe I was off on another planet like that while Mum and Dad have had so much to think about. I would never have acted like such a selfish cow going on and on about me and Ian."

34

"Kate, believe me, the thought of your wedding has really cheered them up. Your news came at *exactly* the right time."

"I feel like an idiot. I should have guessed."

"There's no point beating yourself up," said Tess. "We're not going to know anything for certain until Mum gets the results, so we've just got to keep calm and carry on. And keep Mum and Dad distracted."

"How can we do that? I feel like Pollyanna talking about anything but Mum's health right now."

"How about . . ." Tess suggested that a trip to a bridal-wear shop might cheer their mother up.

"What? Today? I haven't really thought about what I want to wear yet," Kate protested.

"Well, there's no harm in seeing what's out there. It's just an outing. We could go to Bride on Time."

"The prom-dress place above the supermarket? You're kidding. Ian and I aren't planning a wedding with a trailer-park theme."

But Tess insisted. "I hear that's where all the local brides go. Apparently, it's not as tacky as it looks once you get upstairs. There's a woman there used to work for Vivienne Westwood."

When Elaine heard the plan, she clapped her hands together and a proper smile appeared on her face for the first time that day.

"I've always wanted to see you in a wedding dress."

Kate was suddenly acutely aware that at thirty-nine, she had kept her mother waiting longer than most.

"OK," said Kate, resigning herself to the idea. "We'll go to Bride on Time."

Still, as she made the call, she crossed her fingers and prayed there would be no chance of an appointment before she had to go back to London. No such luck. As it happened, there had been a cancellation. Melanie Harris and her team would be delighted to see Kate that very afternoon.

CHAPTER
SEVEN

Diana had long since decided that she would be getting her wedding dress from Bride on Time. It was where her best friend Nicole's sister, Gemma, had bought her dress — a fabulous hand-embroidered number called Evangeline that cost more than her first car. Diana's cousin Grace had also bought her dress there. And Grace's sister-in-law. And Diana's next-door neighbour. And Diana's colleague Jane. Everyone who was anyone within a fifty-mile radius had to be a Bride on Time bride. All the girls recommended Melanie Harris in particular.

"You have to make sure you get an appointment with *her*," said Gemma, "the boss. Or Heidi, who used to work for Vivienne Westwood. You don't want one of the juniors, who don't know what they're doing."

Diana duly booked an appointment with the boss for 29 October.

It was the first in a series of wedding-related appointments in Diana's diary. She had pencilled most of them in even before the weekend at Cliveden. She had also, unknown to Ben, been collecting cuttings from wedding magazines and Sunday supplements for years. The length of time that had elapsed since Diana began her "wedding folder" was evidenced by the changing styles of the dresses she had clipped. In the past couple of years, Diana had been erring towards simple shapes that were almost more evening dress than traditional wedding gown, but there were genuine meringues among the dresses Diana had picked out over the decades. And of course there was the iconic wedding dress worn by her princess namesake.

29 July 1981

Diana Ashcroft was born on the day that Lady Diana Spencer married her prince. Diana's mother, Susie, watched the wedding on a TV set wheeled into the delivery room by the midwife, who was determined not to miss a minute of this historic occasion for any birth, no matter how difficult. For a long time the procession of guests arriving at St Paul's took Susie's mind off her labour, which had been going on for twenty-two hours by the time the princess-to-be and her father appeared at the cathedral in their carriage. Unfortunately, Susie and the midwife missed most of the ceremony itself, as Baby Ashcroft chose that exact moment to make her appearance to a soundtrack of Kiri Te Kanawa singing Handel and her mother's best collection of swear words. She was bald as an earthworm and bore an uncanny resemblance to her paternal grandfather, but Susie pronounced her new daughter at least as beautiful as the newly minted princess.

"I'm calling her Diana," Susie told her husband when he finally came to pay his respects two whole hours later. Dave had been watching the wedding in a pub, or rather, he had been sitting at the back of a pub sinking lager and stuffing sausage rolls from the complimentary royal wedding buffet the pub's landlady had put on for her regulars. He hadn't seen a moment of the ceremony.

"You can't call her bloody Diana," he said, realising simultaneously that this name nonsense must mean he had a daughter and not a son. Bang went his plan to be allowed to buy a Southampton FC season ticket and an enormous Scalextric track.

"I'll call her what I bloody well like. You didn't have to squeeze her out through your private parts. Where the hell were you, anyway? You were meant to be holding my hand. Ten minutes you said you'd be gone. Ten minutes! I bet you were in a bloody pub."

"It's a day of national celebration, sugar." Dave tried to soften his wife up with her pet name. "I was toasting our future queen."

"How about toasting your first-born, you tosspot? It's been two hours since she was born. Two bloody hours! I didn't know where you were. You might have been run over by one of the floats in the royal wedding parade for all I knew. You had better make this up to me," said Susie.

Dave promised that he would, and he did. As soon as the shops reopened after the national holiday, Dave bought his wife a new charm for her treasured bracelet: a little golden bootee studded with pink crystal to mark the birth of a girl. He bought his new daughter, his first-born, a charm bracelet of her own. In silver. Susie sent him back to the shop to change it for a gold one.

"She's your daughter, Dave, your only child."

"My first child."

"Your bloody *only* child if I have anything to do with it. And from now on your daughter wears gold."

It was the first hint of the long list of expenses to come: private school, a pony, a car . . .

The fact that Dave would be bankrolling the whole project did not, however, mean that he would have much, if any, say over the wedding preparations. He certainly wouldn't be allowed to join the first excursion to Bride on Time. Choosing a wedding dress was women's work. Diana would be accompanied by her mother and by Nicole, her newly appointed maid of honour.

In any case, by the time his darling Diana got engaged, Dave had been divorced from her mother for almost eleven years. They didn't even speak. He had cited unreasonable behaviour. Susie promised she would never forgive him. Neither would she ever tire of making Dave's life a misery. Thus Susie was right behind her daughter's plan to have the biggest and the best of everything, especially if it meant that Dave couldn't spend that money on Chelsea, his second wife.

"I want you to have the dress I was never able to have," Susie told Diana as they drove to Bride on Time.

When Susie and Dave got married, Susie had had to wear a maternity dress. She had wanted to wait until after Diana was born to have the wedding, so that she could slim down and wear a proper bridal gown, but Diana's maternal grandfather had insisted that the marriage came before the birth. He would not countenance an illegitimate grandchild.

"So I missed out on everything," said Susie. "I had to wear a nylon sack and have my reception in a working men's club. Your wedding is a chance to have the day I always wanted."

"Trust me, Mum," said Diana, "my wedding is going to be the best wedding in the world. No expense will be spared." She pulled out her phone. "I'm just going to remind Dad he needs to transfer five grand to my account for the deposits."

CHAPTER
EIGHT

Kate didn't know what she had expected the atmosphere in a bridal shop to be like. Actually, she did know what she had expected. She had expected it to be like a wonderful girls-only tea party, full of excitement and anticipation. Full of happiness . . .

Well, there was to be no tea. That was quickly established. There was a sign on the wall as you walked into the self-consciously styled salon saying, "No beverages or food whatsoever." Beneath it was a picture of a teacup scored through to underline that such things were strictly verboten at Bride on Time. Kate understood that a spillage among so much white silk would be very expensive indeed, so no tea, but she was surprised that there didn't seem to be much happiness going on either.

There were three brides-to-be in the shop that afternoon. All of them, Kate included, looked as though they were waiting for a dental appointment rather than to choose a wedding dress. As she hovered with her mother and sister, and waited to be told what to do next, Kate worked out that she was the eldest bride by at least a decade, though one of the others had two children in tow. Kate heard that particular bride discussing the children's part in the wedding with a woman who could only have been her mother. They had the same pinched expression on their faces, as though constantly smelling something bad.

"Jayden's dad says he's not going to let him come to the wedding at all, but I told him that I am Jayden's mother and he will be there whether his father likes it or not. Anyway, after this wedding, Terry will be his father, won't he? Darren won't have a say any more."

Kate winced at the thought of the custody battle brewing there.

The other bride, with her long, glossy hair and her beige patent Louboutin courts, seemed unnaturally poised for someone so young. She was accompanied by her mother, Kate guessed, and a friend or sister, who buzzed around her like a handmaiden. The younger bride gave Kate a very obvious once-over. Kate withered under her gaze.

"Kate Williamson!"

Kate raised her hand as her name was called.

"Oh," said the middle-aged woman with the clipboard. "I thought you were one of the mums."

"I'm already not enjoying this," Kate whispered to Tess.

Heidi was going to be looking after Kate that afternoon.

"She's the one from Vivienne Westwood," Tess whispered.

Heidi didn't look like she'd started her career in a top designer atelier. She was five feet tall with hair the colour of overcooked red cabbage. Her cheap purple skirt suit, which strained over her stomach and hips, clashed violently with her badly dyed hair. All in all, Heidi's appearance did not inspire much confidence in her ability to help Kate look beautiful on her wedding day. Still, according to Tess, women came from miles away for the benefit of Heidi's expertise, and she seemed professional enough as she explained how the session would proceed.

Heidi handed over five plastic rings — each with a slit — that Kate was to place over the hangers of the dresses that she wanted to try on. She encouraged Kate's mother and sister to help make the choices and advised that it really was a good idea to go "a bit crazy" when picking out the first five. So many brides came in with a fixed idea of what they wanted and were horrified at the thought of trying on anything else, but with Heidi's "five-in-a-day" plan, they were forced to consider the alternatives and quite often they went home with something they would have turned their nose up at had they seen it in a bridal magazine. Heidi said she saw it all the time.

"Fact is," she told Kate, "very few people have a proper idea of what they really look like. They come in here wanting a column dress when they would look so much better in a fuller skirt. Most women look better in a fuller skirt. Hides a multitude of sins, a big skirt does."

Kate was sure that Heidi glanced at her thighs as she said that.

"You a twelve to fourteen?" Heidi asked.

"Ten to twelve," Kate protested.

"You sure? I think you're on the larger side myself. Choose from the dresses in this section."

Twelve to fourteen.

Kate decided she hated Heidi already.

"Off you go."

Tess, who had been sitting on a velvet chaise longue while the instructions were issued, leaped into action. She was delighted to have been given a mandate to pick out something for her sister to try on. Elaine, too, seemed excited.

"I don't want strapless," Kate reminded them both, remembering how she and Tess had only recently roared with laughter at the bridal supplement of the local paper. Every bride in strapless, no matter whether they had arms like sticks or biceps like hams. Strapless was to the 2000s what the puffball sleeve had been to the 1980s, even if arguably it wasn't quite so flattering.

"We'll find you something lovely," Tess promised.

Tess and Elaine circled the room like two lionesses scouting out prey ahead of the pack. Kate took just one ring and advanced towards a rack of dresses as though she were approaching a rabid hyena. The other brides and their entourages were circling too. When the two other brides landed on the same dress at once, there was venom in their "After you's. It happened several times. Each time, the bride who capitulated shot evil looks at the back of her competitor as the winner triumphantly placed her ring on the hanger. Kate supposed she could be thankful that shopping among the "larger" rails meant she didn't have to compete.

★ ★ ★

Prior to entering Bride on Time, Kate's criteria for a wedding dress had been simple. It just had to *be* simple. In the brief time since their engagement, she and Ian had selected Marylebone Register Office as the venue for the ceremony and booked a slot for early March, the earliest Saturday available. As the register office of choice for London's glitterati ever since Mick and Bianca Jagger made it famous, it was hardly the place to turn up looking like a crocheted loo-roll cover. In fact, Kate hadn't intended to shop for her wedding dress at a wedding specialist at all. She had, in her rare wedding daydreams, imagined a knee-length white dress by Azzedine Alaïa, with matching coat, nipped in at the waist. She wanted to look chic for the wedding and have half a chance of wearing the outfit again afterwards. Looking for a Cinderella frock in a size twelve to fourteen was a complete waste of time.

But Kate was in Bride on Time because her mum needed cheering up, and what cheers the average woman up more quickly than the spectacle of thousands of Barbie-style frocks in one place? There was no harm in trying them on if it made her mum happy. It might even be a laugh. In that spirit, Kate finally placed her single blue plastic ring round the hanger of a dress so enormous a bear could have hidden beneath its skirts. The bodice was covered with big fabric flowers. The back was laced up with three different coloured ribbons. All in all it looked like something that even Katie Price might have declared a bit too rich for her taste.

"I've chosen mine," Kate announced with relief. "It says it's by Giovanni Lucciani. That's a made-up name if I ever heard one."

"Oooh, yes," said Tess, in the *Coronation Street* accent she used to denote a joke, "that's really *lovely*."

Now the reason for all the ring-hanging became clear. The dresses looked so light and fluffy — all that tulle — but the accusation that they were "meringues" was true in one sense only. They may have looked as though they had been spun from sugar and air, but they definitely didn't feel like it.

"Don't even attempt to help me," said Heidi when Kate moved to unhook the dress she had chosen. "I've had years of practice at this. You need to have the right technique so you don't do your back in. I reckon this dress is three stone."

Kate could only gawp in horror as she contemplated trying on a dress that weighed as much as her niece.

"Three stone. Perhaps I'll go for something simpler," she said. "I only picked this one out as a joke."

"No," chorused her mother and sister. "We like it. You've got to try that one."

Kate had the feeling she was doomed.

CHAPTER
NINE

Unlike Kate, Diana already knew the ropes at Bride on Time. She had accompanied three other brides to their first dress fittings. This time was going to be so much more fun, now that she was no longer the bridesmaid but finally, thankfully, the bride. She didn't know if she would ever forgive Ben for letting her think that she might make it to thirty without an engagement ring.

Anyway, here she was at last. She was slightly frustrated to see that there were two other brides in the "salon" that morning but was soon reassured that she would be the centre of attention regardless. After all, Diana was being assisted by Melanie Harris, the proprietress herself. Add to that the fact that Diana was much more beautiful than the rat-faced woman with her equally ugly children and so much younger than the other bride. How old was that one? In her forties? Diana was surprised that a woman of *that* age was even considering a traditional wedding dress. Wouldn't she be better off in a nice tailored shift dress with a matching jacket to cover her arms? Diana shared that thought with her mother, who agreed.

"Thank goodness they do a good line in boleros," said Susie.

Melanie handed Diana her five plastic rings. Diana said she didn't need any instructions.

"Do you know what sort of thing you're looking for?" Melanie asked.

"I know *exactly* what I want," Diana assured her. "I thought with my complexion, I should go for an off-white. I'm having pale pink flowers. Tea roses. They're a type of rose named for Princess Diana, which I thought would be appropriate."

Susie Ashcroft agreed. "She was named after Princess Diana," Susie explained to Melanie. "And a right little princess she's turned out to be."

"Oh, Mum," Diana chided her mother playfully, "you don't mean that. In any case, who isn't a princess about her wedding? Doesn't every girl deserve her special day to be exactly as she wants it?"

"Yes, especially if her scumbag deadbeat father is paying."

"How about this one, Mum?"

Diana fingered a strapless dress in duchesse satin with a cathedral-length train.

"Isn't a cathedral-length train going to be a bit much?" asked her friend Nicole.

"Not if you're getting married in a cathedral, like I am."

Nicole shrieked at the news. "You're not . . ."

"It's true."

"How on earth did you swing that?" Nicole asked.

"Daddy did the bishop's kitchen. He got a discount; I get a cathedral wedding."

Susie nodded. "It's about time Dave turned out to be useful for a change."

"Oh my God, Diana," Nicole was almost hyperventilating, "your wedding is going to be so grand."

"Where are you having the reception?" Melanie asked.

"Well, it's going to have to be somewhere special to match up to the ceremony, isn't it? Cliveden's too far from the cathedral, which is a shame."

"Yeah. Pity."

"Can you believe Dad suggested that gastro-pub that overlooks Osborne House? I told him that if he thinks I'm going to have my wedding reception in a flippin' pub, he can bloody well think again."

"It was probably his slut of a second wife's idea," said Susie.

"So anyway, I said if I can't actually have my reception at Osborne House, then I'm having it at the Queen Victoria."

"The country club? That place is expensive."

"Yes, but can you imagine the pictures we'd get on the golf course?"

"Oooh, yeah," said Nicole.

"Have you made your mind up about bridesmaids?" Melanie interrupted. "We can dress all shapes and ages."

"She's narrowed it down to seven," said Susie. "I think that's just about right."

"So a cathedral train will be no problem," said Diana, "with seven pairs of hands to handle it."

"Are you having a veil?" Melanie asked.

"God, yes! Bring it on."

While Melanie went in search of a cathedral-length veil for yet another distinctly un-virginal bride, Diana began her dress hunt in earnest. She snatched two dresses from beneath the nose of the rat-faced girl with the snotty kids. This was going to be fun. Fifteen minutes later, it started to get more frustrating, spotting a possible contender only to find that Rat Face was going for it too. Diana felt the urge to slap away the other girl's nicotine-stained hands when she saw them reaching out to touch the pristine fabric of the wedding gowns. Ugh. Mostly it was embarrassing to think that someone who looked so trashy could possibly share Diana's taste.

"You have got the same LV handbag," Nicole dared to point out.

"Mine's real," Diana snapped back at her.

What kind of wedding was Rat Face planning to have, anyway? Where would she wear her cathedral-length train?

"At her Big, Fat Gypsy Wedding," Susie whispered in her daughter's ear after Diana won the face-off for a third time.

"My, that Marilyn strapless is popular," said Melanie when she saw that the two younger brides were in competition. "And the Meribel and the Ernestine. You ladies will have to take it in turns to try those three dresses. But you don't need to worry about not being able to have the frock that you want," she assured her colleague's client. "These are just our samples. Every dress is ordered in new."

Diana knew that, of course, but it still didn't stop a little bubble of anger from rising in her throat as Rat Face was first to find the fourth dress on Diana's hit list. At least she did not face the same battle with the other bride. Diana and Rat Face were fighting over the size eight to tens. The geriatric bride would be lucky to squeeze into a twelve. Did Bride on Time even carry size-twelve samples? Diana supposed they must. Very few women were as lucky with their figures as she was. Except that it wasn't really luck. Diana went to the gym five times a week. Rat Face obviously kept her figure by living on nothing but fags and booze.

"Finished."

Diana hung her final plastic ring on a dress by Giovanni Lucciani.

"Oh, that's nice," said her mother, admiring the multicoloured ribbons at the back of the bodice. "Really classy."

Diana turned to Rat Face with a velociraptor smile. "Of course, in the end, the way a dress looks is really all about the class of the bride."

CHAPTER
TEN

While Rat Face and Diana had their wedding-frock face-off, Kate was already being helped into her first gown. Heidi explained that they would try the least voluminous dress first and gradually build up to the monster frock that Kate had only really chosen to make her mother smile and her sister laugh out loud.

"We have to do it that way, otherwise you'll be too shocked by the girth," Heidi explained.

Kate was pleasantly surprised by gown number one, which had been chosen by her mother. It wasn't really much more extravagant than the average evening dress. Had it been in black instead of off-white, Kate might have thought it suitable for her law firm's Christmas ball.

"This is nice," said Kate as the skirt settled around her feet.

"Come out into the main room," said Heidi.

"Oh, no . . . I thought that . . ."

"Your mum and sister want to see the dress, don't they?"

"I suppose."

It was the other brides and their families that Kate didn't want to show off to. Still, she shuffled out into the main salon. Her sister and mother made approving noises. The two other brides' supporters seemed pleasantly surprised too.

"I chose that one," said Elaine proudly. "I knew it would suit her." The other mothers praised Elaine's taste.

But Heidi was shaking her head. "Makes you look enormous here and here" — she indicated Kate's thighs with the aid of a stiffened tape measure — "and yet you're like a Biafran up here." She indicated Kate's décolletage. Kate looked down at her chest in disappointment. She knew she wasn't exactly blessed in the breast department, but . . .

"Now that you've got this dress on, I can see that your figure is what I would call a wooden spoon. You're skinny as a stick down to your waist. Then . . . whoompf." Heidi made the sound of a hot-air balloon inflating prior to lift-off. "Completely out of proportion. Do you know what I mean?"

"I get the idea," said Kate. "I'll try something else, shall I?"

"Yes. Bigger round the bottom," said Heidi.

Kate was just grateful that the third bride, the one that Tess had dubbed the "Mean Girl", hadn't been around to hear such a damning assessment.

Heidi refused even to let Kate out of the changing room in dress two.

"No, no, no, not with your saddlebags."

Saddlebags?

Heidi made what she must have thought was pleasant chat as she helped Kate get back out of that frock. "Doesn't matter how much you exercise, I know — you can't get rid of them. I've got a friend who had liposuction. It's the only thing that works."

"I'm sure," said Kate.

"She still didn't have the figure to get married in a straight skirt, but I didn't dare tell her. I always try to be honest with my clients about their figure faults, though. I don't want you coming back here and saying, 'Heidi, you let me look like the back end of an elephant on the most important day of my life.' I may sound harsh, but it's for your own good. You've got to keep imagining what you'll look like from behind."

"Thank you," said Kate.

Kate refused to show anyone dress three, which was practically see-through. Dress four, which passed the saddlebag test, was nonetheless met with instant disapproval by Kate's sister.

"Makes you look three months pregnant," said Tess.

Kate's mother pricked up her ears.

"I'm not," said Kate, as hot embarrassment crept up her neck.

"Ah, well," said Heidi, "there's plenty of time . . . or IVF. I know a girl who had triplets on her eighth try."

Kate couldn't wait to get back into the changing room.

Meanwhile, the girl with the pointy face and the Mean Girl were preening side by side in the floor-length mirror. Though they were objectively both pretty enough girls, their attitudes made them look like Cinderella's two ugly sisters getting ready for the prince's ball. Kate didn't even bother to try to get a better look at the dress she was wearing, to see if Tess was really right. She followed Heidi back to the changing room feeling enormous relief that the next dress was to be her last. She'd try it on, whip it off and hurry to get back into her jeans. Then she was outta here. Why had she ever let herself be talked into this in the first place? There was only so much she could put up with in the interests of making her mother happy and her sister snigger.

Ian had texted. **Are you having fun?** he asked.

While Heidi prepared dress five, Kate responded. **Oh, yeah. This is about as much fun as being back at school.**

Kate had told Ian about the cool girls who had made her teenage years a misery. Even over twenty years on, the thought of them could still make her shoulders slump. The past hour in this stupid bridal shop, with Heidi commenting so candidly on her figure and evil looks from the other brides, was having the same effect as an afternoon in the school gym. The confident Kate her work colleagues knew had all but disappeared.

Kate lifted her arms at Heidi's instruction while the dress was slipped on over her head.

"OK," said Heidi, surveying dress five, "your saddle-bags are covered, but we're going to need the crate."

The crate.

Moments later, Kate found herself standing back outside in the salon on the crate in question — just a plain plastic bottle crate — while Heidi and another assistant fussed around the enormous skirt of the

Giovanni Lucciani dress like a couple of busy elves. Kate, meanwhile, was having an out-of-body experience. Heidi had laced her in so tightly that she could barely breathe.

"You're lucky you've no back fat to speak of," Heidi said when the lacing was done.

Elaine and Tess were less damning in their praise.

"Oh my God," breathed Tess, when she returned from a loo break to see Kate in the final outfit.

"It's amazing," said Elaine.

Kate, too, was stunned by her reflection. She looked like Cinderella in the last picture in the Penguin fairy-tale book she and Tess had shared as children. At least, from the neck down she did. Her waist was tiny.

"In comparison to the skirt," Heidi kindly pointed out.

"The back looks wonderful," said Kate's mother.

"Like I said," Heidi chipped in, "no back fat."

"You look like a princess," said Tess.

"It's ridiculous," said Kate. "You know this dress weighs almost three stone?"

"It's my favourite," said her mother.

"I'm getting married in a register office."

"I always tell my ladies," interrupted Heidi, "that no matter where you're getting married, you want to make sure people know you're the bride."

"I don't think anyone would make a mistake if I wore this frock. It's much too much for me. Even Lady Gaga couldn't pull this one off."

"Oh, Kate!" Elaine suddenly sobbed. "It's so wonderful!"

Kate and Tess looked towards their mother. The Kleenex were out and the waterworks were off. Tess wrapped her arms round Elaine, but Kate, stuck on that stupid crate in a dress that weighed three stone, was powerless to move. She didn't dare.

"Oh, Mum," she said. "Mum. Please. Please don't cry. It's supposed to be a happy occasion."

"I'm sorry," said Elaine. "I am happy really. It's just that I've always wanted to see you get married. It means so much to me to know that someone's going to promise to care for you for the rest of your life. I can end my life in peace. I've got cancer," she explained to Heidi.

"What?" said Kate.

The definitiveness with which their mother announced her diagnosis was a shock for both Kate and her sister. Weren't they supposed to be waiting for the results of the biopsy? Now Tess burst into tears too.

"I've never seen so much crying," said Heidi.

"You look like an angel in that dress, my love. You have never looked more beautiful. I think that's the one," Kate's mother added before making a trumpeting snort into a fistful of tissues.

"It is the one," Tess agreed through her tears. "Definitely. You've got to have it."

And that was how Kate came to be the proud owner of a genuine meringue.

Kate and her family were so busy being emotional that they didn't notice Diana step out of her changing room in the exact same Giovanni Lucciani dress. Diana's eyes narrowed as she took in the familiar coloured ribbons on the back of Kate's bodice. She had assumed something so expensive and intricate could only be a one-off, but no, there was a sample in a large size too, goddamnit. Diana could barely contain her annoyance. First Rat Face and now this. Was it really too much to ask for something unique?

All the same, Diana allowed Melanie to help her step up onto another upturned crate to better show off the skirt. She stood with a dancer's poise as Melanie pulled the ribbons at the back of the bodice as tight as they would go.

Diana asked her mother for a hair clip from her handbag. With it, she gathered her chestnut hair up into a loose chignon that showed off her well-toned shoulders. Thank you, Pilates. She turned this way and that, checking her reflection from all angles. Susie and Nicole cooed their approval.

"It's beautiful with your skin tone," said Nicole.

Melanie stood on another crate in order to be able to fasten the cathedral-length veil, the perfect accessory.

"Ben isn't going to know what hit him," said Susie.

"Especially if I can get those Swarovski Louboutins to go with it," Diana agreed. "They cost well over a grand."

"Your dad will be delighted to get you those shoes, I'm sure."

"How much is this dress again?" Diana asked Melanie.

Diana didn't even blink when Melanie answered, "Two thousand pounds . . . It's more expensive than the others you've just tried on because of the flowers on the bodice. Each one of those roses has to be stitched together by hand."

"So you're telling me that even though that other girl is wearing the same dress, they're not *exactly* identical."

"That's right."

"OK."

Satisfied that she was wearing a dress better than the older bride, Diana told her mother, "This is the one for me." While Melanie scuttled off to gather the paperwork, Diana posed for a while longer on her crate, basking in what she perceived to be the envious looks of the other women in the salon. Rat Face, skinny from years of worrying and smoking, could come nowhere near this sort of perfection. Meanwhile, the older bride slunk back into her changing room and emerged in a pair of ill-fitting jeans that showed her big arse in all its glory. Round one of Bride Wars to Diana Ashcroft.

CHAPTER
ELEVEN

30 October 2010

Back in London, Kate wondered what on earth had possessed her to put down a deposit for a dress Richard Branson might have filled with hot air and taken to the moon. She didn't dare tell Ian what had happened. Though both of them made good money — great money, in fact — she had a feeling that he would be unimpressed by the idea that she had spent the cost of a damn good holiday on a dress she would wear for at best half a day. They were supposed to be getting married at a register office in March and following that with lunch at one of their favourite restaurants. If she told Ian about the dress, he would think she had gone mad. Ian's theory, casually aired to Kate's brother-in-law, that inside every girl was a Bridezilla just waiting to come out would be proved to be true.

In any case, there was more to think about than a dress. Kate had just a month left in her current job. There were an awful lot of loose ends to be tied up before she could go on gardening leave. And now there was her mother's biopsy to think about too. If the news turned out to be as bad as Elaine seemed certain it would be, Kate had a feeling she would be spending much of her gardening leave in Washam. All that seemed far more real than planning a wedding.

It still hadn't quite sunk into Kate's brain that she was going to get married. Perhaps it was simply that work and her mother's health were much more pressing, but perhaps it was that Kate was finding it hard to shake years of not even daring to dream that she would one day find herself engaged. After she and Dan broke up for the last time, Kate had rather given up on the idea of ever being in a long-term relationship again, let alone getting married. But then she met Ian, and now she was going to have a wedding, albeit a full decade later than "the norm".

"Has hell frozen over?" asked one of her college friends when she telephoned to tell him the news. Even her very best female friends — Helen and Anne, who had known her since the three of them had rocked up at Cambridge, aged eighteen — agreed that they wouldn't have put money on this particular outcome, though they were absolutely delighted, of course.

But no matter how often Kate kept pinching herself, expecting the status quo to be restored at any moment, Ian was still there beside her when she woke up in the morning. He had been beside her for only eleven months but already it was starting to feel as though Kate had never been without him. She certainly never wanted to be without him again. Spending the rest of her life with him should be a breeze.

When people asked how they met, Ian would say, "In a bar." He wouldn't be drawn any further. Ian liked to keep things simple. Plus, he was slightly embarrassed by the truth.

"Your version of events makes me sound like an alcoholic nympho who hangs around in public places waiting for unsuspecting men," Kate protested, but Ian did not want people to know they had met through a dating site.

Kate had no such qualms, though she found that when she said, "We met on Sugardaddy.com," people were generally too amused to ask for the whole truth, which was that she and Ian had found one another on Guardian Soulmates. Perhaps it wasn't as romantic as eyes across a room, but, realistically, where else would she have met her match at such a late stage in the game? The pool Kate could fish from had dwindled dramatically during the four years she had wasted with Dan. She just didn't meet single men any more. She didn't have a wing-woman with whom to go clubbing. Most of her friends had long since paired up and were on to their second, third or even fourth babies. Kate's social diary was all fortieth birthday parties and christenings. She hadn't been invited to a wedding in years. The choice was simple: it was sign up or never have sex again for the rest of her life.

Kate actually passed over Ian's profile the first time she saw it. He hadn't included a photograph and the computer declared them to be just a 20 per cent match. Despite such a damning assessment, Ian wrote to her anyway, and through his emails he soon set himself apart from the crowd. He was polite and thoughtful. There was none of the innuendo that she had come to expect. He didn't seem to be trying to gauge whether she might be up for a one-night stand. Ian said in his profile that he was looking for a serious relationship and he approached their early acquaintance accordingly. Kate was glad. The week before Ian started writing to her, she had become embroiled in a furious email slanging match with a man who accused her of being a "frigid bitch with an agenda" because she asked if she could have his phone number in preference to giving him hers for the sake of personal safety. In that context, perhaps it was easy for Ian to seem refreshingly normal. Whatever, by the time Ian let Kate see his photo, she was already sold. She knew she would definitely meet him.

Ian's behaviour on their first date was equally gentlemanly. He was waiting for her when she arrived at the bar where they agreed to meet for a drink. He said he had been there for fifteen minutes already to make sure she didn't find herself alone. He didn't want her to feel awkward. Kate appreciated that. She had chosen a drink at a bar as the safe option. As a veteran of Internet dates, she knew only too well that what seemed promising online could quickly turn into a nightmare when you brought it into the real world. She was determined not to be stuck spending a whole evening with a man whose conversation began and ended with the Inland Revenue, for example, as had happened the month before.

So Kate had made sure she had another appointment lined up. She had arranged to meet Helen for dinner at a restaurant close by. If this meeting with Ian went badly, then at least she and Helen would have something to laugh about later. So Kate was pleased and surprised to find that she and Ian had far from run out of conversation by the time the moment to leave rolled around. Quite the opposite, in fact; it was hard to drag herself away. Over dinner, she found herself telling happily married Helen that she thought she might have met someone *really* nice.

"Oh, yeah? You thought Dan was 'really nice' at the beginning," Helen reminded her. Helen had held Kate's hand through her many break-ups from Dan, from the first one, which had only lasted for a week, until the last, which had been surprisingly permanent. Kate often wished she'd taken Helen's advice to give Dan up as a lost cause far earlier.

"No, really. He is nothing like Dan."

"Well," said Helen, "I'm glad to see you looking so excited. Just promise me you'll be careful. Take it easy. At least make sure he's not married before you sleep with him."

"He's definitely not married," said Kate. "I think he's just a straightforward nice guy who's been too busy setting up his career to settle down. He's the kind of guy you always said I should look for."

Helen picked up her glass. "I'll raise a toast to that."

The second date, for which Kate allowed a whole evening, was just as lovely. Kate was impressed by Ian's modesty, even though throughout the course of the meal it became clear that he had done some pretty impressive stuff with his life. He was very successful in his career. He was a partner in a big accountancy firm.

He had grown up in Telford and was the first member of his family to go to university. He hadn't forgotten his roots, though. He saw his family often. He doted on his nephews, his sister's boys.

By the end of the second date, Kate knew that she really, *really* liked this ordinary man and would definitely be seeing him again. It was just so easy to be with him. Dates three, four and five totally restored her faith in single men.

With Ian, there was none of the usual trauma she associated with early dates. He called when he said he would. He always wanted to know what she was doing at the weekend. This experience was a world away from the nightmare of the early days with Dan. Kate remembered one horrible Sunday when she and Dan had arranged to have lunch together. He had promised to call first thing on Sunday with the plan. He didn't call until two o'clock, by which time Kate had already made herself a sandwich. Dan blamed his flakiness on the trauma of his divorce.

"I find it very hard to be pinned down," he said.

"It's hardly being pinned down," Kate tried. "If you ask someone to have lunch on a Sunday, they in return expect you to call and tell them when and where before one o'clock on the Sunday afternoon."

Ian had no psychological excuses for bad behaviour because, it seemed, he simply had no intention of behaving badly.

After they'd been dating for about three months, Kate and Ian went on a mini-break to Copenhagen.

They spent three nights in a charming hotel right by the port.

"This is the first time we've spent three nights in a row together," Kate pointed out. "Do you think we could go for four?"

"I think we could go for a whole lot more than four," said Ian.

Kate had forgotten — or perhaps she had never really known — just how easy a relationship could be. Ian was constantly thinking of ways to amuse her. One morning, having stayed over, he left a note in her fridge, on a Post-it stuck to the milk.

"You are lovely," was all it said.

It was such a simple little gesture, but it reduced Kate to happy tears. There were so many moments like that.

Kate hadn't really expected to find love through a website. It seemed too clinical a medium ever to inspire grand passion. She had thought that Dan was the love of her life. Certainly, no one had ever brought out in her such a range of emotions. However, as time passed, she began to realise that as far as Dan was concerned, her overriding emotion had actually been frustration. Frustration that he just didn't seem able to move their relationship forward. Frustration that after four years he still hadn't introduced her to his children, who were by that time seventeen and nineteen, and doubtless had much more to worry about than whether or not their father was dating again.

Ian would not make Kate feel frustrated. At least, not in the same way.

There was only one small seed of doubt in Kate's mind: Ian was very different from the men Kate had dated before. Her preference had always been for tortured, soulful types. By contrast Ian was remarkably simple. His approach to life was in fact so simple that about six months in, Kate wondered if she would be bored, but as Tess pointed out, she'd had an awful lot of practice with the tortured, soulful types and none of it had got her anywhere near the altar.

"Easy is good. Just go with it," Tess had advised her.

Almost a year after their first date, Kate was still going with it and it was working out very well indeed.

For once she was glad she had taken her sister's advice.

CHAPTER
TWELVE

Diana thought that people who had to resort to Internet dating must be profoundly sad. She couldn't begin to imagine how terrible it must be to have to sift for a partner among strangers online. She herself had never had a problem finding a date. At junior school, she was always the first girl in her class to get a Valentine. One year, she had seven. The trend of adoration continued when she moved up to a private secondary school. At the end of her second year there, Diana was voted "Most Beautiful Girl in School" by the boys in the year above.

Diana's only problem was that a girl with as much to offer as she had needed a really special man. During Diana's teenage years, boyfriends were picked up and discarded for all manner of reasons: not good-looking enough, not rich enough, not well connected enough in the nightclubs around town . . . Very few lasted for more than a month. From the age of twenty to twenty-three, Diana dated a nightclub promoter, but she dropped him when he said he had no intention of getting married before he hit fifty. (He was twenty-five.) Diana was not prepared to wait around.

She had hoped that ditching the promoter would be the wake-up call he needed. When he didn't immediately give in to her demands, Diana knew she needed a different strategy. The strategy was to make him jealous. The man she intended to use to make him jealous was Ben.

Diana had been aware of Ben for years. He'd been in the year above her at secondary school. She'd seen him making gooey eyes at her in the corridors. She'd never returned the honour, because back then he just wasn't cool enough to warrant her attention, but now Ben was back in Southampton after three years away at university and three years working in London and the geeky boy she remembered had blossomed into an altogether more attractive prospect. Having gained experience while running the student union, Ben was promoting a new club to rival Diana's ex-lover's. Diana and Nicole went along to the opening night and Diana quickly made her interest known.

Having reintroduced herself to Ben and spent half an hour putting in the spadework of making sure he knew that he might be in with a chance, Diana set about leading him a merry dance, which included insisting on a rendezvous at her ex-boyfriend's club night. Mesmerised by any hint of attention from the most beautiful girl in school, Ben would have followed Diana anywhere. It took three months for him to get her into bed. The very next day, Diana had Ben take her for Sunday lunch at her ex-boyfriend's local. She just about managed to hide her fury when her ex told her, "I'm glad you're moving on."

Faced with that obvious uninterest, Diana convinced herself that she *was* actually moving on. Rather than viewing Ben as a stepping stone to getting her ex back, she started to look for evidence that she had in fact traded up. He was good-looking. He was from a great family. One of his cousins had trialled for the Chelsea youth team. Plus, he was just starting out as a promoter. He had a glittering career ahead of him, she was sure.

But Ben's club-promotion career never quite took off. There were problems with drug-dealing and underage drinking. The police were there night after night. It was possible that Diana's ex had set him up. For whatever reason, Ben decided that the life of a promoter wasn't for him. He diverted more energy into his day job in IT.

When Ben announced that he was retiring from the club scene, Diana was disappointed not to be the girlfriend of a promoter any more, but she decided that being the partner of an IT expert might be just as good. Certainly, Ben made more money at his day job. His bonuses were quite impressive. She was very happy to cruise around town in his big, new Audi. As she entered her late twenties, Diana was increasingly aware of competition in the form of younger girls. It was time to settle down, Diana decided. With her behind him, Ben could achieve great things. They could make it work.

Surprisingly, though Diana had always considered herself to be the "bigger catch", Ben seemed as reluctant to make things official as Diana's ex had been. Eventually, she persuaded him that it was worth their buying a house. Panicked by the seemingly inexorable rise of house prices, Ben had agreed. However, he didn't really have enough to buy the kind of place that Diana wanted. It was with help from Diana's father that they bought a new-build four-bedroomed house at the very height of the market.

After that, Diana concentrated her efforts on getting an engagement ring. She spoke glowingly of the advantages of marriage. She invited her married friends over all the time, as though to prove to Ben that settling down needn't mean an end to having fun. Still Ben resisted. He said they were too young.

The last thing Diana expected was for her big break to come in the shape of Ben's infidelity. Had she known how it would play out, she might have tried an ultimatum before. But perhaps it was the fact that her threat to leave Ben was so very real that this ultimatum worked.

"I was so frightened you'd leave me," said Ben when Diana agreed to stay if and only if they got engaged.

Ben had no idea how frightened Diana had been that she would be the one who ended up on a dating site. She was nearing thirty and she had no intention of passing that milestone alone. She was never going to let him go.

CHAPTER
THIRTEEN

16 November 2010

"Oh my God!"

The busy showroom of Bride on Time was brought to a halt by a scream from the backroom.

"OhmiGod, ohmiGod, ohmiGod."

Sarah, who, at twenty-three years old, was the youngest of the three full-time bridal consultants, came out of the backroom flapping her hands and hyperventilating. She couldn't get her words out. She skipped round the salon three times before Melanie pulled up a chair and pushed her down into it.

"Whatever's the matter?"

A bridal consultant gone loopy would not be good for business. The showroom was packed that afternoon. Four brides and their attendants all stopped and stared.

On the chair, Sarah continued to fight to find the breath to speak. She fanned her face with a Pronovias catalogue. She mouthed words but made no sound.

"Sarah? Sarah? Whatever is up?" Melanie asked.

"You're not going to believe it," Sarah said at last. "They're getting married."

An awful lot of people who came to Bride on Time were getting married, Melanie pointed out. "Who?"

"Prince William and Kate Middleton. There's an announcement on the *Mail*'s website!"

One of the brides being fitted that afternoon had an iPhone. She quickly tapped through to the *Daily Mail*'s website. It was true. The palace had announced the young couple's engagement just that afternoon.

"Oh, that's wonderful," said Melanie. The phone was passed around. There was much cooing over the royal fiancée and her prince. The good feeling generated by the news was palpable. There wasn't a woman in the room who didn't remember Prince William as the child behind his mother's coffin and for that reason alone everyone automatically wished him every happiness.

"It's exactly what his mother would have wanted," said Heidi. "Him marrying a commoner."

"Kate Middleton is hardly common," said Sarah. "She's privately educated. She has millionaire parents."

"You know what I mean. She doesn't have a title. Her mother was an air hostess."

"Nothing wrong with that," said Melanie, quickly remembering that one of that afternoon's brides worked for Virgin Atlantic. "Well," she addressed the crowd, "I think this is cause for celebration. Sarah, there's a bottle of Prosecco in the fridge. Will you bring it out here and" — she did a quick headcount — "thirteen paper cups. Make it fourteen. Thirteen's unlucky."

"But . . ." Sarah hesitated. She glanced at the sign with the scored-through teacup. What about the salon's strict no-food-and-beverages policy?

74

"It's a special occasion," said Melanie, "and I know these ladies will be very careful . . . Open the bottle over the sink."

There was hardly enough sparkling wine for each of the assembled women to have a thimbleful, but Melanie knew it was important to mark the occasion. In her experience, women in love were a superstitious lot and to hear the announcement of a royal wedding while in a bridal salon would doubtless come to mean something for all the assembled brides. It was up to Melanie to make sure they assumed it was a good omen. Good omens meant better sales. While the Prosecco was poured, there was much excited talk about the possible choice of wedding date. Would sharing a wedding date with the royal couple be a good or a bad thing? one of the brides asked.

"It might distract from your day," said another.

"But there'll be a national holiday, won't there? Your guests would get an extra day off and could make a long weekend of it."

"Why don't you let me tell you my experience," said Melanie.

Melanie remembered how excited she had felt when she first learned that Charles and Diana would share her wedding day, 29 July 1981. She and Keith had chosen the day well ahead of the royal couple since, for them, getting married meant saving hard for at least two years beforehand. Melanie's parents chipped in their traditional share, of course, but for the kind of party Melanie wanted, extra funding was required. She and Keith worked all hours to pay for their evening do. They wanted a really big bash.

"We're only going to do this once," said Keith.

When Charles and Diana announced their date, Melanie had whooped with delight. Melanie loved that she was getting married on the same day as the royal couple. The entire population of Southampton really went to town in their preparations to celebrate the future king and his wife, and Melanie was happy to imagine that the flags and the bunting were for her too. For her and Keith. How could having the entire nation in such high spirits have failed to have anything but a positive effect on anyone else getting married that day?

The only problem Melanie and Keith encountered was that one of his elderly aunts was prevented from getting to the church on time after getting lost on the drive there thanks to all the street-party road closures, but even that wasn't too much of a headache. Auntie Mildred had been perfectly happy to spend an afternoon sipping sherry with strangers. Nobody was a stranger that day. The nation was united in the celebration of love.

Mel and Keith's wedding reception was held in a country-house hotel. As a wedding gift, Keith's parents had booked a room there for the happy couple on their inaugural night as Mr and Mrs Harris. Before the wedding breakfast was served, Melanie and Keith sneaked up there for a moment alone. On the television, Prince Charles and his new princess had just appeared on the balcony at Buckingham Palace, where they shared their first public kiss, to the cheers of the crowds lining the Mall.

Melanie and Keith sat on the end of the bed and watched the moment unfold.

"I love you, Mrs Harris."

"I love you, Mr Harris."

"I love you more."

"It was perfect. Any bride who gets to share her wedding day with Kate Middleton can count herself lucky, in my opinion. As far as I'm concerned, getting married on the same day as Charles and Diana really made my wedding," Melanie concluded. "It seemed as though the whole country was wishing us well."

The assembled brides murmured their assent. Melanie thought she was preaching to the choir.

"But look how their marriage turned out," said one of that day's customers, a younger sister who wasn't impressed with being picked as a bridesmaid. She was dressed all in black and had a stud through her nose. She didn't look as though she had much time for anything romantic. "I don't think marrying Charles was lucky for Diana at all," she continued. "If she hadn't married him, she wouldn't have ended up being dead in a car crash, would she?"

The young woman's words had everyone looking pensive. It was hard to disagree with her view that marriage to Charles had been the first step on the path that led Diana to her horrible death. All the same, Melanie made a gargantuan effort to put a happier spin on things.

"Without Diana marrying Charles, lovely Kate wouldn't have her own prince to marry," Melanie pointed out. "The silver lining is those beautiful boys of hers. Her spirit lives on through both of them."

The older women agreed and Melanie was glad she had successfully defended romance again, even though she, more than any of the women present could know, had reason to find Diana's story particularly sad.

"Now, let's get back to work, girls!" Melanie clapped her hands. "You ladies need to choose your frocks and get them ordered before that Kate Middleton comes down here and takes up all our time."

There was a ripple of laughter. As if Kate Middleton would ever set foot in Washam.

Melanie collected up all the paper cups and took them into the backroom. Alone at last, she leaned against the sink for a moment, looking out onto the road down below. Outside, it was dark already, though it was only four o'clock. Melanie wished that it were later so she could close up for the night. She could do without having to go back out into the salon in her role as cheerleader for all those happy, newly engaged romantics. Thinking about Princess Diana never failed to make her feel sad.

Melanie hadn't told many people how much Princess Diana's death had affected her. Sometimes it seemed ridiculous, like crying over the break-up of the Bay City Rollers. It wasn't as though she'd ever actually met the woman. But Diana's death had been a pivotal moment in her life. Melanie had been right there, in Paris, the night the princess died. As crazy as it sounded, Melanie felt almost as though the dead princess's ghost had walked right through her on her way to the afterlife.

Back in the UK after that awful weekend, Melanie had taken a train up to London to pay her respects in Kensington Gardens. She lay flowers with all those other flowers, which filled the air with such a heady scent that Melanie felt faint to be close to them. She had cried all the way back to Southampton. Such a waste of a life. And of love. If a woman as beautiful and lovely as Princess Diana couldn't make love work, then how could anyone else have a chance?

If she'd lived, Diana would have turned fifty in 2011 and Melanie and her husband would have celebrated their thirtieth anniversary. Tuning in to the chatter in the salon, Melanie heard Sarah explain to her client that Melanie's royal wedding story actually had a sad ending.

"She's a widow," said Sarah in a stage whisper that was clearly audible in the backroom.

"Melanie!" Heidi shouted next. "Can we have the cathedral-length veils for Jessica Stott?"

Melanie snapped back to the present.

A cathedral-length veil would make Jessica Stott, who was all of five feet in her heels, look like a child dressing up as a ghost for Halloween, but Melanie always catered to her customers' wishes. She was pretty sure that as soon as Jessica had the first veil on, she would ask for something shorter.

"Coming right out," she said.

Melanie paused by a mirror. She stuck her fingers in the dimples that Keith had always loved.

"Happy face." She smiled, pulling the corners of her sad mouth upwards.

CHAPTER
FOURTEEN

The day of Kate and William's engagement announcement brought much less welcome news for the Williamson family. Elaine's biopsy had confirmed the presence of malignant cells. Cancer. Suddenly, the much-maligned NHS swung into impressive action as the oncologists drew up a treatment plan. There was no question that Elaine would have to have a lumpectomy. After that, there would be radiotherapy and perhaps a whole bunch of other therapies that sounded nowhere near as much fun as the therapies Kate indulged in at the beauty salon near her office.

"This is terrible," Kate said to Tess.

"It's not a death sentence," Tess reminded her. "Plenty of people get through this."

But Kate had never had her younger sister's stoicism. She couldn't just treat the news of her mother's breast tumour as she might have treated news of something like, say, a gallstone. Though in theory you could just as likely die while having your gall bladder removed as a tumour, the word "cancer" was so much more evocative. It was as though the letters of the word themselves were shrouded in the black cape of death.

Having Lily to care for meant that Tess couldn't spend all day dwelling on their mother's illness, but Kate could not think of anything else even while she was in the office. She spent hours online looking up breast-cancer statistics. Her mother had DCIS, ductal carcinoma in situ, which was, according to many of the websites, the simplest kind of breast cancer to deal with. And it had been caught early. There was no reason to believe the cancer had spread elsewhere. Kate printed out a stack of learned papers on the subject and tried to make sense of them in her lunch break. It shouldn't have been hard for a lawyer, right? But Kate's head swam with the unfamiliar acronyms; the difference of one or two letters could mean the difference between twenty more years or just a few months.

At four o'clock, her father called for a chat. The effort of remaining calm and upbeat for the duration of the conversation was tremendous. She told her father that her "extensive research" seemed to suggest that everything would be fine. These days, getting rid of a couple of tiny breast tumours was no more complicated than filling a rotten tooth, she assured him. Survival rates were getting higher and better year on year. She hoped that her father left the conversation feeling reassured, though Kate herself felt horribly drained. And then she had to go straight into a meeting and be her usual impressively professional self. Only she couldn't. For a start, she had spent more time looking up breast cancer than she had reading the papers she should be discussing with her colleagues. Her attention drifted back to her mother whenever she wasn't called on to speak for a while. She gazed out of the window while other people gave their opinions. She managed to make herself cry by imagining her niece's next birthday party. The prognosis for DCIS sufferers was generally good, but what if Elaine fell into the small bracket of people who were unlucky, for whom a lumpectomy didn't work? What if Elaine wasn't there to see her granddaughter turn seven? What if she couldn't make Kate's wedding? It was unthinkable. Elaine was the lynchpin of every Williamson family gathering.

"You OK?" one of her colleagues asked as they left the meeting room.

"I'm fine," said Kate. "Just a bit distracted."

"Already given up on us now you know you're leaving, eh?" The colleague raised an eyebrow.

Kate was mortified. "No. It's not that. It's just that —"

"Keep your eye on the ball, Williamson," was her colleague's parting shot.

Kate fumed. That particular colleague had already suggested "in jest" that Kate was wasting time moving firms since now she was getting married, it wouldn't be long before she had children and quit altogether. It was a stunning comment, especially coming as it did from an employment lawyer.

Back in her office, Kate took a call from her mother.

"Your father said you found out a few things about my condition," she said.

Kate's heart fell. She could tell by the tone of her mother's voice that Elaine was hoping for some good news. She also had a horrible feeling that her mother would take more notice of Kate, with her 2:1 in jurisprudence, and her half-day's Googling than she would of her learned physicians.

"I can't say I've found anything out exactly, Mum. I just read a few papers online. One was written by your consultant, Mr Calil. He seems to be pretty well respected in the field."

"Oh, I'm glad you think that. I know it sounds silly, but it's just . . . it's just he looks so young! I can't believe he's really done all that training."

"He's not that young, Mum. He's a year older than I am. He's got more letters after his name than most of the professors at my college ever had."

"OK. Well, if you think he's qualified . . ."

"He's definitely qualified. You don't get to be a consultant without taking exams year after year. You have to train your entire career." Kate made that last bit up, but it sounded right. Possibly it was right.

"There was an article in the *Daily Mail* about a man who impersonated a doctor. He ended up running a whole hospital in Utah."

"That's the States, Mum. I'm sure they have different criteria there. That would never happen on the NHS."

Or would it? While her mother chatted, Kate typed "fake surgeon" into the Google search box. It produced a horribly large number of hits.

"I've got to go, Mum. I've a meeting in ten minutes."

"Oh, I'm sorry, sweetheart. We know you're busy."

That made it worse. Kate wasn't really too busy. She didn't really have another meeting that day. She just didn't think she could continue to hold it together, and the last thing her mother needed right then was to hear Kate cry.

That evening, she couldn't wait to get back to Ian's flat, which was where they had been spending most nights since the engagement. (They were properly living together for the first time. Kate would be moving the rest of her things into Ian's flat when her gardening leave began, leaving her own place empty and ready to be put on the market.) Unfortunately, that night, the Tube conspired against her. Random delays held her underground for far longer than most people could stand. Kate, full of worry for her parents, thought that she might have to scream. When she got to the flat, Ian was already home, sitting at his PC, comparing the price of one package of accountancy software to another ostensibly identical package. Ian could occupy himself for hours with such a seemingly pointless endeavour. Internet prices rarely differed that much from site to site any more. Still, Ian was absorbed. He didn't look up as Kate walked by his office door on her way to the kitchen. She had never quite got used to that. She'd told him that it bothered her the way he didn't say, "Hello," unless she said it first.

"Don't you want to know who's come into the flat?" she asked him. "I could be anyone. I could be a burglar. Why don't you at least look up?"

"Because I know it's you," said Ian simply. "I can tell by the way you sigh when you're hanging up your coat."

That night, Ian went one better. While he did not call out, "Hello," as Kate walked down the hall, he did decide, five minutes later, that it was appropriate to shout out, "What's for dinner?"

The floodgates opened. Of all the evenings when Kate really needed a hug upon her return to the flat, Ian could not have chosen a worse one to fail so absolutely to anticipate her needs.

"You can sort out your own bloody dinner," she shouted. She threw a dirty mug into the cold water in the sink and left it there. When Ian eventually came to look for her, Kate was face down on their double bed. She hadn't even taken her shoes off. And she was crying like a child. When Ian touched her, she flipped over onto her back so that he could experience the full horror of her fear and premature grief. She didn't feel like hiding it from him. She wanted him to know just how miserable she was. She let her mouth fall open and she bawled.

Ian's face was a picture of panic.

"What's the matter? What's happened?"

Kate just continued to bawl.

"I don't know what to do," Ian said, when it was clear that she wasn't about to stop crying. "Is it something I did? Is it something I said?"

"No," said Kate. "No, of course it's not."

"Then what am I supposed to do? What should I say?"

"You could have just given me a hug when I walked through the door instead of asking me what's for bloody dinner. My mum has cancer, Ian. Actual bloody cancer."

"But isn't it early stage?"

"That doesn't make it better! I've had a terrible day. I can't take it any longer. I just need a hug."

"I can give you a hug." Ian held out his arms to give her the hug he thought she'd asked for, but Kate just shook her head.

"It's too late now. I want to be on my own. Go away."

She sent him out of the bedroom. Ian lost more points by not even trying to stay.

Kate was still in a foul mood when Ian came to bed three hours later. Not even the cup of tea he brought with him could shake her out of it. He brought more disapprobation upon himself when he managed to fall asleep in an instant, leaving Kate wide awake and utterly unable to persuade her racing brain to switch off.

As he had got ready for bed, Ian had asked her to tell him about the diagnosis, but she hadn't felt able to. She didn't want to have to say the ugly words out loud again. Now she was angry with him for not having *insisted* that she get the whole story out there. It might have helped. He might have lain awake too. As it was, he was sleeping like a baby, as usual. Nothing was worrying his big, fat head.

Kate rolled away from Ian's body, irritated by even the sound of his breathing. It was only then that she saw the small black box on the bedside table. Her engagement ring had arrived.

CHAPTER
FIFTEEN

What interested Diana most about the engagement of Kate Middleton and Prince William was that they had actually become engaged on the same day as Diana and Ben. That meant that Diana had a special interest in all the astrological websites that posted charts for the auspicious day, twenty ten, twenty ten. Diana was very pleased to see that she and Ben had become engaged under such good stars.

There was, of course, still the question of the actual wedding to come. Diana pondered the suggestions the press put forward. The royals would choose a summer wedding, surely, the better to cash in on the boost to tourism such a special occasion would bring. God knows the UK needed such a lift.

Diana also closely examined the outfit Kate Middleton had chosen for the couple's engagement announcement. She wondered if Kate's hair was its natural colour. Did she have extensions, or was her long, glossy mane simply the result of good breeding and great nutrition? Diana bought every newspaper she could lay her hands on in the hope of finding a clue. She made notes of the names of Kate's hairdresser and facialist, and began to plan a trip to London to engage their services herself. She pencilled a date on the chart she had bought especially for the purpose of wedding-planning.

Susie agreed that the news that Diana and Prince William had become engaged on the same day was auspicious. She told her daughter that she had always been convinced that the spirit of Princess Diana was looking out for her. "I mean, think about it, sweetheart. You were born on the day that she married and became engaged on the same day as her son. That doesn't seem like a coincidence. That seems like karma. The princess will make sure your wedding is every bit as good as Will and Kate's."

Diana shared this view with Ben as they settled down to sleep that night.

"Wouldn't it be amazing if they chose to get married on the same day as us? That would be proof that Princess Di is on our side."

"They're unlikely to get married in April," said Ben. "That's nowhere near long enough to plan a big wedding."

"We're planning *our* wedding for the end of April," Diana pointed out. "Our wedding is going to be big too."

"Yes," said Ben, "but for us it's just a matter of booking the venue and sending out the invites. They've got to close down a nation, mount security for heads of state from all over the world, have some special coins minted . . . Kate Middleton has got more to worry about than her dress."

There was a pause of the sort that Ben had come to recognise as a harbinger of trouble. He heard Diana's sharp intake of breath and knew he had somehow offended her.

"Is that all you think I've got to worry about? My dress? Do you think that finding a venue for the reception and thinking up a colour scheme and finding a caterer and booking a band and making sure it goes to plan is going to be easy?"

"I didn't mean that, but —"

Diana sat up in bed and switched her bedside lamp on. "That is what you think, isn't it? You think that all I have to do is buy the dress and get my hair done. Do you have any idea how stressful this wedding-planning is for me *already*? I'm going to show you my chart. Do you know how much I have to get done in the next five months?"

"We could always push it back a bit," said Ben, slightly too eagerly.

"No way," said Diana, already out of bed and looking for her A3 pad. "Absolutely no way. But I do need as much time as I can get, Ben. In fact, I think I might have to leave work."

"What?"

Now Ben was sitting up in bed too.

When, a few days later, the royal wedding was set for 29 April 2011, the day before Ben and Diana's own big day, Diana's mind was made up. Kate Middleton would not be working in the run-up to her wedding, so how could she, Diana, be expected to hold down her job, run their home and plan a wedding too?

"Kate Middleton is marrying the freaking heir to the throne," Ben pointed out.

Diana deferred to her mother and father, who both agreed that Diana should take a small career break for this most important day of her life.

"You are my princess, after all," said her mother.

That was good enough for Diana. Ben would just have to get used to it.

CHAPTER
SIXTEEN

27 November 2010

Kate had no idea what planning a wedding involved. While Diana was already letting the stress bubble up in her, five months in advance, Kate hadn't thought beyond booking the slot at the register office for a Saturday in mid-March. She assumed that once she was on gardening leave, it would be relatively easy to pull together a lunch party for forty. (A honeymoon would have to wait until Kate had been in her new job for a little while.) And of course she already had the dress. That stupid dress. Over a quick lunch to celebrate Kate's engagement, Helen and Anne had dissolved into tears of laughter when Kate admitted that she'd accidentally put down a deposit on a meringue. There was, Kate hoped, still time to let her mother down gently over that. Maybe that weekend. And maybe, just maybe, Bride on Time would not yet have put her order through so she could get her money back.

Kate had often felt guilty that she didn't spend enough time with her parents since they had retired, and now her mother's diagnosis made it seem important to spend all the time she could with them.

Luckily, the wedding made it possible for her to drop down to Washam without making it obvious that she wanted to keep an eye on her mum and see how her father was coping.

The weekend after the definitive cancer diagnosis, Kate was at her parents' place again. They were going to visit a wedding fair held at a local luxury hotel.

"It will cheer Mum up," was Tess's reasoning when she announced the plan. "Plus, you might get some ideas."

"For what?"

"For what you absolutely don't want to do."

Ian had declined to go with them.

"Aren't you worried I might come home having spent all our money on sugared almonds?" Kate asked.

"No," said Ian. "I know you wouldn't do that."

"How do you know?" Kate asked him.

"I trust you," he said, and gave her a hug. He had been giving her an awful lot of hugs since the night Kate had her freak-out over the cancer news. She had cried pretty much all night. For her mother, for herself and because she had been so vile to Ian, when all the time he could have — and might have, were he less subtle or more clever — pulled out the engagement ring in an attempt to shut her up. She loved him for not having done that. She loved him even more when he finally did put the ring on her finger the next morning.

The solitaire, with its simple gold setting, glittered against the steering wheel as Kate drove down to the south coast on her own again. She dropped her car off at her parents' house and got into the back of her dad's car for the short trip to the hotel. Her sister had leaped upon the excuse to leave Lily with her father, Mike.

"It's a long time since I got to go to a wedding fair," Tess said.

Kate didn't remember having accompanied Tess to anything like a wedding fair. It was possibly because at the time that Tess got married, she and Kate weren't as close as they had become in their thirties. Kate had thought Tess was old before her time, getting married at twenty-five. She was sure that Tess looked down on her and thought her flat-sharing, single life quite tragic. And Kate wasn't wrong about that. At the time that she got married, Tess did feel rather sorry for her older sister, but now, twelve years and one daughter on, Tess didn't mind admitting that she wished she could have experienced some of Kate's freedom. She wished she'd travelled. She wished she'd lived alone for a while. The grass is always greener.

Kate was glad that Tess was coming with her and both their parents to the bridal fair. Tess could always be relied upon to fill an awkward silence with some tale about her child. Just that morning, said Tess, Lily had walked into the kitchen at breakfast time and addressed her parents with the cheery line "Hello, old people." When Mike had pointed out that wasn't very nice, Lily had amended her greeting to "Hello, poo people."

"Lily would have liked to come to this bridal fair," said her proud grandmother Elaine.

"She'd have had her sticky fingers into everything," said Tess. "It would have cost me a fortune in damages."

Tess and Elaine remembered an afternoon when Lily had climbed into a bedding display in the enormous branch of Marks & Spencer at Hedge End. The shop assistants had smiled indulgently as Lily pretended to snuggle down for the night. They were a little less pleased when Lily climbed back out of the bed, leaving a streak of brown on the bottom sheet. Tess still shuddered as she remembered trying to persuade the shop assistants that it really was just chocolate.

"You're right. It's not a good idea to let Lily anywhere near a wedding dress," Elaine conceded.

"I will make sure she doesn't have any chocolate on your big day," Tess told Kate.

"She's going to make a lovely bridesmaid," said Elaine.

"I don't know if I can have bridesmaids at the register office," Kate pointed out.

"Of course you'll be allowed to have bridesmaids," said Elaine. "I've seen pictures of bridesmaids coming out of the register office in Southampton. Besides, you're going to need help with that skirt."

"Ah, yes, about that dress —" Kate saw her moment but failed to take it before she was interrupted.

"Lily has already asked me if she's going to get a new dress too."

"She'd make a beautiful bridesmaid," said John from the driver's seat.

"All right," said Kate. "I'll ask Ian."

The online advertisement for the bridal fair had suggested opulent surroundings in the form of the

Grange Hill Hotel. The photograph of the hotel used to illustrate the ad showed a smiling couple walking out through an ivy-covered doorway to a Rolls-Royce parked on an immaculate gravel drive. As soon as John turned off the dual carriageway at the first sign for the hotel, Kate had a feeling that the website had somewhat oversold the event. The official wooden sign, which could have used a coat of paint, had been embellished with a plain sheet of A4 paper, on which someone had written, "Bridel Fayr," in Magic Marker.

"Can't get the staff these days," John commented as he took in the mistake. Two further signs drawing punters towards the hotel advertised the bridal fair with different variations on the spelling of the words: "Bridle Farye" and "Bridul Faire." Kate was ready to ask her father to turn the car round then take them to a pub on the seafront.

But Tess and Elaine were determined. They had planned the whole afternoon around this bridal extravaganza. They would look around the first half of the fair — the advertisement had promised more than three hundred exhibitors — then they would break for lunch in the hotel's garden room, which was trumpeted as the ideal venue for a top-class wedding reception.

"We should definitely check that out," said Tess.

"But we're getting married in London," Kate reminded her sister.

"It's still useful to have a comparison."

"Yes," said Elaine. "In any case, today they're doing two main courses for ten pounds. We could have Sunday lunch for twenty pounds. I don't think I could cook a roast for that if I bought all the ingredients from Marks & Spencer."

"I'm hungry already," John agreed.

They had reached the gravel driveway of the Grange Hill Hotel. There was no romance to it. John feared for the bodywork of his new Passat and refused to drive at anywhere near the recommended ten miles per hour. A queue of traffic built up behind them like a funeral cortege as John stuck to two miles an hour so that any gravel thrown up by the wheels would not damage the shiny red paint of his pride and joy.

Kate, sitting in the back with her sister (just like old times), blushed at the thought of the traffic behind them, though unlike drivers in London, none of them resorted to blowing their horns. Still, the thought that other people might be wondering what on earth her father was thinking took Kate back to a great many incidents in her childhood, when her father's idiosyncrasies had made both her and Tess squirm.

At last they reached the car park, which was full to overflowing, and got their first view of the Grange Hill Hotel. There was the beautiful ivy-covered archway, where so many newlyweds had posed for wedding pictures . . . Possibly because there was nowhere else to pose for a decent picture. The archway, which had looked Victorian or older in the photograph on the website, was attached to a block straight out of the 1960s. Less old hunting lodge than Travelodge.

"Not exactly very picturesque, is it?" Kate commented.

"The gardens are supposed to be nice," said Elaine.

98

It was hard to tell. Every spare patch of grass had been commandeered. The reason why the car park was so full was that most of the cars parked out there were in fact for hire. There were Rollers and Bentleys and old-fashioned Mercedes, all polished to glistening and bedecked with ribbons.

"I can do any colour of ribbon you like," a chauffeur told a concerned-looking bride.

There was even a London taxi, tricked out with a white rosette on the bonnet.

"You could have one of those," said John. He picked up a leaflet. "Says here it's four hundred quid for the day."

"Four hundred quid?" said Kate. "Dad, I could hire a real London taxi for less than that. Just about. Besides, getting in a cab isn't exactly a treat for Ian and me."

"How about a horse?" asked Tess.

A dopey-looking grey stood at the end of a row of Rollers, its head hanging heavy. It looked as though it couldn't pull a muscle, let alone a carriage with a bride and a groom and a dress that was three stone in weight.

"Remember Kerry's wedding," was all Kate needed to say.

The girls' cousin Kerry had hired a horse to take her to her wedding. While she was in the church saying her vows, the horse had expired right outside the door. The wedding guests, including the bride and groom, had to be held inside the nave until the knacker's van came to take poor old Dobbin away.

"Besides, you're not getting me in a horse and carriage in the middle of London. I'm not Kate Middleton."

Kate Middleton fever had already infected the wedding industry. Right inside the doorway was a sign proclaiming, "Kate Middelton dress's upstairs." Kate rolled her eyes at the multiple errors, but Tess insisted that they see the frocks anyway. Alas, the signwriting skills of the stallholder were reflected in the quality of the product. The opulent blue silk of Kate Middleton's engagement dress had been translated into a searing electric-blue polyester. Still, the dresses seemed to be flying off the hangers. Kate and Tess watched three brides fighting over the last size twelve.

"Do you think they're planning their own engagement pictures?" Tess asked.

"Do ordinary people have engagement pictures?" Kate mused.

She was about to find out.

CHAPTER
SEVENTEEN

Diana Ashcroft coolly reached over the heads of three much fatter brides to pick up a Middleton dress in a perfect ten. She held it against her body and twirled in front of the mirror like a little girl playing dressing-up.

"Oooh," said Susie, "that's lovely."

"Isn't it?" said Diana. "I'm going to get one for our engagement photos."

"Now that's a good idea."

"I'll try it on."

Moments later, Diana emerged from the makeshift changing cubicle in that dress, wearing it with such aplomb (and such a frighteningly smug expression on her face) that the three other brides all gave up the fight for the size twelve and drifted off in the direction of the nearest free cupcake.

"I don't think I've seen that dress look so good on anyone today," the stallholder said obligingly.

"Ben is going to love it," Diana said, as she smoothed the fabric over her hips. "I'll take it. How much?"

"It's two hundred pounds," said the stallholder.

"Two hundred?" Susie exclaimed.

"It's made in the same factory where Issa have all their dresses made," the stallholder explained. "I've got a contact there. So you could say it's a genuine Issa dress without the label."

Though in fact there was a label sewn into the back of the dress Diana tried on. It said, "Isa."

"I've got to have it," said Diana, handing over the card from the joint account. "Ben is going to be so amazed that I managed to get hold of one. I only hope he's got a decent enough suit to play his part. I think the one grey suit he's got is a little bit shabby."

"He's got more hair than Prince William, though," Susie pointed out.

"Oh, yeah, that reminds me I need to choose a hairdresser. I mean, these pictures are going to be around for ever."

"We'd better find you a photographer first."

Diana had a list of possible candidates gleaned from other brides, but she happily led the way into the photography section of the wedding fair, where fifty jobbing snappers vied for her attention. She browsed their portfolio albums with the cold eye of a magazine editor looking for the photographer who would shoot that year's Christmas cover. She didn't mind who she offended with her snap appraisals of the photographers' strengths and weaknesses. In fact, she told her mother that she thought they would be grateful for her feedback because it would give them an idea of what they needed to change if they wanted to get more business.

"Too old-fashioned," Diana pronounced one photographer's samples. "Though perhaps it isn't the photography that's old-fashioned but the bride. She's got that frizzy-haired kind of look that's very 1980s."

Diana was unaware that she was commenting on a photo album the photographer had produced for his sister and brother-in-law. The photographer just stood there and took the criticism on the chin. He needed all the work he could get. He even agreed that perhaps the bride wasn't the most photogenic he had ever had the opportunity to work with. It would be so much easier to get a good angle with someone as classically beautiful as Diana.

"You know what," he told her, "you might want to consider going for a more old-fashioned approach yourself. With the classic lines of your face, you should go for something timeless."

"Hmm." Diana put a finger to her cheek while the photographer pretended to frame her profile. "Perhaps you're right." She let the photographer explain his fees.

In the end, however, Diana chose a photographer who claimed that he had worked with Victoria Beckham.

"Before she was in the Spice Girls," he admitted when Diana pushed, "but they were great photos. One of them was used in her autobiography. The early years."

"Have you photographed any other celebrities?" Diana asked.

"Fern Britton," the photographer told her.

"I bet it was hard to get a good angle on that," Diana laughed.

"I'll have a much easier job with you."

Diana called her father and had him give the photographer his credit-card number. Pete, the photographer, tapped Diana's big day into his diary and they set up the engagement shoot. Diana put a big tick next to "photographer" on her to-do list.

CHAPTER
EIGHTEEN

This is such a waste of time, was the thought that ran through Kate's head as she trailed her sister and mother around the first room. Her father, claiming fatigue after the previous evening spent babysitting Lily, had excused himself to the hotel bar for a cappuccino. He was now sitting on a sofa in the hotel lobby, listening to one of eight wedding singers who would be performing that day, belting out Whitney's "I Will Always Love You". How Kate wished she could join him, but that wasn't possible. They were here to find inspiration for *her* wedding, after all. She had given up protesting that all this guff was just irrelevant for her simple register-office do.

Prior to visiting this, her first ever wedding fair, Kate had been under the impression that getting married really shouldn't be too difficult. She had never understood those brides who complained of "wedding stress". Why should joining your life with that of the man you loved be stressful? she'd asked herself.

Perhaps it was the chair accessories that did it . . .

Kate had visited the Grand Bazaar in Marrakech, but nothing had prepared her for the atmosphere in that first room, which was dedicated to everything you needed to host a wedding breakfast. In the stark conference room with its beige wallpaper and equally beige prints, a hundred vendors faced maybe thirty brides. Kate felt like she had a mark on her forehead.

"Have you thought about your cake?" someone asked her.

"Have you hired a cake stand?" asked somebody else.

"Have you considered how you're going to be dressing your chairs?"

"Dressing my chairs?"

While her sister and mother aimed doggedly for a tower of cupcakes, looking neither to the left nor right as they moved, Kate had made a rookie mistake. Fascinated by the idea that chairs needed dressing, she had accidentally engaged with one of the vendors. Now she would have to listen to the spiel.

"People commonly overlook one of the most important details of any wedding day," the vendor explained. "You've paid thousands for your dress, your bridesmaids' dresses, the flowers, the cake, the three-course meal at the reception . . . You get to the hotel and you realise . . ." The vendor clapped her hands to her mouth. "Oh my God! I've forgotten the chairs!"

"Don't most venues provide chairs?" asked Kate naively.

"Oh, yes, they provide chairs. Of course. But have you seen the kind of chairs they provide? Tatty, dirty, possibly not even matching. And even if you're lucky and the chairs are not that bad, do you really want to risk getting red-velvet upholstery when you've gone to

106

such an effort with your simple salmon-pink scheme? It's a nightmare."

"I'll take your word for it."

The vendor carried on. "I can make sure that chairs are no longer a worry." She directed Kate's eye to the three chairs arrayed behind her. They were all draped in plain white cotton covers. The vendor flourished a handful of ribbons.

"Have you chosen your colour scheme? Name your colour."

"I don't know . . ."

"Go on. Any colour."

"Purple," said Kate.

The vendor pulled out an imperial-purple band. She looped the ribbon round one of the white-covered chairs and tied it in a wonky bow. "Ta da! Now isn't that better than red velvet?"

Kate nodded.

"It's the finishing touch that will make all the difference. And at just fifteen pounds for a chair, you can hardly afford not to do it."

Fifteen pounds didn't seem like an awful lot of money for a chair, Kate agreed.

"Not for the whole chair," the vendor explained. "Fifteen pounds for the hire of the chair cover and the ribbon. And an extra five pounds per chair if you don't want to have to tie the ribbons yourself."

"So twenty pounds per chair is what you're really saying?"

"It depends on the ribbon. If you want a difficult colour or you also want some tulle . . ."

Kate shook her head. "I don't want to waste your time," she said.

"You don't want to think about chair-dressing?"

"I really haven't decided if we're having chairs at all. Maybe we'll do a Moroccan theme," she ad-libbed.

"We can also provide floor cushions." The vendor was undeterred.

Kate backed away trying to calculate that woman's fee per hour. As a lawyer, Kate often found herself having to justify her hourly fee, but twenty quid to fling a cover over a chair and tie a piece of silk round it? That was just spectacular. It wasn't even as though the woman had much talent when it came to making bows.

"I just had the most ridiculous conversation about chair accessories," she whispered to Tess, who had joined a circle of brides round a cupcake stand. "Twenty quid a chair. I tell you, I'm giving up law."

Tess nodded.

The cupcake vendor was explaining her own tariff of extraordinary prices. "The price is per cupcake and varies according to how many you have. They start at seven pounds fifty per cake. Hire of the cake stand is extra."

"This is insanity," Kate said without moving her mouth. "How much does it cost to make a cupcake?"

The samples were passed around. Tess politely nibbled on a cake iced with a picture of a shoe.

"And a shoe? For crying out loud," Kate hissed. "What's this obsession with grown women and shoes?"

The vendor must have heard.

"You can have any design you like. I've done shoes and handbags and sweet little dresses on padded hangers."

"For weddings?"

"Yes, for weddings. Of course."

"I don't think shoes and handbags are quite my fiancé's style."

"Oh, you're the bride! I thought perhaps you had a daughter getting married," said Mrs Cupcake.

Kate took the woman's leaflet, but the moment the conversation was over, she dropped the leaflet on the floor. And then promptly felt guilty and picked it up again. To alleviate her guilt, she made a show of reading the leaflet's opening paragraph. Apparently, Mrs Cupcake had given up a "high-powered job in the City" to indulge her "passion for baking". Kate wondered which bank had let such an obvious asset go. Seven pounds fifty for a flipping cake you could pick up for twenty pence at a Brownies' bring-and-buy sale. If that woman was really as busy as she claimed, she had found a way to turn flour into gold.

Kate was ready to leave the bridal fair long before her mother and her sister, but they insisted on the scheduled lunch in the hotel's restaurant. Kate tried to make her excuses over the roast lamb.

"Want to get back to London before the traffic gets bad," she said.

She just wanted to get the hell out of there. If she heard one more version of "(Everything I Do) I Do It for You", she thought she might scream. Not even the restaurant was safe. A Prince Charles impressionist was making the rounds of the tables, explaining how he could bring a bit of class to any ordinary wedding reception by announcing the speeches in the style of the future king.

"Keep that man away from me," Kate hissed to her sister.

As if lunch wasn't stressful enough, the strain of not mentioning the cancer was telling on everyone. Kate knew that her father wasn't just tired from having looked after Lily. He was exhausted from all the bad news. Despite having plastered on the make-up, Elaine was looking grey with worry. Tess's forced jollity was bordering on insanity. And somehow, pretending to be excited about bloody cupcakes just made the whole thing worse.

Diana and her mother were having an altogether better time. The Prince Charles impersonator who had given Kate the creeps was exactly what Diana was looking for.

"We've got to have the Prince Charles impersonator, Mum, to tie in with the royal-wedding theme."

Susie agreed that it was an excellent idea. It would fit in with the theme. Plus, Prince Charles's £500 fee was one less pair of Louboutins for her ex-husband Dave's new wife.

"Quick lunch?" Diana suggested. "Then I want to talk to someone about chair-dressing."

CHAPTER
NINETEEN

While Kate was enduring the strained happiness of lunch in Washam, lucky Ian had spent the afternoon watching West Ham play Wigan. Ian was nuts about West Ham. He had been a season-ticket holder ever since he could afford it and attended home matches without fail. He had quite a group of mates among the regulars in his stand. They met for lunch before a match and went for a few beers afterwards. Kate could smell the beer on Ian's breath as he hugged her when she got in.

"How was the bridal fair?" he asked.

"A bit like my worst nightmare. I had no idea what a performance planning a wedding could be."

"Do you think so? It's not going to take over my life," said Ian.

Kate sighed. "I feel like it's already taking over mine. I don't know why I let Tess persuade me to go. Can you believe there was some woman charging seven pounds fifty for a cupcake?"

"Is that good?" Ian asked.

"Of course it's not good," said Kate.

"I could eat a cupcake now," said Ian. "Is there anything in the fridge?"

"I don't know," said Kate. "It doesn't have a see-through door. Why don't you have a look?"

"Can't be bothered," he said.

Kate frowned. She knew he would have eaten something had she put it right in front of him. He was just too lazy to fix something for himself.

"Shall we watch some telly?" Ian asked. "I'll even let you watch a fascinating documentary about Prince Charles's 'other mistress' if you're good."

"I can't think of anything worse," said Kate.

"Football highlights it is."

Kate sat beside Ian on the sofa, but her mind wasn't on the football. Instead, she carried on a text conversation with Helen, bringing her up to speed with Elaine's treatment plan and telling her all about the horrors of the bridal fair. Helen responded in kind with the horrors of a Saturday spent ferrying small children to swimming class and ballet practice. Her youngest child had vomited in the pool. These texts were what Helen called her "mummy moans".

One day, when you've got a house full of screaming toddlers, you'll look back on that bridal fair and long for those simpler times, Helen assured her.

Stop it, Kate responded. **You're making me want to get unengaged.**

Don't you dare, said Helen. **I haven't been to a decent wedding since 1998.**

That was the year Helen, their mutual friend Anne and Kate's sister got hitched. Kate had been bridesmaid three times.

That night, Kate had a dream about the last flat-share she lived in before she could afford to rent a place on her own. The dream did not bring back happy memories and when she woke up, she found herself thinking about the end of that particular period of her life and it filled her with fresh sadness.

It had all come to a head over the August bank-holiday weekend of 1997.

Kate was used to being woken in the middle of the night. The grotty Lavender Hill flat she shared with two Italian language students and an Australian beautician had a bus-stop situated right outside it. When the 345 to South Kensington via Clapham Junction stopped there, as it did several times an hour, the rumble of the ancient Routemaster's diesel engine shook the entire building like a six on the Richter scale. When Kate took the single room in the flat, which was all she could afford on a trainee lawyer's wages, she told herself she could live with it. And most of the time she could. But after a year, she was aware that she hadn't had a full night's sleep since she moved in. It wasn't just the rumble of the buses; drunken revellers tumbling off at the stop showed no consideration as they shouted their goodnights.

So when she heard someone scream at five o'clock in the morning that Sunday of the August bank-holiday weekend, Kate was not unduly disturbed. She rolled over to face her sleeping partner for the night. He was snoring lightly. His name was Jake, or Jack; she wasn't entirely sure. She did know that she'd met him at the

Sofa Bar, a funky wine bar further up Lavender Hill towards the Junction, furnished with old sofas that left you itching. Jack or Jake had been drinking there with someone she vaguely knew from law school. The connection made it seem safe to bring him home.

Why had she done that? Was he so good-looking? She couldn't really tell in the soft orange glow of the streetlight through the cheap window blinds. Had he kept her in stitches all night? She couldn't remember him having been particularly funny. Was it just that he had shown some sign of wanting her? That, Kate was beginning to understand, was pretty much the only connection between the men she had brought back to her flat in the previous six months. There had been five of them. Five lovers — if you could call them that — in the six months since she broke up with Matt, the boyfriend she'd had since her first term at university. Now Matt, a junior doctor, was engaged to an intensive-care nurse and had apparently just bought a family house in Edinburgh. Kate was . . . Well, Kate was twenty-six years old, working all hours, living in a shared flat, where there was never enough hot water for four girls to take four showers in the morning, and bringing home God only knows who in the hope they might turn out to be the One.

"Are you the One?" Kate asked the man sleeping alongside her. Fragments of the previous evening came back to her now. His name was Jack, definitely. He worked for Arthur Andersen. He came from somewhere up north. He liked rugby. He was wearing an England shirt. He had been drinking, unusually, sambuca. He told Kate that the three coffee beans in the bottom were supposed to bring you luck: health, happiness and prosperity. Or had he? Kate thought that perhaps one of her Italian flatmates had told her that instead.

Kate lay back down on her pillow. She knew she should get up and have a drink of water. Her hangover was already coming together nicely. But she didn't want to clamber over Jack. Having agreed to three sambucas of her own after four large glasses of dog-rough red wine, she wasn't certain she could make it without throwing up. If Jack was the One, it would hardly be the best way to cement their relationship. And so Kate tried to avert the worst of the hangover by lying very still and listening to the sounds on the street outside.

Down by the bus-stop, someone actually wailed.

"Diana!"

Kate closed her eyes tightly. If someone was being murdered outside her flat, she didn't want to know.

At eight o'clock, thirst forced Kate out of bed at last. Giuliana was already in the kitchen, making a cup of proper coffee with the pot that her mother had sent over from Milan. As Giuliana turned from the hob, Kate saw at once that her flatmate was red-eyed from crying.

"She dead," said Giuliana. "She dead. She 'ad a car crash."

The radio, tuned to Radio One as usual, played incongruous classical music. And then a news bulletin. Kate sank down onto one of the kitchen chairs and accepted an espresso as she took in the full story. Giuliana had never offered to make her coffee before.

"She so young," said Guiliana. "Her little children."

Kate expressed her disbelief and was surprised to find tears springing to her own eyes. It seemed impossible that the woman who had blossomed from a shy nursery worker and royal fiancée into the most famous woman in the world could actually have died. Then, as the flatmates were sharing their sympathy for the children left behind, Jack wandered in. He had his shoes in his hand as though he had been hoping to sneak out without waking anybody. He locked eyes with Giuliana over the coffeepot. There was a moment of confused silence.

"Jack?" she asked.

"Christ," said Jack. "I thought this flat looked familiar."

That's how Kate discovered she had inadvertently brought home her flatmate's ex-fiancé. And that's why, whenever anyone asked her if she remembered where she was when she heard Princess Diana died, Kate would say, "I'd rather not."

It was an awful day, one of the worst, but no matter how terrible it was, that day did mark the end of a particularly bleak period in Kate's life.

Giuliana would not forgive Kate her mistake. As such, it was impossible to stay in the flat, and a couple of weeks later, Kate moved out of the shared flat and into a tiny bedsit on her own. She had no choice. She couldn't face another flat-share with strangers. Her best friends, Helen and Anne, were already both living with their future husbands. It was the first time Kate had lived alone, and she liked it. At the same time, Kate cut down on her drinking and resolved to stay away from one-night stands. Freed from the tyranny of regular hangovers, she started taking her job more seriously, setting herself on the path to early partnership. Pretty soon she was earning enough to put down a deposit on a little flat in Stockwell.

In a way, Princess Diana's death had focused Kate's mind as much as Giuliana's fury. We don't know how much time we have, was the message she took from Diana. Just as important as taking her job more seriously and cutting back on the booze, Kate would not waste another moment mourning Matt.

Of course, Kate had lapses. Her love life was not entirely successful from 1997 on. She had certainly wasted a long time on Dan, but at last, thirteen years after that awful weekend, her life could safely be said to have come together well. She had Ian now. If only her mother could get through the cancer, life would be pretty much perfect. Waking up the day after the bridal fair, Kate prayed that everything would be all right.

The last time she had prayed so hard was January 1997, when Matt left her. It hadn't worked then. Making coffee later that morning, Kate wondered what had happened to the man she used to love.

CHAPTER
TWENTY

3 December 2010

"Darling, please. Just for me. You said I could have whatever I wanted."

Diana stuck out her bottom lip. Ben knew she was doing it deliberately, playing the little girl whose father could refuse her nothing. Ben had seen Diana's father crumble in the face of that look a thousand times. Well, Dave wasn't being asked to dress up like bloody Prince William for an "engagement shoot". Ben wasn't going to crumble for that.

"What do we need an engagement picture for, anyway?" Ben had asked. "I've never heard of that happening."

"All the best photographers offer an engagement shoot these days," Diana was only too happy to explain. "It's not just a freebie. It's an ideal way to get to know the bride and groom ahead of the day. Get to see what angles they look best from. Hear more about their vision for the day itself."

"Vision?" Ben echoed.

"Yes, *vision*. And I envision our wedding as the best day of our lives. I want the photographs to match and that, Ben, means taking it seriously from the start. You can't expect the photographer just to turn up on the morning of the wedding and get it right."

"But dressing up as Kate Middleton and Prince William? That's not what I call taking it seriously. That sounds like a joke."

"Ben," Diana snapped, "why do you have to question everything I ask of you? I want to recreate that engagement shoot because I think we will look great in it. Everyone says I've got something of Kate Middleton about me and you are much better-looking than Prince William. Besides, it will be fun." Diana linked her arm through Ben's arm and laid her head on his shoulder. "And it's appropriate. We got engaged on the very same day as them, didn't we? And we're getting married the day after the royal wedding. They've been going out for about the same length of time. That makes their story really relevant to ours. I think it would be a nice touch to have a picture like their engagement picture."

"Are you going to make me pose like Prince William when we get married too?"

"Of course not. Our wedding day will be entirely unique. This is just for a laugh. We'll do the Kate and Prince William pics, but we're going to take lots of engagement pictures in our own clothes as well."

"Lots? How long is this going to take?"

"I already told you you're going to need a whole day off," said Diana.

"I don't have a day to take before the end of the year. Not since I took three days off for your birthday." And especially not since Diana had announced that she wanted to leave her "unsatisfying and overly demanding" part-time job at the end of January. Though she had gone quiet about it for a while, Ben still wasn't sure he had persuaded her against that particular idea and the thought that he hadn't and that from 1 February he would be entirely responsible for all their bills was giving him sleepless nights.

"I thought you said that you were important in your office. Surely someone will cover for you. They know how important this wedding is to you."

Ben said that he would do his best, though he doubted that anyone in the office would consider an engagement shoot to be important. Not when there were deadlines to be met. In the end, he had to call in sick.

The day of the engagement shoot was every bit as busy as a shoot for a high-end advertising campaign. Not only would the wedding photographer and his assistant be in attendance, Diana had also insisted that her top choices for wedding hairdresser and make-up artist be there. It would be a good opportunity for them to try out her wedding look and for Diana to be certain that she wouldn't have to look elsewhere. Never mind that having the hairdresser take a whole day out of her usual salon schedule would cost the best part of £300.

"You could just go into the salon in the morning," Diana's father suggested when she told him how much he would need to transfer to her bank account.

"Do you want a nice photograph for your mantelpiece or not?" was Diana's response.

Neither was it just a matter of ensuring that the bride-to-be looked as good as possible. Ben was sent off for a haircut, while Susie, who had also taken a day off at her daughter's insistence, helped to "dress the set". The set that day was Susie's living room. Though she lived in a house that was built in 1989 from a design based on four shoeboxes, Susie's decorating taste tended towards the baroque. With its heavy velvet curtains and dark wood bookshelves (which housed a collection of leather-bound DVDs), her living room could easily pass for a stateroom in a palace. To add to the effect of opulence, Diana had ordered enough cut flowers to make a bee reach for the antihistamines. There were roses in every colour imaginable. Diana and Susie spent an hour deciding which shade of flower would match the fake blue Issa dress, only to come to the conclusion that none of them quite worked and, when he came back from the barber, Ben would have to go in search of some plain white roses that were a whiter white than the white roses Diana had already rejected.

"Surely a rose by any other name," Ben mused when Diana told him what she wanted.

"What are you on about, Ben? Get to the florist's before they all go. People are waiting."

Finally, two hours after it was scheduled, the shoot was able to start. Pete, the photographer, made a good job of hiding his impatience as his subjects got into position. The "royal" poses were first. Diana had studied the newspaper cuttings carefully and was able to get into character right away. Ben found it altogether more difficult. He really had very little in common with the heir to the throne other than that they were both male and liked rugby. He was happy, sort of, to stand alongside Diana with his best "regal" look on his face, but he drew the line at having to look more William-like, which would, as far as he could see, involve getting a bigger set of teeth.

"Come on," said Diana. "It won't work if you don't put your all into it."

"I am not going to pull a *Prince William face*," Ben insisted. "I can't."

"You can," said Susie. "Look. It's easy. Look at this picture again."

Susie did her own heir-apparent impression. It was frightening realistic.

"Perhaps he should just smile naturally," said Pete. "Everyone will get the idea. In my experience, pastiches work much better if there's a little hint of difference, a touch of the real couple coming through."

Diana disagreed. "But he's not trying at all. You can't stand like that, Wills."

"Wills? My name is Ben, for God's sake. Now you can't even call me by my own name."

"I'm sorry," said Diana, blowing little kisses in his direction. "You look so princely I just forgot. One more time. Just one more time, please. I'll be nice to you all day."

"All right," said Ben. "Just for you."

Diana draped her arm through Ben's so that her engagement ring was perfectly on display. At least, a ring was on perfect display.

122

"Where's your engagement ring?" Ben asked, as he clocked a very different-looking bauble on his fiancée's ring finger. The extravagant diamond ring that had cost him so dearly had been replaced by a dazzling blue sapphire in a collar of diamonds. It was a replica of Princess Diana's engagement ring with a central stone so big it could only be a fake. He hoped his Diana had put her real diamonds somewhere safe. Ben was still paying for them, after all.

The new ring wasn't a fake.

"They did a part exchange," Diana explained. "But what you'd already paid didn't quite cover it. It was three hundred pounds more. You can pay me back later."

"You said you didn't mind what engagement ring I chose. I chose that other ring for you."

"I know, but . . . this is what I've really always wanted. I didn't know it until I saw Kate Middleton wearing one, but I really love it. It's so unusual."

Unusual? There were probably thousands of rings exactly like it circulating the country right now.

"But I thought you loved that other ring?"

"Isn't it a girl's prerogative to change her mind?" asked Diana.

"Am I allowed to change mine?" Ben muttered under his breath.

Pete had seen many things, but he had never seen anyone look quite as uncomfortable as the groom he was photographing that morning. The results were not good. The bride — a real Bridezilla — really knew how to pose, but in just about every picture her fiancé looked as though he would rather be eating his own feet. After half an hour, during which Ben did not loosen up, even with the application of a glass of cava from the celebratory bottle that Pete always brought along to engagement shoots, it was time to give up on Diana's royal dream.

"I think we should try some shots of you guys in your own clothes now," Pete suggested.

Diana scowled at Ben. "You didn't make any effort at all."

However, the other photographs were not much better. For the rest of the afternoon Diana was in a sulk and barely addressed a word in Ben's direction. Sure, she turned on a megawatt smile whenever the camera was pointed in her direction, but she had no smile for her fiancé's benefit. Instead, Pete thought with a slight chill, she seemed to be directing all her best expressions at him. Pete hated it when a bride flirted with either him or his assistant. It really wasn't right. But then misplaced flirtation was far from being the only thing that wasn't right with this particular pair.

The phrase "The camera never lies" was rarely far from Pete's mind when he first met a new couple. A micro-expression caught on film — or digitally, as it was these days — could reveal a whole different story behind a so-called happy event. While Diana had her make-up touched up for a fourth time, the photographer and his assistant went through the frames they'd already captured and shared a knowing glance when they came to a picture in which Diana's face was frozen in an unfortunate tooth-baring expression that brought to mind the American serial killer Aileen Wuornos en route to her trial.

"Delete?" suggested the assistant.

"No, I think I might keep this," said Pete, transferring the picture into a file that he would not show his clients but which might raise a smile from several of his photographer friends. "It's Kate Middleton meets *28 Days Later*."

"I'm ready," Diana announced. Ben got wearily to his feet again.

"We've got about three hundred shots to work from here," Pete tried. "If you're feeling tired, then there's really no need to keep snapping away. I'm sure you'll be pleased with the results we already have."

"But we haven't recreated the iconic pose from *Titanic*," said Diana. "I definitely want some shots of that."

Ben assumed another pose and thought of England. Everyone present, apart from Diana, gritted their teeth and thought of England as the shoot went on for the best part of another hour.

CHAPTER
TWENTY-ONE

The following day — a Saturday — brought another engagement shoot. Kate and Ian were about as excited by the idea of spending an afternoon having their photographs taken as Ben had been. They tried to wriggle out of it, but Trudy, the photographer, persuaded Kate that it was important to go through this particular trial.

"I want to get to know you both properly," she said, "so that I can take the best pictures possible on your actual wedding day."

"I'm sure you'll do fine without the practice," said Kate.

"What kind of professional would I be if I didn't do everything in my power to bring you wedding-day perfection?" was Trudy's retort.

Then Ian's mother said that she wanted a picture of the happy couple for her mantelpiece. And so did Elaine and John. They couldn't wait until the wedding.

"I'd like one too," said Tess. "You can pose as Kate Middleton and Prince William."

"We are not posing as Kate Middleton and Prince William," said Kate, "no matter how much it would make you laugh."

"You're so boring," said Tess. "I was going to get it printed on a tea towel for your Christmas present."

"Thanks but no, thanks."

Luckily, Kate knew that Ian would agree with her. There was no need for some silly pastiche. They would just be themselves. To that effect, they both dressed as they would have ordinarily dressed at the weekend. No ball gowns or tuxedos for them. They both wore jeans. Kate washed her hair but didn't spend an especially long time styling it.

Because Trudy was based down on the south coast — Kate had picked her at random from the photographers at the bridal fair — Ian and Kate were going to travel down to meet her there. It seemed like a good idea. For a start, it would give Kate another opportunity to see her parents, who were in need of buoying up as the day of Elaine's surgery grew nearer. Plus, there would be far more beautiful venues there than in London. Kate had no outside space at her flat. Ian's scruffy little garden was overlooked by half a dozen other flats and neither Kate nor Ian relished the thought of the neighbours seeing them prancing around in front of a camera. They would think they had gone mad.

Unfortunately, Trudy was not of quite the same mind. After Kate explained that they wanted to keep things classy, she reminded Kate and Ian that her speciality was "quirky" wedding photographs. She wanted to give each bride and groom she worked for a wedding album that would keep them smiling into old age.

"For that you need something different. I'm going to tune into your deepest desires," she promised, "and give you a set of photographs you never dreamt possible."

"Really," said Ian, "some simple poses would be OK."

Kate agreed.

"But that's so boring!"

"Please," Kate pleaded. "He's right. It's not as though we're kids. We're not quirky people. Some simple, classic, casual poses will reflect the way we are just fine."

"As you wish," said Trudy.

Kate should have guessed the moment she saw Trudy at the bridal fair that a photographer with bright green dreadlocks was hardly going to take a traditional approach, but Trudy tried her best to achieve the look Kate was after.

The trio walked down to the beach. It was bare and stark in the winter, but Trudy approved of the light reflected off the water. She said she liked to shoot with natural light wherever she could.

"What about my wrinkles?" Kate asked to break the ice.

"I can Photoshop them out if you wish."

Kate made a note to stop joking about things like wrinkles and saddlebags, since it was becoming clear from people's responses that these days she actually had them.

"We'll start here," said Trudy.

Ian scouted out a large piece of driftwood that would make do for a seat. He and Kate sat down at either end.

"Snuggle up a bit."

"It's not very well balanced," Kate explained. "If we move closer together, we might fall over."

"But you don't look very romantic."

Ian reached out his hand. Kate took it.

"Better?"

"Just about."

Trudy quickly ran through fifty frames.

"There's not a lot of dynamism here, folks. Laugh with each other. Ian, tell Kate a joke."

"Why is it that being told to make a joke chases just about every funny thought I ever had right out of my head?" Ian complained.

Kate forced a smile at his observation.

"I am hating this," she told him.

"You look lovely," Ian reassured her.

"Come on! You look like you're advertising health insurance," said Trudy, "and this is the picture to show how you're getting on with real life after your breast-cancer diagnosis."

Kate bristled.

"Was it something I said?" asked Trudy. She carried on snapping without waiting for an answer. "Don't look at the camera like that, Kate. It's even worse than before."

Ian shook his head slightly to let Kate know that there was little point telling Trudy she'd come a bit close to the mark with her breast-cancer comment.

"Hmm. I think we need to try something different," Trudy sighed when she saw her results. "It's just so wooden."

"I'm sorry," said Kate. "We're neither of us used to this modelling lark."

"Then why don't you let me make some suggestions? I know you didn't like the sound of it, but I've found that quite often when I get people posing like they're in a scene they already know, such as the royal-engagement pictures or something from a film, it helps them to put their inhibitions aside. If you know that you're only mucking about, you start to have a bit of fun. Will you try it? We're by the sea, so how about we go for the scene from *Titanic* where Winslet and DiCaprio are on the front of the boat? That 'I'm the king of the world' bit. You do know it . . ."

"I suppose we could," said Ian.

"You want me to be Kate Winslet?" Kate asked.

"For the first few shots," said Trudy. "Then you can swap over. Even funnier. Come on. You might enjoy it. Let's do it here."

Gamely, Kate and Ian did their best to do as Trudy asked. They climbed up onto the sea wall and leaned over the rusty old railings. Kate grimaced as Ian leaned his weight against her and her hip bones pressed into the metal. Not only was the metal painful, it groaned ominously and Kate could picture herself face first on the shingle.

"How long do we have to hold this pose?" she asked.

"As long as it takes to get the right expressions on your faces. You're supposed to look ecstatic. You're in love. You're together. Feel the exhilaration of the wind in your hair, the sea breeze on your face."

"I'm bloody freezing," said Ian.

"Then snuggle up," suggested Trudy. "Come on, guys. I want to feel the love coming out of the pixels."

"Ian," said Kate, "you're going to have to lean back a bit. I can't breathe."

Ian obliged, but he leaned so far back that he tumbled from the wall and turned his ankle as he landed.

"Shit." He sat down heavily on the pebbles.

Between them, Kate and Trudy helped Ian to his feet.

"Have you broken anything?" Trudy asked anxiously.

"I don't think so," said Ian.

Kate seized the opportunity to say, "But we should probably call it a day for now. I'll get Ian back to my mum and dad's place and stick a bag of frozen peas on his ankle before it has a chance to swell up."

Trudy tutted. "And you guys were just starting to loosen up."

"Well, that was an experience. How are you feeling?" Kate asked in the car. She was watching Trudy's little red Mini in the rear-view mirror, hoping that the photographer would turn off soon. It wasn't as though she could hear them, but Kate still felt observed.

"I'm fine," said Ian.

"You're not in any pain?"

"Not at all."

"It looked like you landed badly."

"I was acting. Anything to get out of having to be Kate Winslet."

"Are you sure?" Kate asked. "Because it looked like you landed badly."

"Completely sure," said Ian. "I landed like a cat."

"Then you don't need the peas."

"I do need a pint, though. Can we stop off at that pub your mum and dad took us to that time?"

Kate wasn't going to argue. Anything to put off the moment when they went back to her parents' place and the conversation turned to hospitals again.

The lumpectomy was just a few days away now and it was overshadowing everything. In some ways, thought Kate, it was better that they didn't have longer to prepare themselves for the awful day. In the few short weeks since Elaine got her diagnosis, she had seen her parents age years. No matter that the doctors kept reassuring them that Elaine's was a relatively contained cancer and was unlikely to turn much nastier overnight, Elaine and John swung between pessimism and outright despair. Within minutes of picking up the phone to them Kate was feeling equally drained. Being at the house was worse. They rehashed their hospital conversations endlessly, asking Kate for a close reading of everything, as if her law degree might be any use at all when it came to unscrambling medical talk.

Kate hated this sudden shift in perspective. She hated feeling that her parents were looking to her to find the answers. This wasn't the way of things. Despite the fact that she was nearly forty, Kate wasn't sure she felt ready to move into the position of responsible adult as far as her parents were concerned. She still felt she had so much to learn from them. She still wanted to be able to turn to them when she wasn't sure about something. To find herself having to reassure her mother and father about something so important was simply horrible.

Still, she was ready to do her bit. Thank goodness Kate's gardening leave was about to start and she wouldn't have to worry about getting time off work to help out. In that respect, the timing could not have been better. The plan was that she would spend the days after her mother's surgery in Washam. There was no fixed timescale. Kate said she would be there for as long as it took. Though her parents insisted that there was no need for Kate to decamp to Washam for the duration of Elaine's recovery, Tess confirmed that Kate's decision was the right one. Elaine was relieved that Kate would be there to "look after Dad", the main reason being that after forty-seven years of marriage to an excellent chef, John couldn't cook anything more complicated than a Pot Noodle. The fact that Kate was hardly any more qualified in the kitchen didn't seem to matter.

"You're a woman," said Elaine. "You don't think it's beneath you to read the instructions on the label. Your father would put a steak and kidney pie in the microwave in a foil tray and burn the place down."

"What's wrong with putting a foil tray into the microwave?" Ian asked.

★   ★   ★

Back in London after the disastrous engagement shoot, Kate worked doubly hard to make sure that all the loose ends were tied up before she left her job. Though she didn't feel much loyalty to the firm that she was leaving, the world of employment law was a small place and Kate knew it was just a matter of time before she found herself working alongside her old colleagues again. It was best to leave on a high note. She was, however, irritated to have to cancel a long-awaited and much-anticipated girls' night out with Helen and Anne in her efforts to make sure everything was done to perfection. With children and husbands and careers to juggle, it could be months before all their schedules coincided again.

With work tidied away, Kate turned her attention to home. She even did an early Christmas shop, filling the freezer at Ian's flat with almost everything they could possibly need for the holidays ahead and ordering the rest on Ocado. Not knowing how long she would have to be in Washam, she didn't want to risk having to brave Waitrose on Christmas Eve. She made sure that Ian inputted the arrival of the Ocado van in his BlackBerry, just in case she wasn't back in time to receive it.

Ian was being surprisingly sulky about Kate's upcoming stay with her parents. When she told him that she didn't know exactly how long she would be away, he said that he understood, but Kate recognised that he wasn't happy. Ian didn't have to say anything to express his disappointment when Kate told him that she would have to turn down an invite to his sister's house, just in case.

"I just hate spending too much time apart," he said.

To soften the blow, and since the operation was to take place on the Friday, Kate suggested that Ian join her over the weekend. There was plenty of space in her parents' house. She told him she'd love to have him there; plus, she figured that he could help keep her dad occupied with talk about football and *Top Gear*. Men's stuff. Given that he had pouted over their upcoming separation, Ian surprised her by making his excuses straight away.

"It doesn't make sense for me to come down as well," said Ian. "Your mum and dad have only got a small place. I'd be in the way."

"You won't be in the way. Besides, it will only be me and Dad rattling around. Mum will be in hospital. I could do with the moral support."

"I've got quite a lot on at the office. If you're not going to be around, I could go in on Saturday, get some work done."

"Oh, Ian, you don't want to go into the office on a Saturday."

"Of course I don't *want* to, but if I go this weekend, then when your mum's out of hospital and our life is back to normal, we can spend more time together without me worrying about work."

He seemed adamant.

After asking him a second time, and receiving the same answer, Kate stopped trying to argue her case. Much as she had wanted his support, maybe Ian was right. Maybe it would be easier not to have him around. Kate knew her family's idiosyncrasies. It might be stressful for Ian and her father to have to share the same space when they didn't really know each other that well, especially under the circumstances. If Ian found it upsetting when Kate cried, how on earth would he cope if his future father-in-law was overcome with emotion too?

I must not be upset, Kate told herself as she packed a suitcase. To Ian, this makes sense. He'd be there if he thought I really needed him.

All the same, she couldn't help wondering why he was so determined to stay in London for the weekend if he really did hate to be apart from her as much as he claimed. She emailed Helen, who thought that Ian probably really did think he would get in the way, but later that afternoon, on a hunch, Kate tapped a familiar web address into her browser and discovered, not entirely to her surprise, that West Ham were playing that Saturday. At home.

"Saturday in the office, my arse."

Kate didn't reveal her discovery to Helen. She was too embarrassed. Neither did she say anything to Ian about it — he certainly didn't mention any home game — but Kate brooded until Thursday morning, when she got in her car and left for the south coast while Ian was still in the shower. She didn't even kiss him goodbye.

CHAPTER
TWENTY-TWO

"Oh God, no!"

Diana exclaimed with such anguish that Ben immediately feared the worst. He stopped mid-shave and barrelled downstairs, almost slipping in his hurry, to find Diana sitting at the kitchen table with her iPhone. Her face was crumpled. She looked distraught, as though she'd just received news of a death.

Ben raced to be by her side. He fell to his knees beside her chair and lifted her face so that she was looking right at him.

"What's the matter?" he asked. "Tell me what's happened."

"This," she wailed. She shoved the iPhone into Ben's hand. Diana's browser was open to the *Daily Mail* online. She could never start the day without a strong dose of gossip.

Ben looked at the article she had been reading uncomprehendingly.

"I thought they had done their engagement pictures," Diana sniffed. "Nobody told me they were going to have Mario Testino."

Ben focused on the photograph of Kate Middleton snuggling into Prince William's arms. It was a lovely photograph, if you liked that sort of thing. It was a little bit too cheesy for Ben.

"They look nice," said Ben, handing the phone back to his fiancée.

"But they're wearing different outfits!" said Diana. "She isn't wearing the blue dress. Oh God, I might have known. We're going to look like complete idiots because we're in the wrong clothes. Unless . . ."

Ben knew what was coming next. She couldn't . . . Surely she wouldn't suggest that they do more photographs. He had to pre-empt her. He stood up, pulling her up from the chair as he did so. He pulled her close to him and held her tightly.

"Don't worry about it. We don't need to look like Kate and Wills," he said. "We're Diana and Ben. I don't want you to look like anyone else. I just want you to be a hundred per cent pure you."

The sentiment was wonderful. Ben was certain that he'd headed off disaster, but Diana recoiled in disgust.

"For God's sake, Ben, you've got shaving cream on my shoulder. You're so bloody selfish. I can't believe it. This dress has to be dry-cleaned. I might as well throw it out."

Diana did throw the dress out. And after Ben went to work, she called in sick. She spent the rest of the day driving from mall to mall in search of the cream Reiss dress that Kate Middleton was wearing in the Testino shots.

CHAPTER
TWENTY-THREE

10 December 2011

There is a reason why people have a phobia about hospitals, thought Kate as she accompanied her father to the local general on the morning of her mother's lumpectomy. Elaine had been on the ward since the previous night. Kate had dreaded having to wake early enough to see her mother again before she went into theatre. She thought she might sleep through and had set three separate alarms to ensure she didn't. In the event, Kate got hardly any sleep at all. She could hear her father pacing around the house throughout the wee small hours. She knew that he had hated having to leave Elaine alone overnight and he was determined, even if it meant sleeping outside the hospital doors, to be there well before she went into surgery the next morning.

Well, there was no way he was going to be sleeping outside the hospital doors. The country was shivering through the coldest December for seventeen years. Scotland and the north of England had just had another dose of snow. The weather forecast had warned that the south would soon be getting its share.

Fortunately, when Kate dared look that morning, the ground outside was still snow-free. The gods were with them. When she dragged herself into the kitchen, she found her father had already made breakfast: three rounds of toast that were so cold and hard Kate guessed he'd made them at least half an hour before she woke up. He hadn't touched anything himself.

"Have a piece of toast, Dad, please."

"I can't eat anything this morning, love. Not while I'm thinking of your mother in that place on her own. Not while she can't eat anything herself."

Of course. Elaine had been on nil by mouth since midnight in readiness for the operation ahead.

"She's going to be OK, Dad. They do operations like hers every day of the week."

"I don't care about all the other people they've operated on. Your mother's the only one I'd miss."

They were on the road to the hospital at seven. John insisted on driving and Kate let him, even though she wasn't sure it was the best idea. She had never seen her father quite so distracted as he was right then and the motorway was surprisingly busy, even at that time in the morning. Kate received a text from Tess, who said she had already been up for hours. That wasn't unusual for her. Lily was still a horribly early riser. Tess said she couldn't wait for Lily to become a lazy-arsed teen. Helen and Anne likewise had sent their best wishes for the day ahead. There was nothing from Ian. He was probably still asleep.

At the hospital, the working day was already well underway. The daytime nurses had long since started their shifts. The consultants were making their rounds. Elaine was sitting up in bed. She was staring into space with a blank expression on her face as John and Kate walked onto the ward. Catching sight of them, she plastered on a smile and flicked through the pages of a magazine as though she wanted them to think that she had been happily amusing herself with the antics of the *X Factor* contestants.

Kate noticed at once that the magazine her mother held was upside down.

John placed a kiss on the top of his wife's head. Kate gave her mother a squeeze.

"All set?" John asked.

"Oh, yes," said Elaine, as though they were discussing a hairdressing appointment. "They should have me in by half past nine. Have you spoken to Tess this morning? Is Lily going in to school, do you know?"

Tess had mentioned that she thought Lily might be coming down with a cold.

"Lily's fine, I think," said Kate.

"And how's Ian? It's a shame he can't come down to keep you company this weekend. He works very hard."

"Yes," said Kate, through slightly gritted teeth. "So hard that he's going into the office on Saturday."

"Oh, he is a good man. You are lucky to have him to look after you."

It wasn't the right time for Kate to express her annoyance. She just nodded.

The ward sister came to tell Elaine that the orderlies would be along to fetch her in the next ten minutes.

"I'll leave you two to it," Kate said. "Dad, I'll wait for you by the nurse's station."

Kate felt that it was important that her parents had this moment together. Elaine may have been Kate's mother, but she was John's *world*. She was his wife, his lover, his best friend. They had vowed to be each other's everything. If, in the very worst-case scenario, this was the last time they held each other, then they deserved to be alone.

Out in the corridor, Kate felt a lump rising in her throat. Had she just said goodbye to her mother for the last time? Almost certainly not. She knew that. A lumpectomy was a fairly routine procedure. Ian was certainly treating it as such, but what Ian didn't seem to appreciate was that this was the first time anyone in her family had even had a general anaesthetic. What if Elaine turned out to be allergic to the sedatives they used on her? What if she just gave up? The Williamson family had been so lucky so far. Not so much as a broken toe. It was so disconcerting to see her strong mother look so weak. Was their luck about to run out? Kate dabbed at her eyes. She wished that Ian was there to tell her how silly she was being, but Ian still hadn't so much as texted, "Good morning."

At last, Kate's father shuffled out into the corridor. He looked shockingly bent and old, as though the cancer were taking over his body too.

"Everything OK?" Kate asked uselessly.

"They've taken her down to theatre."

142

"They know what they're doing, Dad. They really do."

Kate hated herself for using the matter-of-fact tone she might have used with a client.

CHAPTER
TWENTY-FOUR

Hospitals had come a long way since Kate last spent any time in one. She figured that must have been when her school friend Emma had her appendix taken out. The girls in their little gang had taken it in turns to visit Emma every evening of her hospital stay. Back then, in the mid-1980s, visiting hours were strict. There was no question of hanging around all day. And the distractions on offer for a bored friend or relative were limited to say the least. There was a single kiosk selling magazines, get-well cards and flowers for the unprepared, plus a hospital "friends" stall providing homemade cakes and well-stewed tea. This much newer hospital had a concession of Costa and a proper branch of WHSmith.

"I've got a feeling we're going to get to know this branch of Costa rather well," said John as he carried two small lattes to a table.

John wouldn't leave the hospital, not while Elaine was in the operating theatre, though he kept insisting that Kate should go into town and do some Christmas shopping if she wanted to. Shopping? How could she think of that now? Kate told her father that she wasn't going anywhere. She was perfectly happy to sit at a table in the coffee shop. She had her laptop and the toggle that gave her an access code so she could log on when she was out of the office. She could do some work. Except, of course, there was no Wi-Fi to be had. Even the phone signal was terrible. Kate had to walk right out of the hospital lobby to pick up her messages. It wasn't much fun. The hospital doors were ringed by smokers. A man puffed his way through two B&H while a drip fed something more useful into his arm.

God, the place was depressing. It was at moments like this that Kate realised that working at her law firm in London had kept her somewhat cushioned from real life. At Ludbrooks, the staff were uniformly young and fit, as though they were part of some future world where all disease and ageing had been wiped out, but this was true life. Everyone gets old. Everyone dies in the end. Kate thought of her mother on the operating table. She thought of her father, grey-faced under the artificial light of the Costa concession. She wanted to go back to London and get away from the horrifying spectacle of people filing in to the hospital to be cured or just to die comfortably. She felt guilty for even having that thought, and guilty with the knowledge that she could still walk away if she wanted to.

Kate asked the guy on a drip if he could spare her a cigarette.

He obliged at once. "These things are killing me, anyway," he said.

Kate lit up. It was the first cigarette she had smoked since 1997, so in retrospect, perhaps it was fitting that, while Kate was squinting through the smoke, a vision from that terrible year should appear.

"Kate? Kate Williamson?"

Kate waved the smoke away and swiftly crushed the cigarette beneath her heel.

"Yes."

A man in a white coat stood before her. Someone from the oncology department, she assumed. Why had he come to find her? It could only be bad news.

"Is Mum out?" she asked urgently. "Did everything go OK?"

"Oh, no," said the doctor. "Your mum is in there? What happened?"

"What do you mean?" Kate was confused. "What have you come to tell me?"

"God, you really don't know who I am, do you?" The man shook his head in disbelief. "Well, I know I've put on a bit of weight and I've lost some hair." He took off his glasses.

"Matt Hogan?"

Kate recognised at last the man she had dated for six years through and right after university.

"The very same."

He went to kiss her on the cheek just as Kate aimed in the wrong direction. They banged noses.

"What are you doing here?" Kate asked him.

"I work here. What are *you* doing here?"

"Mum. Lumpectomy. At least, we hope that's all she'll have to have. She's got DCIS."

146

"Oh dear." Matt nodded his understanding. "I'm sorry to hear that."

"It should be straightforward, they said."

"She's certainly at the best place."

"That's what I said to Dad. I just came out to . . ."

"Have a fag." Matt shook his finger.

"Check my messages, actually. There's no signal inside."

"Thank God. Can you imagine what it would be like if all the patients were on their phones in there?"

"But it's so depressing out here. I don't know what possessed me. I had a sudden urge for a puff and I haven't had a cigarette since 1997."

Since the night Princess Diana died and I brought home my flatmate's ex-fiancé and finally realised that my "work hard, play hard" lifestyle was getting out of balance on the "play" side, was what she didn't say.

"So . . ." Kate peered at Matt's face. He wasn't joking about having put on some weight. His brown eyes peered out at her like raisins in a bun. "How long have you . . .?"

"Been here? We moved down here in 2004."

We. Was he still with the intensive-care nurse?

"It was Rosie's idea. She wanted to be close to her parents."

Rosie was the name of the nurse. Kate remembered having cursed it once. Or maybe a hundred times.

"I wasn't too keen. I liked being up in Scotland."

So it was true that he'd moved back to Scotland too. That was where his family came from.

"The agreement was that we would give it two years and if I still didn't like it, we'd move back to Edinburgh. Two years later, I still didn't like it, but by that time Rosie had left me for a dentist and now I'm stuck down here for ever if I want to see the kids."

"Oh, no," said Kate. She wished she had another fag so she had something she could fiddle with to hide her embarrassment.

"Yep," said Matt, "that's my life. The job's all right, though."

"What did you specialise in in the end?"

"Gynaecology."

"Just what you always wanted."

"And you?"

"Still a lawyer. Can't you see my horns?"

Matt grinned. They'd had many arguments back in the day about the relative moral values of their career choices. "You look well. Is there . . .? Do you . . .? Are there any children?"

"Not that I know of," said Kate. "Though I am getting married, can you believe?"

Kate found herself stretching out her left hand to show off her ring as if to prove it.

"Only now? I thought you would have been snapped up years ago."

Kate raised her eyebrows. She didn't remember Matt having expressed that kind of opinion before. In fact, when they were breaking up, he'd told her that no one would ever want a mad-eyed neurotic like her. Still, she accepted the compliment.

"Working too hard on my career, I guess."

148

Matt looked at his watch. "Talking of which . . . I've got to go. My eleven o'clock."

"Of course. Can't keep her waiting."

Matt hesitated. "Can I . . . can I have your number? I mean, it would be nice to catch up. If you're down here for a few days because of your mum and you're at a loose end, we should go for a drink. In any case, let me know how your mum gets on."

Matt searched in his pocket for a card. Kate took it.

"You look amazing, Kate Williamson." Matt winked at her as he left. "You look every bit as beautiful as I remember."

Did she look amazing? Kate found herself checking out her own reflection as she walked back through the revolving doors. Then she checked herself. She wasn't at the hospital to flirt. Her mum was on the operating table.

Kate found her father sitting in the exact same place she had left him, now nursing an empty coffee cup.

"It's eleven o'clock," said Kate. "We should go up and see how Mum's doing."

John followed her to the lifts. Kate wondered if she should tell him about Matt to fill the silence. She decided against it. John didn't seem to be in the mood for small talk. It was as if he was in a daze.

When they got to the ward, they were greeted with the news that Elaine was in recovery. There was not much more information than that.

"Did the operation go OK?" Kate asked.

The nurse on duty shrugged. "They don't tell us. All I know is that she's in the recovery room. She'll be back on the ward in an hour."

"That's good," Kate assured her father. "I'm sure it is."

CHAPTER
TWENTY-FIVE

That night, Kate stayed with her father again. He was a little less anxious than he had been the night before. The surgeon had come to check Elaine's progress while Kate and John were still on the ward, keeping her company. He reassured them all that the operation had gone well. He was happy that he had removed 99.9 per cent of the malignant tissue, if not all of it. The radiotherapy would squash anything he'd left behind. He was pleased with the neat incision he'd made and was sure that, when the time was right, the reconstruction of Elaine's left breast would also be simple.

"This is as good as it gets," he explained.

When visiting hours finished at eight, Kate drove her father home. She insisted on taking the wheel, though she knew he hated the thought of his new car in anyone else's hands. Kate wasn't sure John would have got them back in one piece. He looked every bit as tired as his wife. Back at the house, he ate a couple of sandwiches and fell asleep in the chair. Kate chose that moment to catch up with Ian.

Their phone conversation was brief. Ian was monosyllabic on the subjects of work and weather and what he had eaten that day. Kate was reminded of conversations with Ian's nephews, who could barely be persuaded to grunt if they were engaged with a DS or an Xbox. That night, she had a feeling that Ian was watching the television at the same time as trying to talk to her. She felt her annoyance bubble up again. Of all the days when she needed him to pay her a little bit of attention he could just about be bothered to mutter "Mm-hmm" in response to her news. It was as though he was punishing her for something. Still sulking about her being away, as though she were on a spa break rather than looking after her dad.

"Have you changed your mind about the weekend?" she asked.

That seemed to capture Ian's notice for a moment.

"I've got a lot to do before the end of the year," he responded.

"Like watch West Ham?" Kate asked.

"Are they playing?"

Ian's attempt to feign ignorance of his beloved team's fixtures was unconvincing. Ian had a photographic memory for West Ham facts.

"Like you don't know. Goodnight," said Kate. "I've had a long day and I'm going to bed. I'll call you tomorrow."

Kate ended the call, but for a short while she remained sitting on the end of the bed, holding the phone in her hand as though she expected Ian to call back and ask what was up with her. He didn't. When

152

her phone next sprang to life, it was with a text from Helen, asking how the operation had gone.

Fine, Kate responded. **And you'll never guess who I bumped into at the hospital. Matt Hogan.**

OMG, texted Helen.

He's working down here. He's looking fat and getting a divorce.

Karma, texted Helen.

Kate didn't reply to that. She could use some good karma of her own, for Elaine. It didn't seem right to be gossiping about Matt Hogan. She ignored Helen's entreaties for more information and put her phone away.

Back in the living room, Kate placed a blanket over her father's lap. He would probably have been more comfortable in bed, but she decided against waking him, in case his head filled with worries and he was unable to drop off again. Kate washed their two sad-looking plates in the kitchen sink. She drew the blinds for the night. She hung her coat, which had been draped across the back of a chair, in its proper place. Then, suddenly remembering that morning, she reached into her coat pocket and pulled out Matt's card.

She looked at it closely. So many years had passed since their last fraught conversation, in 1997. She had thought she would never see him again. At least he hadn't aged as well as George Clooney. That would have been too much to bear. Still, she was surprised to find that seeing Matt again had brought a little of the sting of rejection back. She couldn't help thinking how much he must have loved Rosie to follow her down to Southampton. Kate would have followed Matt anywhere. Would she have felt differently if someone had been able to show her the currant-bun face and receding hairline he would have by the time he turned forty? Who knew?

Kate held the card in both her hands, ready to tear it in two and consign Matt back to where he belonged, in history. She hesitated.

No matter what Matt had said or done back in 1997, that morning he had been pleasant enough. He had seemed delighted to see her, like any old friend should be. He didn't seem to be remembering the anguished ending of their relationship when he bounded up to her. His presence at the hospital had been a very welcome distraction while her mother was in the operation theatre. He had asked her to let him know how the operation went. Surely common courtesy required she at least send a text.

Kate typed a brief message with her thumb. **Mum's op went fine,** she wrote. **Take care.**

Kate went to bed at eleven o'clock. When she woke briefly at three in the morning, she heard her father pacing around again. He couldn't sleep without her mother beside him. Kate wondered if she would ever feel like that about Ian. Would she be holding his hand at the very last moment of her life? Would she pace the floor if she didn't know when he was coming home? It was hard to imagine, if he was really going to choose West Ham over giving her moral support that weekend. She checked her phone to see if Ian had sent her a goodnight text message since she'd been asleep. Ordinarily, he would. There was nothing, but there was a text from Matt.

It was SO good to see you today, he wrote. **You looked every bit as beautiful as I remembered. It's as if the years since we last saw each other fell away. Please call. It would be great to catch up properly if you can.**

Next morning, John knocked on Kate's bedroom door at six thirty. He came bearing a cup of tea.

"Dad, it's half six."

"I'd like to get in to see your mum as soon as possible," he explained.

Kate dragged herself to the bathroom. Far from her usual habit if woken too early, she found herself putting on make-up. She told herself that it was nothing to do with Matt, of course. It would simply be unfair to the world to force her bare face upon it at such an early hour. She always looked like death warmed up before nine. Still, knowing that Matt might be watching, she was definitely a little more self-conscious than she had been the previous day when she and her father crossed the car park.

Elaine was sitting up in bed when they arrived. Her breakfast was half finished. She said she was feeling good, if a little sore.

"I'm glad that damn thing is out of me at last," she said. "It's only going to get easier from now on."

155

"You'll be wanting to get back to London," said John to Kate. "I can look after myself. Your sister will bring Lily round to keep me company at the weekend."

"No," Kate insisted. "I want to stay with you until Mum is back home."

John protested, but she could tell that he was glad she'd made that decision.

Leaving her parents alone while she went to fetch coffees, Kate used the opportunity to call Ian to tell him her plans.

"You could still come down on Sunday," she said. "Just for the day."

"No," he said. "I don't want to be in the way. Oh, have we got any more toilet rolls?"

"I believe you can get such exotic things in Waitrose," Kate replied.

Well, if Ian really wasn't going to come down to keep her company, then Kate decided she would have to make her own amusement. She could go for that drink with Matt for a start.

CHAPTER
TWENTY-SIX

Diana had got over the shock of discovering that the royal couple's official engagement pictures were very different from the poses she had persuaded Ben to lampoon. There was nothing that could be done about it. Pete, the photographer, said that he was absolutely chock-a-block with assignments every weekend between now and the wedding. Ben said that he could not take another weekday off without risking his job, and since Diana was going to give up her job . . . She had to give up her job. There was so much to think about. Planning a wedding really was incredibly stressful.

While Ben was out at work, Diana vented her frustrations on online bridal forums. She was signed up to eleven different forums, using the name "theother-princess" for each. However, she spent most of her time on Nuptialsnet.com, a forum based in the United States. Diana liked the forum's format. It was ever so easy to set up a profile complete with a "wedding countdown", which ticked off the days until the big day. Diana chose a picture of two unicorns with their horns entwined for her avatar photo. Unicorns held special significance for Diana. The very oldest item in her secret wedding folder was a drawing she had done at the age of six. In it, two unicorns (or, more specifically, two pink rectangles with spindly legs and horns) pulled a coach that would have made Cinderella's fairy godmother proud. Now, almost twenty-four years later, that picture had talismanic properties for Diana. She carefully unfolded it to remind herself of her childhood fantasy whenever she was stressed.

But what Diana liked best about Nuptialsnet was not the countdown calendars or the unicorns; she liked the feeling that American brides took the whole business of getting married more seriously than their English counterparts. Thus they were far more sympathetic towards Diana's wedding-planning woes.

Top of Diana's current woes was the fact that Ben seemed uninterested in the minutiae of the wedding-planning.

"Last night," Diana wrote on the forum, "I asked him to look at three website links to wedding-cake companies and to give me his honest opinion. He was on the Internet for the best part of two hours, but when he came to bed, he told me that he'd 'forgotten' to look at the three websites I specifically asked for his opinion on. What can I do to focus his attention on our important day?"

The solutions came flooding in. Had Diana considered offering to get a wedding cake made in the colours of his favourite football team? Not bloody likely. Southampton FC and Princess Diana roses were far from a perfect match. Had she thought about getting samples from each of the cake-makers, then blindfolding her BFH (beloved future husband) and feeding him the samples in bed? "No way," Diana typed back. She never ate in bed. What a disgusting thought. No wonder that particular Nuptialsnet bride was still trying to lose a stone with less than three weeks to go.

"I would suggest withholding sex," came the third answer. "Once a man has easy access to sex, you can bet that he will give up trying in just about every area of life. That includes your wedding-planning. Sex is the reason why so many non-Christian marriages fail. If you have sex before marriage, you are setting yourself up for disaster, but you can go some way to setting things right if you abstain from sex starting right now until your honeymoon. Think of it as renewing your virginity. What man doesn't want to marry a virgin? And in the meantime, your BFH will take much more interest in wedding cake, believe me."

Hmm, thought Diana. Now perhaps this was something she could work with. Renewing her virginity. It sounded quite romantic. And if it had the side effect of piquing Ben's interest in planning, then so much the better. Diana was going to save herself for the big day. She'd tell Ben that evening. Meanwhile, Diana would offer some of her own wisdom to the other brides on the board.

Under the heading "Very confused", a young woman lamented that despite having become engaged to her boyfriend of two years, she was having feelings for someone at work, who was also in a relationship. So far she hadn't acted on her feelings, but should she break off her engagement and tell her colleague how she felt?

Diana responded, "You are a slut and a bitch. You should break off your engagement anyway, because no man deserves to be with a slag like you. Then you should leave your colleague the hell alone. He belongs to another woman. I hope one day that someone steals a man off you, you thoughtless, selfish cow."

Diana then advised a girl whose maid of honour had just announced that she couldn't take a whole week off work for the hen party to dump her friend.

"Cut her out of your life. Who needs a bitch like that for their bestie? If she can't see how important this is to you, then screw her. She's probably jealous or a lesbian."

Diana pressed "post". Job done. She loved the sense of community she got from Nuptialsnet.

CHAPTER
TWENTY-SEVEN

Out of his white coat, Matt looked a little more like the man Kate remembered. Off-duty, he still favoured the way of dressing he'd had all through university: a nicely ironed shirt, a pair of chinos. He hardly ever wore jeans, even as a student. He'd looked a little oldfashioned back then. Now, however, the look suited him perfectly. That evening, he was wearing a pink shirt. Pink had always been a good colour for his lightly tanned skin and thick hair. Though his hair was a lot less thick now and he didn't look as though he'd been out in the sun for a while. As Kate walked towards him through the pub he had chosen, she wondered if he really did think she looked as good as ever. Time had taken such a toll on Matt it didn't seem possible that she had escaped its worst ravages.

"I'm really glad you could make it," he said. "I got you your usual. A pint of Stella?"

Kate shook her head at the pint at her place on the table.

"Ugh. Actually, I prefer to drink wine these days," she said.

"Of course." Matt jumped to his feet. "I'll have it. I thought getting you a pint would be a bit of a laugh, that's all — remind you of all those nights in the union bar."

"Some things are best forgotten," said Kate.

Matt went back to the bar and returned with a glass of chilled pinot grigio. It was somewhat inappropriate for the freezing weather outside, but Kate accepted it gratefully nonetheless. It was as good as you could expect a pub wine to be: so sour that it made her mouth pucker.

"I so need this drink," she said, glad that she had decided on a taxi rather than driving herself. Seeing Matt again like this, away from the hospital, was like seeing him for the first time. Kate was surprised at how nervous she felt. Was this evening going to be excruciating?

"Tough day?" Matt asked.

"Tough week. I can't believe how much Mum's cancer has taken out of us."

"Ah, yes. Tell me all about it."

It wasn't much of an ice-breaker, but it was helpful to be able to talk to Matt about her mother's condition. While Elaine's consultant had been friendly enough, he had very little time built into his schedule for the pastoral care of his patients. Mindful of that, John and Kate dared not ask the questions they hoped to ask and had thus come away with a bunch of half-heard and less than half-understood information. Though it was not his area of specialisation, Matt was able to cut through a lot of the jargon the oncologist had used.

"Is that really all it meant? I feel so stupid," said Kate as the mysteries unravelled.

162

"Don't," said Matt. "It's easy to forget when you're dashing from one patient to the next that they don't understand all the bloody acronyms. It sounds to me as though the operation went exactly as it was supposed to. Trust me, if it hadn't, you would know about it. One thing the NHS is good at is responding to a real emergency. Thank God."

"Thanks, Matt. I feel like an idiot having to ask you all these questions. It's been a difficult time. I've felt so stressed out worrying about Mum and Dad. Especially Dad. I don't know how he'd cope if he lost her. More to the point, I don't know how my sister and I could cope with *him*. I hope you don't think I'm being overly dramatic. I know that there are people in far worse shape than Mum in that hospital."

"But they're not *your* mum," said Matt. "You don't have to care as much about them as you do about Elaine. You're not being dramatic at all. You're being every bit as concerned as a daughter should be."

"Really? Only, when this all started, I felt as though I was interfering when I wanted to ask questions. The registrar told me I shouldn't believe everything I read on the Internet. That made me feel like a real fool."

Matt snorted his amusement. "You know how arrogant doctors can be," he said.

"Ugh. Well, this is all very gloomy," said Kate. "Shall we move on?" She raised her glass. "Happy Christmas."

"Happy Christmas," said Matt.

"Are you doing anything nice for Christmas this year?"

"I thought we were moving off gloomy subjects. Don't ask about Christmas, for God's sake."

They talked a bit about Matt's life in Southampton. Matt explained that he would be spending his Christmas alone. He'd have spent the day working if he could. His soon-to-be ex-wife was taking their children skiing with her new man. It was to be the first time he had not been with his children on Christmas Day.

"The worst of it is, I don't think they care half as much as I do. Not now Richard is taking them to Verbier."

"And he's a dentist?"

"Yes. I should have guessed when my beloved wife came home with a mouthful of veneers."

"You must be gutted."

"I was. I thought Rosie was the love of my life. When I married her, I was convinced that I would never look at another woman. I certainly didn't think she would ever look at another man. Marriage is hard bloody work. I can understand why you haven't bothered until now. What's he like, anyway, your fiancé?"

"Oh, you know."

"I don't know. Is he good enough for you?" Matt frowned like a concerned father.

"He's great. He's an accountant, but he's not boring."

Matt laughed. "So he's nice and steady. That's good. How did you meet him?"

"In a bar," Kate lied about it for the first time.

"Good old Katie," said Matt. "Keeping the British brewing industry going."

164

"I really don't drink as much as I used to," Kate reminded him.

"I believe you, though I'm sad you won't end the evening by dancing on the table. But tell me about your man. What's he passionate about? Apart from you, of course."

"West Ham," Kate deadpanned.

"Can you believe my eight-year-old son supports Chelsea?" Matt rolled his eyes. Matt was a die-hard Celtic fan.

"It's only a game," said Kate.

"Never say that . . . Tell me more about your man. What else do you like about him?" asked Matt. "What do you guys do together at the weekends?"

"Why all the forensics? Tell me about you and Rosie. After all, she pinched my boyfriend."

Matt shook his head. "You don't want to hear that."

Kate smiled to let him know that he really could tell her. Thirteen years earlier, she had wanted to know because she wanted to work out whether she had any chance of stealing Matt back. Now she was just curious. It no longer made any difference to her, did it? She was getting married.

"What can I say? I felt like I didn't have a choice. Rosie walked into my life and everything seemed to fall into place around her. It wasn't that I didn't want to be with you any more; it's just that the pull of attraction from Rosie was so strong that I decided it must be because she was the One. My destiny."

"I didn't think you were superstitious."

"I'm not, but you know what it's like when you meet someone and in the first second they smile at you, you feel like you've come home. You feel like you've known them your whole life and everything feels right. You must have had that with Ian."

Kate was distracted by a group of teenagers who had just tumbled through the door of the pub. They must have been celebrating the end of the school term. They were drunk and arguing about who was sober enough to convince the barman to serve them. Their high-pitched disagreement made it all but obvious that they were underage.

"Do you know what I mean?" Matt asked her again. "About just knowing? I bet Ian felt exactly that when he asked you to marry him. I bet meeting you made everything suddenly make sense."

Kate came back to the conversation. "What? Well, I suppose so. He's not the kind for big, sweeping statements like that."

"I didn't think I wanted to get married until I met Rosie. With her I had no problem committing to anything. I couldn't wait for the rest of my life to begin. It happens when it happens. You can't fake it."

"I'd nearly given up waiting."

"I really don't know how you got away with staying single for so long."

"I think I do," said Kate, remembering all the guys who had followed Matt through her heart. The one-night stands. The weirdoes. The ever-noncommittal Dan. Since meeting Ian, it had crossed Kate's mind that perhaps she had subconsciously chosen men who wouldn't commit to her because she didn't want to commit to anyone either. "Perhaps I just wasn't ready," she concluded.

"And now you are," said Matt.

"I hope so."

Matt clinked his glass against hers.

"So here we are again. You know it's been twenty years since we first met."

"It can't be."

"It is. September 1990. Freshers' Week. You had that terrible accent."

"Hang on . . ." Kate protested.

"You did. You sounded like a farmer. You soon got rid of that burr."

"If only you'd got rid of those mustard-coloured jeans you used to wear as quickly."

"I've still got them. I'm saving them for Tom."

"They must be able to walk on their own by now."

"They'll come back into fashion. Like that jumper you're wearing. Didn't you have something exactly like that at Cambridge?"

"This *is* the Cambridge jumper," Kate admitted. "Mum and Dad had it at their house. It was the only thing I could find to put on. I hadn't expected it to be so cold down here."

"When are you going back to London?" Matt asked.

"I'm not sure. Maybe tomorrow if I think that Mum and Dad will be able to get by without me. You know, it's really shaken me, this whole thing. It's like I didn't believe my parents were mortal until now. And this is

167

just the first hint of the frailty to come. It's bloody frightening."

"It happens to us all at some point."

"I know you're right. I guess I've been lucky so far." Kate struggled to keep a lump from her throat.

"It's great that you've got Ian by your side to help you through it."

Kate made a little noise of agreement. There was no point telling Matt that Ian would rather be at the football than lend her his support that weekend.

"You know you can call me anytime you like to ask questions about the things Mr Calil has said. If you want, next time your parents are in the hospital, I could even go along to an appointment with them if you give me some notice."

"Would your colleagues like that? I mean, wouldn't it look as though you were interfering?"

"Possibly, yes, but it's you and your parents I care about. If it would make you feel more comfortable to have my 'expert' opinion, I'm there." He put a heavy jokey emphasis on "expert" that made Kate remember how much she had liked his self-deprecating humour when they first met, twenty years before.

"That's kind of you. Really, it's made a difference to be able to talk to you about it."

Matt took her hand across the table. He squeezed her fingers.

"I am so glad you came here tonight. All the time that's passed. You're getting married. I'm getting divorced. But I feel as though underneath we're still the same people, don't you? I've missed you over the years, you know."

Kate nodded.

"But now we've found each other again. Promise you'll keep me up to speed with your mum's progress, and promise you'll call me next time you're in town."

"I promise," said Kate.

What did you do tonight? Ian texted just as she was going to bed.

Stayed in and watched TV with Dad, Kate lied.

I miss you, Ian told her.

I miss you too, texted Kate.

But did she? Back in her parents' spare bedroom right then, it was hard to imagine that Ian even existed in her life. Perhaps it was the nostalgia kick. Her brain was confused by going back over old times with Matt. So much so that when Kate woke up the following morning, she had the distinct impression that she was back in her old room in college and at any moment Matt would be hammering on the door, asking if she was ready to go down for breakfast.

That intense moment of recollection was followed by a rush of guilt when she discovered that another text from Matt was waiting on her phone alongside Ian's habitual "Good morning."

Would be really nice to see you again, Matt had written.

Yes, Kate replied. **Hope to introduce you to Ian soon.**

CHAPTER
TWENTY-EIGHT

Elaine was allowed home a few days later. Kate had the distinct impression that the hospital staff tried to get rid of as many patients as they could before Christmas to help them arrange holiday leave. She wasn't convinced that her mother was ready to leave the ward, but Elaine said she couldn't wait to get home. Her recovery would be much faster, she was sure, if she could do it in her own front room. She had to get strong again ahead of the radiotherapy she would have in the new year.

When she saw how much happier her mother seemed to be back in her own bed, Kate felt guilty for having tried to persuade her to stay at the hospital. Kate was aware it might have been more to do with her fear that John would not be able to cope with her care than that Elaine wasn't well enough to be moved. Both John and Elaine insisted that it was time for Kate to return to London, to work and her fiancé.

Back in London, Kate was faced with the usual round of last-minute Christmas chores and social obligations. She attended Ian's company party. He accompanied her to a dinner at the firm she would be joining the following February. Neither evening was a glittering success, with the party catering reflecting the strict austerity budgets that both companies had adopted. Plus, Kate felt a lingering resentment towards Ian for having avoided the whole business of the hospital. She didn't say anything, but she had to bite her tongue when, while making small talk at his office party, he inadvertently let slip, in front of Kate, that he had been at the West Ham home game that Saturday. Just as she suspected. Kate smiled at the revelation. At least it made her feel a little less guilty for not having mentioned seeing Matt. She hadn't even told Helen about their catch-up drink.

But there were more frustrations. In Kate's absence, Ian had run down the supplies in the flat. Not only was there just half a loo roll left, Ian had started on the food that Kate had stashed in the freezer for Christmas and — this was the real kicker — he had cancelled the Ocado order in Kate's absence because he "didn't know what to do when the van arrived".

Meanwhile, the bad weather meant that the supermarkets had been hit by panic-buying. There was a real danger that they would have nothing festive to eat come Christmas Day. Kate's resentment went up another notch as she pushed a trolley around Waitrose. Why was Ian so clueless when it came to running a home? How had he survived before he met her? Kate fumed as she restocked the freezer when she could have been doing 101 more useful things. Why was filling the freezer her job, anyway? She hoped it was just because she was on gardening leave that Ian seemed to assume she would play housewife. He definitely shouldn't get used to it.

Kate ranted to Helen via text. *Welcome to my world,* was Helen's deadpan response.

While Kate had been in Washam, Trudy, the photographer, had sent Kate and Ian a link to the private members' area of her website, so that they could see the results of the engagement shoot. When she finally found a moment, Kate clicked through and tapped in their password, which was "Eiffel", their password for all things wedding-related.

Trudy had suggested that Kate and Ian might like to use one of the photos from the engagement shoot on their wedding stationery. Her site provided a link to a website where they could turn the photos into calling cards. Kate wasn't sure that was her sort of thing, but in the event, there wasn't a single picture from that engagement shoot she would have wanted to send out in any case.

Kate grimaced at the first three shots, taken sitting on that rickety log. She and Ian looked like strangers who had just been dragged out from a supermarket and told to pose together. Ian had his eyes shut in one of them. The "walking along the beach" shots were not much better. Kate and Ian were holding hands, but their bodies were miles apart. They looked as though they would have preferred to be holding on to two ends of rope for a little extra distance.

The *Titanic* shots were the worst of all. Kate remembered how physically uncomfortable that pose had been, with the railings digging into her belly, but she was surprised to see how anxious both she and Ian

172

looked. Was it just the thought of the drop behind them? Despite his brag that he had landed like a cat, Ian had had to hold off on his habitual Sunday run because his ankle hurt too much.

We don't look right together. Kate was shocked by the thought that popped into her head. Once she had acknowledged it, she couldn't help comparing in her mind these pictures with the photographs she had taken over her time with Dan, for example. She and Dan had looked right with each other. In fact, when they were breaking up for the last time, Kate had shown some of those photographs to Tess for confirmation that two people who looked so good together couldn't possibly be splitting up for real.

Kate knew that Ian was a very different man to Dan. He was by no means as vain. Ian had lived for years without even having a mirror in his bathroom. If Kate hadn't insisted he bought one so that she had something to look into while doing her make-up whenever she stayed over, she suspected that Ian might never have got around to buying one. Likewise, when he was shopping for clothes, Ian had two criteria: does it fit, and is it comfortable? Kate had often told him that it was a good job he came to their first date straight from work. If she'd seen him in his weekend clothes before she got to know him, they wouldn't have got past date one.

Given that he paid so little attention to his appearance, perhaps it was unreasonable to expect Ian to look as though he was having a good time at a photoshoot on a beach in front of members of the public, for heaven's sake.

Still, Kate couldn't silence the little voice in her head that held some store by how comfortable a couple looked when they were photographed together. Somehow, the digital images of Ian holding her as though she were a small child who might pee on his shoes at any moment had made tangible Kate's suspicion that he really didn't feel connected to her at all. His decision to stay in London and go to the footie while she was dealing with her mother's operation certainly didn't seem like a connected thing to do.

Was Ian just getting married because he felt it was time to? Had he chosen her simply because she was a suitable girl: good job, no obvious baggage, similar background? Was there any passion there at all? Lately, Kate was starting to think that Ian was marrying her because it would be cheaper than getting a housekeeper.

"What do you think of the pictures?" Ian asked when he called to say what time he would be home that night so that she knew when to start cooking dinner.

"They're OK," said Kate in a guarded way.

"I think they look fine," said Ian. "I think Mum would like the first one from the series where we're sitting on the log."

"Not a *Titanic* shot?" Kate asked.

"She didn't like that film," said Ian, taking it literally, as always.

"OK," said Kate. "I'll email Trudy. I'll get the same picture for my parents as well."

She couldn't imagine it being on their mantelpiece for ever, she realised with a jolt.

Something had definitely shifted.

CHAPTER
TWENTY-NINE

Diana was delighted with all the photographs in her online engagement album. The effort she had put into her hair and make-up had definitely paid off. She clicked the tick of approval next to almost every shot. Of course, she would incorporate one of the photographs into the wedding stationery. It was hard to choose just one. In the end, she chose the first of the "royal" photographs. So, they weren't the Testino shots, and Ben didn't look exactly comfortable, but Diana had never seen her hair look quite so good. Also, her expression was just right. She looked remarkably like the princess in waiting.

"Please," Ben begged her, "don't tell me that we're going to have one of those royal photos on our invitation."

"Oh, Ben," Diana wheedled, "everyone will love it."

"No way."

"Fine," said Diana. "Then we'll have this one instead."

She picked out a photograph of herself in a floor-length gown and Ben in a rented tux.

"Why do we have to have a photo of ourselves on the invitation at all?" Ben asked. "Isn't it classier to have something plain?"

Diana considered that thought for a moment. She consulted one of her half-dozen wedding-etiquette books before admitting, "You're probably right."

Still she was determined that as many people as possible should see the engagement pictures. What was the point of having them otherwise? She ordered a dark-brown leather-bound album to be made of all the shots she had approved of. She ordered copies of the album, in a slightly less expensive finish, for her mother and Ben's mum and all four sets of grandparents. She ordered two framed photographs for her father. They would make perfect Christmas presents. That really didn't spread the news of Diana's triumph far enough, though. While Ben was in the sitting room, watching *Match of the Day*, Diana fiddled around with the wedding-stationery options on the photographer's site. She chose a picture of herself and Ben dressed up as the royal couple and set it on a white card with a fine silver border. She played with the typesetting, choosing a swirling, extravagant font that looked like the very best calligraphy. The card she created, complete with matching silver-tissue-lined envelopes, was surely oozing with class.

But in a rare show of deference to her future husband's wishes, Diana did not press the "order" button on her wonderful invitation design. If Ben wanted plain wedding invitations, then that was what they would have.

Christmas cards, however . . .

Three days later, Diana was very pleased to see how good her favourite photograph from the engagement shoot looked on the custom-printed Christmas card. On the inside of the card, she'd had printed, "Merry Christmas and happy New Year from the other couple getting married in 2011." Nicole and Susie thought the cards were great fun. Very witty. Ben could hardly believe his eyes.

"Tell me we are not sending this card to anybody I know."

"Why not?"

"Because we look like a pair of idiots, that's why. Is it supposed to be a joke card?"

"No," said Diana, "of course it's not a joke card."

"That makes it even worse. I'm not sending this card out. I'll get another box from Tesco."

"We have to have a joint card. We're engaged."

"You can send it to anyone you like on your side of the family, but I don't want my friends to think I've gone soft in the head."

"Oh, Ben, it's just for a laugh. Here . . ." She reached under the chair and pulled out an enormous envelope. "I haven't forgotten. This is especially for you. I had it made at the same time."

"Thanks," he said.

"You can put it up now if you like. Did you get me one?"

"What?"

"A card."

"Hang on," said Ben. "It's upstairs."

He returned with an envelope. Diana ripped it open. Her face fell. Her lip curled as she took in the picture of a robin sitting on the handle of a spade. "What's this?"

"It's a Christmas card."

"I can see that."

"And?" Ben was confused.

"Couldn't you have made a bit more effort? I'm your *fiancée*, Ben. This is the only Christmas in my entire life that I will get to spend as someone's fiancée. They do make fiancée Christmas cards, you know."

"They do?"

"Yes." Diana sniffed. "Open my card."

Ben opened the card Diana had designed for him. On the front, two teddy bears with their faces cuddled under a piece of mistletoe. Above them were printed the words "Happy Christmas to my wonderful fiancé."

"I thought we could put our cards side by side on the mantelpiece to make a special focal point, but this is just like something you would have given somebody at the office. In fact, you probably did give a certain somebody at the office exactly the same card!" Diana snorted into her handkerchief.

"I haven't given her a Christmas card," said Ben, knowing at once who Diana was referring to. "I swear."

"You better not have. Is she going to be at your office party? I don't think you should go if she is."

"She's not going to be at the party. She's already gone back to Australia for the holidays, to see her family. She's taking two weeks off."

"How do you know in such detail what her plans are?" Diana's eyes narrowed.

"I'd hardly say that was detailed knowledge. I work in the same office as her. Of course I know when she's not coming in."

"Can't they get her moved?" Diana asked. "I hate the fact that you're still working alongside her, after what she did to me." Diana took a deep breath through her nose. Ben recognised it as the precursor to a bout of sobbing. He couldn't face it.

"She's leaving," Ben lied. "She's going freelance."

Diana's face brightened. "Well, that's the best news I've had all day."

Later that day, Ben called his future mother-in-law to see whether she had any idea what Diana really wanted for Christmas.

"She needs new tyres for her car," he said. "I thought I could get that sorted out."

"Oh, Ben," said Susie.

"She said she was going to put them on her Christmas list."

"She didn't mean it, you doughnut. You don't get your fiancée tyres for Christmas. Not unless you don't want to get married."

Ben was tempted to click straight through to the Kwik Fit website.

Susie chuntered on. "You've got to get a girl something sparkly for Christmas, something in a Tiffany box. Get her a charm for her bracelet at least."

That bracelet. Ben hated it. He hated the way it jangled around. He especially hated the way it got caught in his hair, which he wore longer than he liked just to please her, when she grabbed hold of his head in moments of passion. Not that there were many of those any more. Ben had almost choked when Diana told him that she was "renewing her virginity" by swearing off sex until the big day. What was that about? Ben had mentioned that to his best friend, Ed.

"Well, don't think you'll be getting any on your wedding night either," Ed told him. "My missus told me about some statistic that says nine out of ten brides are too exhausted by the big day to put out until halfway through the honeymoon."

It seemed that none of the married people Ben knew had a good thing to say about it, but then he would see an old couple holding hands across the table in the café in Marks & Spencer, which is where everyone in Ben's office went for their lunch, and the sight of such enduring love would fill him with a sense of warmth and contentment. That was what he was getting married for, so that someone would want to hold his hand when he got old. But could he stand the rest of it for long enough to get there?

CHAPTER
THIRTY

That Christmas, Ben's office party was a pretty scaled-down affair out of respect to the colleagues who had lost their jobs earlier in the year. Still Ben expected a very eventful evening.

He had lied to Diana about Lucy having left to go back to Australia. In fact, Lucy had decided that it wasn't economically viable for her to go Down Under that Christmas, not when she would have to be in Australia the following May for her big brother's wedding. As a result, Lucy was still very much in Southampton and she was very much intending to be at the office party. When he overheard her telling one of the secretaries that she had bought a "knockout" dress for the occasion, Ben got the distinct impression that he was the intended recipient of any fatal blow, but Lucy was not at the party when Ben first arrived. He accepted a glass of some cheapo fizz from his boss and toasted their continued success as a department.

"You're looking good," said Mary the office manager, noting Ben's new jacket. "Did Diana buy that for you?"

"I chose it myself," said Ben.

"Sure you did," Mary laughed.

Ben tried to focus on the original compliment. He was looking good. That was what he wanted to hear.

"And how is your lovely fiancée? Still keeping you in line?"

His phone beeped. Diana had texted him.

Remember we've got to go to B&Q in the morning, she wrote. **Don't get too drunk.**

Ben reached for another glass of the cheap bubbles and knocked it back. No sex and no booze? No way. She couldn't tell him not to get drunk that night. It was his bloody office party.

"Line up another one," Ben told the barman.

Lucy arrived about half an hour later than everyone else. The transformation from "Lucy by day" to "Lucy by night" was amazing. Obviously, Ben had previously noticed that his colleague had some pretty impressive charms, but he was used to seeing her in her work clothes. Even on the evening when they finally got it together, Lucy had been dressed in a dull grey suit, having come straight from the office. So though he had seen her in her underwear, he had never seen her in a dress. And certainly he would not have imagined, looking at the dowdy two-pieces she wore most weekdays, that she would ever own something quite as spectacular as the red velvet number she was wearing now.

"Va-va-voom," muttered Tony, Ben's boss. "That can't be our Lucy. I didn't know she had tits."

Ben knew, of course, but now it was obvious to everyone that Lucy had a pair of breasts as big as two babies' heads. Knockout?

"She'll give someone two black eyes before the evening's out," said Tony.

Lucy's figure was shown to absolute perfection by the dress, which was as heavily engineered as a suspension bridge. She paused at the doorway to the party and let her coat fall from her shoulders. She knew exactly how to make an entrance. Ben hadn't known that about her.

The moment was slightly spoiled in that no one rushed forward to take Lucy's coat. The boys were too awestruck, and the girls were too busy calculating how much Lucy must have spent on that evening's ensemble and who exactly among their colleagues she was investing all that effort in. Ben didn't dare go anywhere near her. Lucy hung her coat on the overloaded rack with everyone else's.

She sashayed over to the bar. Ben watched her face. He didn't think he had ever seen her wear that much make-up either. She had lined her eyes with heavy black kohl so that they brought to mind a 1950s starlet like Liz Taylor. Her lips glistened as though she had just licked them. Her hair was piled high on top of her head.

"She looks like that one out of *Mad Men*," said Tony. "Those were the days, eh? Back then, you could ask your colleagues for a quickie without risking a lawsuit."

Ben was just dumbstruck. As Lucy crossed the room, he was sure that she was making a beeline for him and his heart quickened accordingly, but instead she bypassed him and headed for Andy and Mary. Andy? What was she doing talking to that prat?

Lucy talked to Andy for a very long time that evening. Ben knew he had no right whatsoever to be jealous, but he still couldn't stop himself stealing a glance in their direction from time to time, more and more frequently according to how much he drank, to see whether they were still locked in conversation over the chicken teriyaki. It went straight to Ben's heart when he heard Lucy laugh loud and long at something Andy said. What exactly was it he'd told her? Andy wasn't that funny. Lucy herself had told Ben she found Andy irritating. Now she was eating out of his hand.

At last, Andy excused himself to go to the men's room and Ben dashed across to take his place. Not that he wanted Lucy to know that was what he was doing. He claimed that he was looking for a glass of water.

"Are you having a good time?" Ben asked.

"Well, it's not exactly Christmas at the Ritz. I feel a little overdressed, but yes, I suppose it's not as bad as I expected."

"Andy seemed to be making you laugh. What's funny?"

"Why do you want to know? You're not jealous, are you?"

Ben had been rumbled. "No."

Lucy just smiled into her cocktail. God knows how she had managed to get an actual cocktail when everyone else was on cheap cava. She raised her glass to him.

"Bottoms up."

"Is that a mojito?" Ben asked.

"It's a virgin mojito. I want to make sure I don't do anything stupid. Again."

They fell into silence.

Ben did not profess to understand women, but he was glad that Lucy at least had confounded his expectations in one good way: she had given him surprisingly little grief over his engagement. She'd simply started to avoid him except when work dictated they had to be in the same room. They'd become the equivalent of office best buddies during the project that led to their single night of passion. It had been harder to let go of that than it had been to pass up on the sex. He wondered if she felt the same way. Now he found himself pathetically grateful she even offered him the time of day. Was this the moment to try to build a new bridge?

"I'm really grateful for how you handled the whole Diana thing," he said. "I don't ever want it to be awkward. You know, us having to be in the same office."

"Trust me," said Lucy, "neither do I. But it's not for long now, anyway."

"What do you mean?"

"I was going to tell you all later in the month, but you might as well know now. I know you'll keep it quiet."

"Of course," said Ben. "My lips are sealed." He at least owed Lucy that.

"OK. I'm handing my notice in. I'm going freelance so I can concentrate on doing something I really love."

Ben's lie had come to pass. He was astonished. He'd always assumed Lucy was happy in her job.

"What's that, then?" Ben asked. "This thing you love."

"I'll tell you when I'm up and running," said Lucy. "No, strike that," she corrected herself. "I'll *show* you when I'm up and running." She managed a saucy sort of smile. It was the smile that had convinced Ben he was in love with her during the months they had spent working late. That smile, and the idea that she might one day soon be using it on someone else, almost had Ben telling her that he wouldn't marry Diana any more. But then he thought about the dirty bathroom and his father's pronouncement that all women go off sex eventually so you might as well find yourself a wife who can cook and clean instead. And then there was the joint mortgage. It would cost him a fortune to get out of it.

"Are you going to have a leaving party?" Ben asked in an attempt to spin out the conversation.

"I expect so," said Lucy. "I'll see you there if you think you'll be allowed to come."

"I wouldn't miss it. You look amazing tonight," Ben said.

"I know."

"Listen, Lucy, I am sorry. I can't tell you how sorry I am for what happened between us. I promise you that when I went to bed with you, I was absolutely sure that I was going to leave Diana. It's just . . . it's just she's a very vulnerable person."

"Vulnerable?" Lucy snorted. "That's funny. She's vulnerable like a bloody snake. Please tell her thank you for the Christmas card."

Ben was confused.

"You mean you didn't sign it? Great photo on the front, Ben. If you ever get made redundant, you could have a nice sideline in impersonating the future king."

The penny dropped. Diana must have sent Lucy one of the custom-made cards she had promised his friends would never see.

"You haven't . . .?"

"Shown anyone? Of course not. It's almost as embarrassing for me as it is for you, after all. But I really don't want to get on the wrong side of your sweet and vulnerable fiancée again, so if you'll excuse me, I'm going to cut short our intimate little conversation before someone thinks there's a reason to gossip."

Ben didn't know where to put himself. After Lucy left him at the bar, he felt so conspicuously alone that he was almost grateful when Andy returned.

"Where did she go?" Andy asked.

"Ladies', I think," said Ben.

"Man, she is looking hot tonight. I never would have thought she had it in her, but tonight she looks like that one out of *Mad Men*. Do you think I'm in with a chance?"

"In your dreams," Ben replied.

He stalked to the hotel lobby and called a cab.

All the way home he was fuming. There were so many reasons to be angry with Diana. Firstly, she had promised that no one he knew would ever have sight of that stupid Christmas card. Secondly, she had sent a card to *Lucy*. God only knew what she had written

188

inside it. Thirdly, Ben couldn't even bring the subject up, since as far as Diana was concerned, Lucy should not actually have received the card, having already left the UK for Australia. Ben was so angry he could have thumped his way through the front door.

But when he got in, Diana was acting especially sweet. She was dressed in her pink pyjamas and wearing a pair of huge, fluffy slippers in the shape of white bunnies on her feet. She threw her arms round Ben's neck.

"Have you missed me?" she asked.

"Of course," he said automatically.

"Was anybody interesting there?" she probed.

"Nobody interesting," he lied.

Not even the fluffy slippers could keep Ben from noticing the murderous grand inquisitor in Diana's eyes.

"I cannot wait for Christmas," said Diana in a little-girl voice as she snuggled into bed beside him. "It's our last Christmas before we get married. Have you got me a very big present?"

CHAPTER
THIRTY-ONE

Melanie Harris would be using the Christmas holiday as a time for stock-taking. Bride on Time always saw a bit of a rush in the new year, as those lucky girls who'd found an engagement ring under the Christmas tree started their mad, gleeful dash to the altar. And like most retail businesses, Melanie thought it was a good idea to have a January sale, offering the least tattered of the sample dresses at incredible knock-down prices, sometimes as much as 80 per cent off the retail price.

The January sale always gave Melanie a warm glow. During the two weeks when she offered her bridal bargains, Melanie met a very different set of would-be brides to the ones she met throughout the rest of the year. These were brides who couldn't otherwise afford Melanie's services. More often than not, they were far nicer women than the ones who could.

Melanie wondered if it was her imagination or had the brides she'd dressed over the past few years really become much more demanding. Spoiled.

There were definitely some brides she warmed to more than others. It was quite an effort making sure that she was polite and professional even when she wanted to slap some girl for being such a brat. Diana

Ashcroft was a brat. If it was possible to be a brat at twenty-nine.

Seven bridesmaids! Still that didn't beat Melanie's record. She'd once dressed a bride who had eight bridesmaids, five of whom were her daughters. The bride also had a son, who, at thirteen years old, was understandably resistant to being dressed as Little Lord Fauntleroy. Melanie remembered the poor lad well. She had met him three times when he was dragged along to dress fittings with his Russian-doll sisters. Melanie tried to persuade the bride that a ring-bearer as well as eight bridesmaids might be overkill, but the bride was insistent that her son should play a proper part. That was how the poor sod ended up attending his mother's second wedding dressed as a chimney sweep.

"Sweeps are supposed to bring luck," said the bride.

Her son clearly didn't think he was the lucky one.

From time to time Melanie found herself being invited to her brides' weddings. Each time she acted flattered, though she knew that for the most part they wanted her there because they didn't trust their mothers or bridesmaids to know how to lace up a tricky bodice or loop up a long train for the first dance. After seven years of wasted Saturdays, Melanie made a policy decision that she wouldn't attend any weddings except those of people she knew outside work. Too much drama. And then there was the fact that Melanie no longer felt quite so optimistic about marriage herself.

She just sold dresses, she said to Heidi and Sarah sometimes. She didn't sell dreams. She certainly couldn't make dreams come true.

If it were possible for dreams to come true, Melanie would not be spending Christmas Day on her own, but that, as usual, was the plan. Since her last Christmas with Keith, back in 1996, there had been more than a few lonely Christmases for Melanie Harris. To start with, she had spent her newly single Christmases with her parents, flying back to the coop at the age of thirty-seven, but that was depressing. They weren't like the Christmases of her childhood. In many ways, a Christmas alone was preferable to a Christmas spent watching the Queen's Speech with her mother while her father snored by the fire. She always seemed to get into a fight with her mother by teatime.

The first Christmas alone was the worst, but only for the first hour or so, when Melanie woke up on Christmas morning and her loneliness seemed like a physical ache in her chest. The trick was to remember that it was just a day. It lasted twenty-four hours, like any other day. When you thought about it like that, it wasn't so hard to endure. Now she looked forward to a couple of days of peace and quiet away from Bride on Time almost as much as she had looked forward to her first married Christmas with Keith.

How naughty it had felt to tell both sets of parents that they would be having their first married Christmas alone together in their half-furnished marital home. Other newly married couples they knew had tossed coins to see who would be the "lucky one", whose family they would visit on the day itself. Keith and Melanie circumvented that dubious contest. They were delighted at the thought of a Christmas spent exactly as they pleased.

The day started wonderfully well. Keith made Buck's Fizz, the very height of sophistication for 1980s Southampton. They opened their presents. Having both come from families where only the children were allowed to open Christmas presents before lunch, they revelled in the wickedness of opening their gifts to each other in bed. Melanie had bought Keith a radio. Keith had bought her a pair of pearl earrings from Argos. Melanie adored them and put them on at once.

However, Christmas lunch was an absolute disaster. Though Melanie had watched her mother cook a turkey every Christmas for twenty-one years, her own first attempt at the most important roast of the year was barely edible. She had underestimated how long it would take to defrost the damn thing and even after two hours in the oven, it still came out pink and cold in the middle. Melanie blamed Keith. If he hadn't insisted on buying the biggest turkey he could find, despite the fact that they were only two, she might have had a fighting chance.

"It doesn't matter," he tried to reassure her. "The legs will be OK."

The vegetables were equally awful. Though Melanie did everything she thought she had seen Cynthia do, the parsnips came out soggy. The roast potatoes, too, wouldn't seem to go crisp. Meanwhile, the Brussels sprouts were hard enough to be classified as dangerous weapons. The gravy, which Melanie tried to make from a proper recipe, using the juices from the undercooked turkey, ended up less a sauce than a series of dubious-looking blobs in mucus. Food poisoning in suspension. Melanie started to cry when Keith said that he would rather have Bisto in any case.

"You think I'm useless," she said.

"I don't," he promised. "I really don't."

"Oh, yes, you do."

Melanie got her chance to laugh when Keith set fire to his new tie (a gift from his parents) while trying to ignite the Christmas pudding.

"It's not funny!" Keith bellowed from the kitchen as he soaked his ruined tie in the sink.

"For God's sake, Keith, you were supposed to be lighting a pudding, not a barbecue."

"I could have burned to death!" Keith shouted. "Still, it's better than dying of food poisoning, I suppose."

Keith's attempt at humour went unappreciated and the newlyweds didn't talk to each other for most of the afternoon.

As was becoming usual in their fledgling marriage, it was Keith who broke the ice during the playing of the national anthem after the Queen's Speech. He was standing up for "God Save the Queen", a habit instilled in him by his dad. Melanie was lounging on the sofa.

"Do you think the queen wears a paper hat for her Christmas dinner," Keith asked, "or do you think she lets the rest of the family try on some of her real crowns?"

"Are you talking to me?"

194

"No, I'm talking to the bloody draught excluder. Who do you think I'm talking to?"

"I didn't think you were talking to me."

"What do you mean? You're the one's been giving me radio silence since lunchtime, Melanie Harris."

"This is the worst Christmas you've ever had. Admit it. I bet you wish you'd gone to your mum's."

"No," said Keith, sitting down beside her. "I only ever wanted to be here on my own with you."

"But the dinner was terrible, wasn't it? I made a mess of the turkey. The sprouts were just awful."

"And I nearly set fire to the house. But it doesn't matter," said Keith. "It really doesn't. We've got the rest of our lives to practise."

Keith and Melanie spent what was left of the day cuddled up on the sofa. They watched footage of the royal family going to church at Sandringham on the news. By that time, the nation knew that the Princess of Wales was pregnant with her first child. She looked radiant as she greeted well-wishers on her way into the Christmas service. Melanie could not have been more delighted if she had been able to announce a pregnancy of her own. That would come soon, Keith assured her. It was just a matter of time.

CHAPTER
THIRTY-TWO

Like Melanie, Kate had spent quite a few Christmases alone. When she got to thirty, she decided that it was just tragic to keep going back to her parents' house: the single daughter still sleeping in her old bedroom with a Duran Duran duvet cover on the single bed. So Kate made certain that each year after that she booked a fantastic exotic holiday for the Christmas week. It certainly helped ease the pain of hearing that Dan would not share his Christmas with her again to know that she would be spending Christmas Day on a beach.

That year would be very different. For a start, she had Ian now, though thanks to his fear of supermarkets, they had failed to score a turkey. Also, Kate's mother's illness had brought it home to Kate that she wanted to spend that Christmas with her family. Tess agreed that they should make that year a proper family affair, with all of them around the same table for the first time since Lily was born. She made it sound like a wonderful, jolly idea. The unspoken reason behind it lurked like the ghost of Christmas Future. The initial relief of hearing that their mother's lumpectomy had gone well had soon dulled with the thought of the radiotherapy to follow. They were still a long way from getting the all-clear.

So, Kate and Ian drove down to the south coast on Christmas Eve. They were billeted at Tess's house to save Elaine and John from having to do extra laundry. When they arrived, Lily was already on the naughty step, bargaining hard to keep her mother from mentioning the latest infringement to Father Christmas. Tess was hugely relieved when her sister appeared.

"Here," she said to Lily, "you can drive Auntie Kate up the wall instead."

Lily did not stop until ten in the evening, by which time all the adults wanted to go to bed themselves. Ian volunteered to tell the bedtime story, allowing Kate a few moments with her sister over the washing-up.

"How's Mum?" Kate asked. "She keeps saying she's fine, but you get to see more of her than I do. What's the real story?"

"She's OK," said Tess. "Tired from the operation, of course, but I think that what's stressing her out more is the idea that she might be having radiotherapy right around your wedding."

"Oh."

"She's putting a lot of pressure on herself in that respect."

"She hasn't said anything to me," said Kate.

"Of course she wouldn't. She doesn't want to upset you."

"What exactly is she stressing out about? She doesn't have to do anything for the wedding except turn up. It's only going to be a small affair. With a stupidly big dress."

"I love that dress."

"You don't have to wear it."

Tess handed Kate another plate to dry.

"Kate, you don't think . . . No." Tess shook her head. "It isn't fair of me to even suggest it."

"Suggest what?"

"No, I can't ask you. It's so soon. It isn't fair."

"Just bloody ask me!" Kate laughed.

"You don't think you could hold back on the wedding for a month or two? To give Mum and Dad breathing space after all the hospital stuff. I know you've waited for a long time for this, Kate, and I wouldn't ask, but . . ."

"It's fine. I understand."

"A couple of months, though? Oh, it's nuts. You're supposed to be getting married in March."

"It's not such a crazy idea. I'll ask Ian."

Though she didn't say it to Tess, Kate felt an odd sense of relief flood her limbs at the thought of an extra couple of months.

Kate asked Ian what he thought of the plan when they got into bed that night. He agreed, of course. How could he not? It wasn't as though Kate was asking to postpone because she needed an extra month or two to lose enough weight to get into her frock. Still, Kate was surprised that he was so chilled out about it.

"Are you sure? The wedding we've planned is only ten weeks or so away."

"Whatever makes you happy," he said.

Kate told her parents the following morning.

The television was on, showing the arrival of the royal family for the Christmas-morning service at Sandringham. Elaine was disappointed by the absence of Prince William and his fiancée, but she approved whole-heartedly when she heard that William was working and Kate was spending a last Christmas with her mum and dad.

"She should make the most of it. Her life is going to be turned upside down. She's going to be even more popular than Diana," said Elaine. "She's got that same glow about her, but she's seen enough of the world not to get swept up in all the hoo-ha."

The news flashed to a shot of Kate and William announcing their engagement again.

"Just seeing those two together warms the cockles of my heart," said Tess.

"I can only imagine what pressure she must be under to organise such a big wedding so quickly," said Elaine.

Kate seized her opportunity.

"Exactly," she said. "And to think I thought we could organise even a small wedding in a few months. Mum, Dad . . . Ian and I have been talking. We've both got a hell of a lot of stuff on at the moment. Ian's busy at the office, and I need to prepare for my new job. I totally underestimated how much I would have to do. So we wondered if you would mind if we put the wedding back a little bit. Maybe until May?"

"Oh, Kate," said Elaine, "why would you want to do that?"

"We just think we could have a far better wedding if we had a little more time to devote to planning it."

"But . . ."

"We've waited long enough, I know, and that's why we're not too worried about waiting for just a few weeks longer. We're only going to do it once, so why not make sure it's really special? And if we have it later, we can take a bit of time for a honeymoon too. I couldn't disappear for a week so soon into my new job if we did get married in March."

"Are you sure?"

"We're sure."

Ian nodded in agreement.

"Well," said John, "I suppose it would give us one less thing to think about for the moment too."

"But it's only ten weeks away!"

"Exactly. Ten weeks and I haven't prepared a thing."

"Haven't you?" Elaine looked stern.

"Except the dress."

"All right," said Elaine. "If you think it's for the best. Your father is right that I've been worrying that I can't help as much as I'd like to because of all the hospital visits, but if you're happy to wait until May . . . As soon as the radiotherapy is over, I am going to properly throw myself into organising a wedding for you."

"Mum, there's nothing much to organise. We're getting married at a register office and then we're having lunch."

"You don't have to have a small wedding because of me."

"Because of you?"

"Yes. I know it's not what you really wanted. You just scaled down your plans because you thought it would be more manageable with me being in and out of hospital."

"That's not the case."

"Kate, I know you. I've known you for your entire life. I knew what you wanted before you even had the words to say it. I know that you don't want your wedding day to be like any other day of the week."

"I'm really happy with what we've planned," Kate insisted.

"Rubbish. Now that you've delayed it a couple of months, why don't you let me put some effort into making it a really special day? We did it for Tess. Don't you remember how lovely her wedding day was? It wouldn't be right if we didn't do the same for you."

"Even though we spent your wedding money on the patio," John chipped in.

"That's why I want to help with the organisation," said Elaine.

"Really, Mum, Dad, I don't want you to worry about anything. I just want you to concentrate on getting well."

"It won't be a worry. It'll be a pleasure. I'll always remember how excited you were when Charles and Diana got married. You were excited about it for weeks before it happened. You were crazy about that dress. You wanted a wedding just like that. And with the dress you've already bought, why shouldn't you have your Princess Diana moment at last?"

"Mum," said Kate, "a year after that wedding, I wanted to be Jayne Torvill."

CHAPTER
THIRTY-THREE

"What do you think?" Kate asked Ian as they were getting ready for bed that night. "Mum and Dad seem determined to get involved."

"Well, let them."

"But they'd like us to get married down here."

The conversation had quickly developed from a discussion of a mere change of date to the planning of an entirely different kind of wedding. Of course, Kate and Ian could have a London register-office wedding if they wanted to, but something on the south coast would be entirely easier for her parents to arrange.

"I don't mind," said Ian.

"I thought you wanted to get married in London."

"I want to do whatever you want to do."

"Really? So you wouldn't mind being married down here?"

Ian shrugged.

"Tell me," said Kate. "Tell me please what your honest opinion is, because I have a feeling that Mum is going to run with this if we let her. If I know her, she's already online looking for a coach and horses."

"I haven't really thought about it."

"Your gut instinct, Ian. That's what I'm after. I don't want anyone to be upset or offended. We've got to tell Mum and Dad what we want and be really clear about it."

"I don't know. I want you to be happy, I suppose."

"And I want you to be happy, but right now I have no idea whether it would make you happy to stick with our original plan or whether you would prefer we got married in a yurt."

"Not a yurt . . ."

"Great. Not a yurt. But what do you think about Mum and Dad taking over? I mean, really taking over. Doing everything?"

Ian shrugged again. "I'm tired. Can't we talk about it tomorrow?" he asked. He rolled over. End of conversation as far as he was concerned. Kate counted cracks on the ceiling and fumed.

"Whatever you want to do."

Kate felt her frustration rising again. Ian thought he was being helpful when he said that, or a variation on it, every time she asked his opinion on what he felt like doing at the weekend or whether he wanted fish or chicken for supper or whether he wanted to sell both their flats and buy a house in between the Commons or splurge all the money on a year-long five-star trip round the world. He couldn't be like that about their wedding too.

By teatime on Boxing Day, the wheels were in motion for a very different wedding than the one Kate and Ian had planned for March. John suggested a family walk to work off some of the food they had been stuffing in during the past twenty-four hours. The walk took them past the golf-course hotel where Kate had endured her first and last wedding fair.

"We could ask if they have availability," Elaine suggested.

"But . . . Mum . . ."

"The food is good and it's ever so reasonable," Elaine said to Ian.

"The food's not bad," said Tess, a little more guardedly.

"Well, let's go and see what they can do for us," Ian responded, ever happy to please.

Kate was open-mouthed.

"No harm in just looking," said Ian.

"Ian," Kate hissed, "you have no idea what you're getting us into. The place looks like a Travelodge."

Ian disagreed. To Kate's astonishment, in contrast to her views, he said he actually liked the aesthetic of the jumble of buildings from different eras, and he was impressed by the Christmas tree in the lobby. It was tastefully decorated. That was a good sign. Ian was swung by the free mince pie offered with every full-priced Italian coffee. "Why don't we just see what they can do, for comparison's sake?"

Elaine was delighted.

"We can do the ceremony and the reception," the hotel manager explained. "If you decide to have both, with a canapé reception between, we can do a very reasonable price. Just fifty pounds per head including half a bottle of wine and two glasses of champagne per guest."

Kate saw to her surprise that Ian was nodding along, encouraged by her mother.

"I like the sound of that," he said. "It would be nice and simple to have everything in one place. What dates do you have available?"

"Well, we're very popular. Most of the summer weekends are already booked up. We could do a weekday, but if you want a Saturday, then the only day we've got before October is the day after the royal wedding, 30 April. We had a cancellation."

"Well, we wouldn't have to worry about getting time off to get ready," said Ian, thinking logically, "not with Easter right before and then the extra bank holiday."

"Oh, it would be so easy," said Elaine, "if you really were happy to get married down here, Kate. I could just take control. You wouldn't have to worry about a thing except turning up on time. You could just concentrate on starting your new job like you need to. And it's so much cheaper than London. You could have so many more guests at this price!"

"My mother would be pleased to hear that." Ian nodded. "I've got a big extended family."

"What do you think?"

"I think that anything that takes the worry off our shoulders is a great thing," said Ian. "I don't want Kate to feel under pressure, especially with the new job."

All eyes were now on Kate, who suddenly felt very much under pressure. Eager and anxious to please, everyone awaited her approval. Kate couldn't find the words.

"Three other brides have been considering the package you're after for that weekend," said the hotel manager to break the silence.

"Oh, you might lose it!" said Elaine, betraying her own wishes in the desperation of her exclamation.

"Then it's settled," Kate said. "We're getting married here, at *a golf-course hotel*."

"I can get a couple of practice rounds in the day before," said Ian, completely missing the sarcasm in Kate's tone. He pulled out his credit card to put down a deposit for a canapé reception and three-course meal for 150 guests.

How had that happened? Kate asked herself that night in bed. How had her simple, chic city wedding become a "country-house-hotel" extravaganza? It was just like the dress. The moment she saw her mother's eager face, she was doomed. Kate could not disappoint her, especially not now.

But it's my day. Wasn't that what Kate was supposed to say? Everyone always bangs on about it being the bride's day, but the fact was, it wasn't Kate's day any more, from the dress to the venue. Even Kate's guest list was under scrutiny. Now that the potential invitees had increased from 40 to 150, her mother had mentioned at least a dozen family friends who would appreciate an invitation. None of this was what Kate had envisaged, and yet she felt that she couldn't complain. Officially, it was her day, but she also wanted the day to reflect Ian's desires. Ian seemed to want to get married on a bloody golf course! And then she wanted the day to make her parents happy too. If, as Tess had suggested, being more involved with the wedding would give their mother something to focus on other than radiotherapy, then how could Kate deny her the opportunity to take control?

"You know that Mum will make sure it's tasteful," said Tess.

Kate had a flashback to her encounter with the chair-dresser at the bridal fair.

It didn't matter, Kate tried to tell herself. Nothing mattered except actually getting married and becoming man and wife. Man and wife? How about woman and husband? Kate thought. OK. Nothing mattered except becoming woman and husband. It really didn't matter if the day didn't reflect Kate and Ian's personalities as long as they signed the register and everybody had a good time.

She rolled over to look at Ian. He was sleeping soundly again. None of this seemed to bother him. He swore blind that he wanted to get married in that golf-course hotel, but Kate had the distinct impression that he would have married in a yurt, just so long as he didn't have to make any effort to plan it. Increasingly, she began to think that Ian didn't want to have to make an effort for any reason at all.

CHAPTER
THIRTY-FOUR

14 February 2011

"How does he love me? Let me count the presents."

That was Diana's mantra on Valentine's Day. For Diana, 14 February was every bit as important as Christmas and her birthday. Not for her the old-fashioned romance of an anonymous Valentine's card. Diana expected a card, a gift (a significant gift) and an evening on the town. Ben knew not to disappoint. It wasn't worth the grief. What Diana wanted, Diana got, starting with a lot more time off.

Diana had, as threatened, given up her part-time job right after Christmas. Since then she had thrown herself into wedding preparations. The blackboard in the kitchen formed the centre of operations. Every day a new to-do list appeared in neat white chalk letters. There was one column for Diana's responsibilities and one for Ben's. Ben couldn't understand how, though he was still very much in full-time employment, he seemed to have easily as many items in his column as Diana did in hers.

"Yours are just little things," she explained. "I don't think you appreciate how much pressure there is on me. I'm not just planning a wedding; I'm planning the rest of our lives."

Certainly, she appeared to have taken to micro-managing Ben's time. They never seemed to have a night to themselves any more. Friday evenings were now taken up with dance lessons for that all-important first dance. They inevitably ended up in a row when Ben accidentally stepped on Diana's toes. Meanwhile, Saturday nights now meant another bloody dinner party.

"I want to share our happiness with our friends," said Diana. "I like having people round for dinner."

Ben liked to go down the pub and stand in a corner with his mates while Diana and *her* mates took up another corner of the room. He liked to go somewhere where it was too loud to tune in to the women's conversations. He did not want to have to sit round the dinner table listening to Diana and Nicole talk about the wedding plans again. Ben was certain that Lucy had arranged a three-day conference for 200 people in Dubai with considerably less fuss.

But Diana wanted to play the domestic goddess. She invited people that Ben had never met before to share their weekends. It seemed the only criterion for an invitation was that the invitees were married.

"Being engaged makes everything different," she explained to Ben. "We can't hang around with all those single people any more. It isn't right you being out with your mates when they're on the pull. Someone might get the wrong idea about you."

Given that his record was far from spotless, Ben could only accept the sentence handed down. No more socialising without his bride-to-be.

210

Diana ordered a hostess trolley from John Lewis online and threw herself into Delia's complete cookery course. The only good thing about those Saturday-night dinner parties was the food. The rest of the week, Diana was on a strict diet.

Oh God, the diet. Ben felt as though he had been put on a diet too. Since the night of their engagement party, Diana had not touched a drop of alcohol. "Pure, liquid sugar," she announced. Neither had there been a loaf of bread in the house, except if they had guests. Biscuits were a distant memory, as were crisps and tortilla chips. It was miserable.

Suddenly, they had to go to the cathedral every Sunday too. The bishop may have been swayed by Dave's excellence as a kitchen-fitter, but that did not mean that Diana and Ben could get away with paying only lip service to the idea of being part of the congregation. Diana did not mind too much. Each Sunday gave her a chance to dress up. She daydreamed through the sermons, imagining herself walking up the aisle to the delighted "Ooh"s and "Aah"s of her wedding guests. It was almost as much fun to walk in slightly late to the Sunday Eucharist.

"Who is that elegant woman?" Diana imagined the usual parishioners, who were uniformly dowdy, wondering.

Ben sat through the same sermons, focusing on the thud of his headache and wondering if he would ever get a Sunday lie-in again. And then, after the service, they would inevitably end up at the shopping centre. There was no end to the list of items Diana absolutely "must have" in connection with the big day. Even Sunday afternoons were no longer sacred. Susie or Nicole would inevitably pitch up at some point, to go over the parts of the wedding machinery that were under their auspices. Ben simply couldn't understand how Diana could have given up her job and yet still need to spend all weekend comparing floral arrangements and different kinds of sponge cake. He could only be thankful that he didn't have to pay for it.

The wedding was going to be a ridiculously big event. Diana's guest list looked set to dwarf that of Kate Middleton and Prince William. Her very first draft list had come to 187. The final cut was nearer 250 on her side alone. Even if Ben only invited his immediate family and closest friends, the list would soon hit 300.

"Do you know two hundred and fifty people?" Ben asked. "I mean, people you don't know through Facebook."

Diana straightened up as she prepared to defend her position. "I do know a lot of people, and you can't ask someone without inviting their other half."

"But that means there will be people that neither of us know at the wedding. I haven't met any of this lot." Ben indicated a group of eight names.

"They're from work. There is no way I can cut these people. You have to understand that my friends come in sets. I can't invite one of the girls from the office without inviting all the others. Likewise, if I invite only half my friends from school, then you can bet that someone will be offended. I don't want to offend anyone, Ben. You never know when you're going to want them on your side."

Ben examined the list again. On it were at least half a dozen women that Diana never seemed to have a kind word for. Now all of a sudden they were people she couldn't afford to offend. It wasn't even as though she had to face them at the office any more.

It wasn't just the cost of it. Dave Ashcroft had made it clear that nothing was too good for his daughter, his only child. As far as Dave was concerned, Diana could invite the whole city. Ben, however, did not really like the idea of such a big party.

"Why not?" Diana asked him.

She didn't seem to think that simply preferring a smaller event, peopled by guests they actually knew and cared about, was a good enough excuse.

"We've got to fill a cathedral, Ben. A cathedral! It's going to look rubbish if we only have people in the front two pews."

Thank God Diana's father had money. The recession didn't seem to have hit him too badly. It was a relief, since he had lent Diana and Ben the deposit for their starter home and Ben was far from being in a position to pay him back.

On Valentine's evening, Ben was acutely conscious of how little he could afford the charm he had bought for Diana's horrible bracelet. She looked at it briefly. "The Eiffel Tower! Does this mean you're taking me to France for the weekend?"

"No," said Ben, "it means it's the only Tiffany charm I could find that you don't already have."

Diana pushed the little blue box to one side.

"Never mind. I've got some good news. Dad says that for our wedding present he's decided to pay off our mortgage."

Ben felt as though Diana's words formed another golden rope round his wrist.

CHAPTER
THIRTY-FIVE

Kate hid her disappointment when she awoke on Valentine's Day to discover that Ian seemed to have forgotten it. He had left for work early that morning, leaving her sleeping. When she got up, Kate saw that he had opened her card to him and put it in pride of place on the mantelpiece. The book she had bought him was on the kitchen table. She could find nothing for her.

Kate went into her new office and put her head down. She had a lot to prove. That was much more important than Valentine's Day. Lunchtime passed. Still nothing from Ian. Kate had thought that he would make amends for having forgotten and perhaps send her an emergency bunch of flowers. No. Kate found it hard not to look disappointed when three enormous bouquets arrived and were distributed among various girls in the office. Ian hadn't even sent her a text to thank her for her card and gift.

"What did Ian get you?" one of her new colleagues asked. That made things even worse.

"Oh," said the colleague when Kate admitted that Ian had forgotten. "That's what men are like! The minute they've got you, they give up trying."

"It certainly seems that way," said Kate.

"I'm sure he'll have a surprise for you when you get home."

"It doesn't matter if he doesn't," said Kate. "It's just a Hallmark holiday." She said it in such a way that she almost believed it.

Then Helen texted, **I hope Ian remembered V Day**.

He didn't, Kate responded.

Mark got me a new filter for cooker hood, texted Helen. **Married life**.

Later that afternoon, Matt called. Kate had fallen into a pattern of speaking to him often since they had gone for their catch-up drink in December. There were plenty of excuses for a chat. She was grateful to be able to discuss Elaine's ongoing treatment. But they had fallen into talking about everything else too. Matt knew all about the politics in Kate's new office, for example. She told him things about her new company that she simply didn't bother to tell Ian. Ian didn't do office politics, and when she had tried to discuss the machinations of her own colleagues in the past, he had simply told her to ignore them. Matt seemed to understand that it wasn't always that easy. Kate was aware that he was becoming quite a confidant.

"Did you get my card?" asked Matt.

"What card?"

"The enormous one covered with fluffy bunnies. It was attached to the hundred red roses."

"Oh, that card," said Kate.

"I expect you couldn't find it under all the other cards you were sent. I imagine Ian bought up Interflora."

"Not quite," said Kate. "How's your Valentine's Day so far?"

"Total bag of shite. It's Valentine's Day and the only thing the postman dropped off at my house this morning was a letter from my soon-to-be ex-wife's solicitor, claiming that I've got much more money than I ever knew I had and she wants half of it. How's your mum?"

"Starts radiotherapy next week."

"You coming down?"

"I expect so."

"Call me. I could do with a night out."

"That'd be great."

Kate was aware as she put the phone down that her mood had improved immeasurably at the thought of seeing Matt again. There was nothing to it, though. Nothing that might explain why she still hadn't mentioned their renewed friendship to Helen, for example.

When she got home, she found that Ian had made a special effort to make up for having forgotten to mark the most romantic day in the calendar. He handed her a bedraggled bunch of roses as she walked into the kitchen.

"I got them from the garage," he said.

"You could at least pretend they're from Moyses Stevens," said Kate.

"Don't want you to think I'm wasting all our money on furbelows."

There was little chance of that. "What's this?"

Ian had laid the table. On both the plates he had put out was a Marks & Spencer ready meal, still in its box. A bottle of wine from no vineyard Kate had ever heard of stood in the middle of the table.

"All this for less than ten pounds."

"Great," said Kate.

"We don't have to eat it here. We can eat it in front of the television."

"Even better."

From time to time, especially when she was with Dan, Kate had craved the simplicity of a television dinner. There were never any television dinners with Dan, unless he was feeling very unwell. At first, that was wonderful, but gradually Kate came to realise that by keeping up the romance, Dan was keeping her at arm's length. He was preventing her from becoming part of his "real" life. By contrast, Ian had never hidden anything from Kate, but sometimes she thought such a total lack of mystique was just as bad as Dan's refusal to let Kate see his "day to day". As she looked at the cheap bottle of red, Kate tried to remember the last time Ian had taken her out. He really did seem to believe that now they were engaged, there was no longer any reason for them to "date".

"Do you know how to cook these things?"

Ian passed her the ready-meal boxes before she had time to take off her coat.

"Thanks." Kate tossed the ready meals onto the kitchen counter. They landed rather more heavily than she had intended. It sounded as though she had thrown them down aggressively.

"What's the matter?" Ian asked. "Have I done something wrong again?"

"Why does it always have to be about you?" Kate asked. "Nothing's wrong. I'm ... I'm getting my period," she lied. She took the ready meals out of their cardboard sleeves. "Twenty minutes at gas mark six. It says on the back."

Ian didn't even move to put the oven on.

Kate had a profound sense of dissatisfaction in that moment. When they first started going out, she thought that Ian had appreciated the stresses of Kate's position as a partner in a law firm. He certainly wouldn't expect her to become a little woman, she was sure. But since she had spent that time on gardening leave, he seemed to completely defer to her in all things domestic. He had even asked her how to turn on the tumble-dryer.

"How did you turn it on before you met me?" she asked.

Ian definitely did not seem to have taken into account the fact that Kate was now back at work. Leaving her in the kitchen, he had disappeared to take a relaxing shower. Kate stared at the two ready meals in front of her. She could tell Ian to cook his own bloody cardboard dinner or she could turn the oven on herself.

Too exhausted from her first fortnight at the new office to argue the feminist position, Kate turned the oven on. Would the next Valentine's gift she received be an extractor-fan filter like Helen's? Was this it for the rest of her life?

CHAPTER
THIRTY-SIX

Melanie didn't want to be going out to dinner that night. She wasn't sure which was worse, to spend Valentine's Day alone, or to spend it with someone she simply wasn't that excited about. The girls at the salon seemed certain that Valentine's Day alone was by far the worse option. They had fussed about their Valentine's dates ever since they came back to work after Christmas. Sarah had been borderline miserable for weeks as she pondered whether or not her fledgling relationship was serious enough to guarantee her a date for the most important romantic date in the calendar. Heidi had limped on with a relationship well past its sell-by date in order to ensure that she likewise wasn't at home alone on the fourteenth.

"I can't stand the thought of having to shag him any more," she admitted to Sarah within Melanie's earshot, "but I'm going to carry on until the weekend after Valentine's, for sure. We've been together for five years. He's bound to get me a good Valentine's Day present, isn't he?"

Melanie could hardly believe such cynicism. And yet wasn't she guilty of the same? She was going out with Phil that night because she didn't want to be alone either. She already knew that Phil wasn't going to replace Keith in her heart. She had known that from the first time they went out together. But he was a decent bloke. He had good manners. From time to time he made her laugh. And it was nice to be taken to the better restaurants around Southampton. It was just . . . she would have to tell him it was going nowhere before she found herself in the position of having to turn him down at the bedroom door. So far he hadn't been pushy, but Melanie was sure that he hadn't been taking her out for almost three months just because he enjoyed their conversations about travel and music.

She made the mistake of confiding in Heidi.

"I wouldn't worry. He might never try it on," said Heidi. "He's what — sixty? His prostate will be shot to pieces by now."

Melanie winced. There were moments when she thought that Heidi was too coarse for a job at Bride on Time, but she was an excellent seamstress. She was worth her weight in gold when it came to making speedy last-minute adjustments. There had been numerous occasions when Heidi had saved the day for a bride who had lost too much weight in the stress of the wedding run-up or, conversely, failed to lose enough. For that, Melanie overlooked Heidi's cruder pronouncements. Even so, Melanie decided she would have to be more discreet in the future.

Should Melanie just have given up on love? No one would bother too much if she did, she was certain. There was something romantic about announcing "I'm a widow" when people asked about her personal life. It

222

was a reason and an explanation in itself. She didn't let people press her for the details. All she said was she was very happy by herself. But she wasn't. Not really. Not any more.

She'd met Phil at a meeting of local business owners. Melanie liked these meetings, usually held in a pub, where small-business owners from the local area got together to moan about rates and rents and the local council's lack of support. She had been seeing Phil at those meetings for years. She didn't know much about him other than that he ran a small company specialising in computer spares and repairs. Then she asked if he might have a look at Bride on Time's IT situation. While he was installing some anti-virus software on Melanie's own computer, they got chatting. She discovered that he was a widower. His wife had died of ovarian cancer two years before. He told Melanie that he was relieved to be able to talk about his situation with someone who understood the pain of being left behind.

Now Melanie found herself glazing over when the conversation moved on to Phil's wife, as it inevitably did after they'd both sunk half a bottle of wine. It was so clear that he'd loved that woman completely. He said that he was ready to move on, but Melanie knew that his readiness really only equated to wanting something, anything, to fill the gaping hole in his life.

On Valentine's Day, the conversation about Sally, as Phil's wife was called, came earlier than usual in proceedings. Phil had chosen a lovely restaurant, full of starry-eyed young couples and a few more established pairs just going through the motions. There were candles on every table. Phil had brought Melanie a rose. One young man proposed to his girlfriend the minute the waiter had taken their order. He said that he had intended to propose after the meal but would have been too nervous to eat if he hadn't proposed first. Melanie couldn't help smiling as she overheard the young couple's excited chatter about where and when they might marry. Should she slip the girl her business card?

Only Phil did not seem buoyed up by the atmosphere in the room.

"This was one of Sally's favourite restaurants," he announced, after the waiter had delivered their smoked-salmon platters.

"Oh," said Melanie.

"It was her second favourite restaurant in the world."

"Which was her absolute favourite?" asked Melanie, playing the game. One of the ways in which she knew Phil wasn't for her was how easy she found it to engage in conversation about his dead wife. She wasn't in the least bit jealous of his enduring attachment to the dead woman's memory.

"La Coupole, in Paris," said Phil. "Do you know it?"

"Actually, I went there once. Just the once, mind."

"We only went there once too, for our twenty-fifth anniversary, but Sally never stopped going on about it. After that, every restaurant we went to was measured against La Coupole. She loved the Frenchness of it."

"It is pretty French," Melanie agreed.

"When did you go?"

224

"Oh" — Melanie speared some salmon — "it was years ago now. I'd rather not talk about it, if it's all the same to you."

For the rest of the meal they chatted amiably about the difficulties involved with the new VAT rate. It was hardly the most scintillating subject. Melanie passed up the offer of dessert. Phil, as ever, insisted that he drove her home. He stopped at the top of the driveway and turned off his engine. This was a new development: Melanie was used to Phil leaving the engine running while she let herself out of the car.

"Let me walk you to the door," he said that night.

"It's fine," said Melanie. "I can see it from here. I won't get lost."

"I'd still like to walk you there."

"OK," said Melanie. She would think of some reason not to let him in when they got there. That was her prerogative. At the door, she took out her keys and hesitated. She did not want to have to offer him coffee.

"It's been a lovely evening," she began, preparing her spiel about an early start.

"Yes," said Phil, "it has."

"So . . ."

Phil took both Melanie's hands.

"Look, Melanie," he said, "you've probably been wondering where this is going. I know I have. It's been three months and we haven't even shared so much as a kiss."

"That's OK," said Melanie.

"No," Phil responded, "it's not OK. A beautiful woman like you. You must be wondering what on earth is wrong with me."

Melanie felt her entire body tense as he squeezed her hands more tightly.

"You deserve to be cherished and desired. You deserve to be kissed all over and made love to day and night."

Now Melanie felt slightly queasy.

"But I know I'm not going to be able to do that."

Melanie's insides dissolved with relief.

"I can't do this any more," said Phil. "I can't keep taking you out and spending half the evening talking about Sally. It isn't fair on you. It isn't fair on her memory either. I'm not over her, Mel. I don't know how long it took you to feel ready again, but two years is nowhere near long enough for me. I don't know if I'm ever going to be over her. I thought I could fill the gap, but . . ."

"It isn't that easy, I know. But it doesn't matter. Really it doesn't. We can be friends, you and I. I will always be there for you if you just need to talk."

"Do you mean that?"

"I do."

Melanie shook her hands free of Phil's grip and gave him a hug instead.

"It will get better, I promise."

"Thanks. I didn't know how you'd take it, but I guess you know what it's like."

"Oh, I'm disappointed," Melanie lied, "but I'm not surprised. You take care of yourself."

Phil nodded his goodbye.

★ ★ ★

That was the problem with really loving someone: the feelings persisted long after the object of your affection had vanished from your life.

As she undressed for bed, Melanie found herself thinking about La Coupole. She and Keith had sat side by side on a banquette in the corner of the enormous room, which was lit so well everyone in it could have been a film star. They snuggled close, their thighs pressed together. After a couple of glasses of wine, they weren't shy about kissing over their steak frites. That was one of the last dinners they had shared as a couple. It was certainly the last truly romantic one.

If Melanie had known on that evening how she would feel looking back on it over the years, would she have done anything differently?

CHAPTER
THIRTY-SEVEN

20 February 2011

The Giovanni Lucciani dresses had arrived at last. Diana immediately made an appointment to go back to the salon and try hers on. As Melanie had warned her, the dress might need some tweaking and Diana wanted to be sure that she allowed as much time as possible for any required adjustments.

Diana could not wait to get her wedding dress on again. She was almost certain that she'd made the right choice, but moving quickly would ensure that if she hadn't, there was time to buy another one. Diana was only going to get married once. She didn't want to look back over her wedding photos and wonder if she'd made a mistake.

"No, this is definitely still the one," she said, as she admired her reflection in the mirror.

"Good job," said Melanie, "because we can't take it back. It's been made especially for you, you know."

"Of course, but if it had been wrong, Dad would have coughed up for something different."

"Good job he doesn't have to, eh?"

"Yeah. But do you still think this is the right dress for me? I mean, do you honestly think this is the best I could look in a wedding dress? Because if you think that I might look even better in something else . . ."

Melanie shook her head. "I don't think I've seen anyone else wear that dress quite so well."

That was exactly what Diana needed to hear. She was still the fairest of them all.

She had Melanie take a shot of her wearing the dress on her iPhone to post on Nuptialsnet later on.

Kate got the call on the same day.

"You need to come in as soon as you can to have another fitting," Heidi told her.

"Really? It's the right size, isn't it?"

Heidi sighed. "We've got to make sure it fits like a glove. There are bound to be adjustments. You don't want to be hoicking the corset up all day long, do you? What kind of bridal consultant would I be if I sent you up the aisle in a baggy corset?"

"OK," said Kate, "I'll have a look in my diary."

She relished the thought of another afternoon in Heidi's company about as much as she relished the idea of an afternoon with the dentist. As she'd left the Bride on Time salon that first afternoon, she hadn't factored in the subsequent fittings at all. Kate looked at her diary. It was packed with meetings related to her new job. There was one day free. Well, almost free. Her new colleagues were fairly understanding when Kate explained that her mother was about to begin radiotherapy and she had wangled some compassionate leave. She could do the dress fitting then. She didn't know which of the two appointments she dreaded more.

"Monday," she said to Heidi.

Monday rolled round.

"Hmm. You seem to have got a bit broader in the beam since you were last here. Someone couldn't lay off the mince pies, I suppose." What a greeting Kate received as she arrived at Bride on Time.

She didn't know how to respond.

"Well, you've got how long?" Heidi asked. She looked at the tag on the dress. "Middle of next month?" she exclaimed. "We'll have to let the bodice out. I don't know if we've got time to do that."

"Actually," said Kate, "the wedding's been put back. It's 30 April now."

"Good job."

Kate must have looked hurt.

"Now, I know that what I'm telling you might sound a bit upsetting, but I really am only saying it for your own good. You've got more than two months. I've seen girls lose a stone a month before their weddings from all the stress. You can do it if you try."

Kate couldn't remember when anyone had last spoken to her in such a patronising tone. When was the last time someone had told her she could do something if she tried, as though she were a child learning how to play scales on piano and work out long division?

"I don't think I'll be losing a lot of weight before the wedding," said Kate firmly. "You'll have to let the bodice out."

"It'll spoil the line," said Heidi.

Kate almost said, "I don't care."

"I understand," she said instead, "but I've got a lot more to think about right now than losing a few pounds for the wedding."

"It's up to you," said Heidi. "It is the most important day of your life, not mine."

Kate balled her hands into fists as Heidi yanked on the ribbons at the back of the bodice again.

"Have you practised peeing?" Heidi asked.

"What?"

"Peeing? I know it sounds funny, but I say it to all my brides. You've got to practise going in your dress, otherwise you'll get yourself into a right old state on the day. You've got a maid of honour, right?"

"My sister, I suppose."

"She's going to have to help you, I'm afraid. If you go into the cubicle front ways, she can hold up the back of the skirt, so you need to practise mounting the loo the wrong way round, facing the cistern. Have you got a long dressing gown? You could have a go in that. Doesn't matter if you get it a bit wet."

Oh God. Kate grimaced at the thought.

"Shall I give you a demonstration?"

Kate looked away as Heidi squatted over a chair.

The list of premarital humiliations seemed to be endless. From the very first dress fitting, Kate had come to feel like an animal being prepared for slaughter. All those people talking about her as if she wasn't there, the pulling and the prodding, the tutting about the size of her waist. Everyone seemed to think that her engagement gave them the right to comment. Was she on a diet? Did she have an exercise plan? They suggested so much preparation: waxing, varnishing, hair practice, make-up practice, even bloody peeing practice now.

Ian was not going through any of this. Kate was pretty damn certain of that. This upcoming wedding had hardly impacted on his life. All he had to do was put on a suit and turn up at the appointed place. Kate knew for a fact that he wasn't even going to get his hair cut.

Peeing practice. It was just too much. To hear Heidi talk about it — and, boy, did she want to talk about it at length — it sounded like an arcane ritual, something akin to foot-binding. It made Kate feel less than the woman she considered herself. She was a bloody partner at a law firm. She owned a flat. She paid her own bills. She was equal to any man and now she was being told how not to get wee on the skirt of a frock. Why was she wearing such a big bloody skirt in the first place? It was bondage, that was what it was.

Kate clamped her jaw shut.

It got worse.

"Don't forget to buy a crochet hook to do the buttons," Heidi continued. "Your sister's going to be at it all day otherwise."

Heidi was oblivious to Kate's expression of horror as she continued to fuss with the hem, arranging it just so.

"Ideally, what you also need is someone to get you out of the dress at the end of the day. Is anyone in the wedding party pregnant?"

"What's that got to do with it?" Kate asked.

Heidi had perfected the drape of the hem over the shoes. She stepped back and admired her handiwork.

"A pregnant guest won't be able to drink and you need someone sober to get these hooks undone. If your husband tries to do it, he'll only pull them all off in his excitement. Not a great start to your wedding night." She gave Kate a faintly obscene wink. "Oh, yes, the number of brides I've had who lost all their buttons . . ." Heidi continued. "If you haven't got a pregnant guest, ask someone like your mum to stay a little bit sober, then she can accompany you up to the bridal suite and hubby can wait outside while you get ready."

Even the word "hubby" set Kate off that morning. She felt a bubble in her ribcage. Was that her stomach lurching in the confines of the bodice? A picture flashed into her mind, a scene from a ballet — she couldn't remember the title — in which a newly married girl submits to having her hair cut off by her older wedded sisters. Only too clearly she imagined herself kneeling at the bottom of the marriage bed being unbuttoned by her mother and Tess while Ian waited outside with a hard-on straining the front of his best suit trousers.

Kate abruptly stepped down from the crate. Heidi's mouth formed a horrified "O" as she raced to check the back of the skirt for damage.

"You could have put your heel through it!" she said. "What on earth are you thinking?"

"I'm sorry," said Kate. "I'm a bit distracted. I've got to get to the hospital for my mum."

"Oh, yes," said Heidi, softening her expression from bulldog to shih-tzu, "now I remember. You're the one whose mum's got cancer."

Don't talk about it, Kate begged Heidi silently. Please don't talk about it now. Heidi launched into a long speech about a friend's husband who'd died three weeks after getting the all-clear.

"It's easier for the man to be left," she concluded. "Men are never on their own for long. Not like Melanie, who owns this place. She's been a widow for thirteen years."

Kate zoned out while Heidi finished unhooking the dress.

That half an hour with Heidi made accompanying Elaine to her first radiotherapy session seem a complete doddle to Kate. At least no one in the hospital was looking at her arse. While her mother was in the waiting room, Kate popped out into the hospital car park to call Ian. She told him what the bitch at the bridal shop had told her, but if she was hoping for sympathy, she was unlucky.

"Well, I suppose most women do go on a diet before their wedding, don't they?"

"Do you think I should go on a diet?" Kate asked.

"That wasn't what I said. It's just that most of the girls in the office . . ."

"If you think I need to lose a few pounds, then why don't you just come out and say it?"

"I don't think you need to lose weight," said Ian. "Unless you do."

It was the wrong answer. Kate hung up on him. And then she called Matt to see if he still wanted to go for a drink.

CHAPTER
THIRTY-EIGHT

That night's quick drink with Matt lasted from eight until closing time. They talked about Kate's mum and the radiotherapy, then moved quickly on to other things. Matt's Christmas: "Just terrible." Kate's postponed wedding: "A relief."

Matt raised an eyebrow.

"I just mean a relief in that I don't have a lot of time to devote to wedding-planning at the moment. There's so much to do at work, and I want to be able to come down and look after Mum, and —"

"You don't have to explain anything to me," said Matt. "I know how stressful these things are, and coupled with your mum being ill and starting a new job . . ."

"Take my mind off it," Kate begged him.

"With pleasure."

Matt brought the subject back to their college days. Kate was relieved to be laughing about old times again. Matt had always had a skill for mimicry and when he impersonated their college friends, it was as though they were right there in the room. He did an especially wicked impersonation of Helen.

Kate felt like she hadn't laughed so hard in a long while. She felt like her old self again. Happy-go-lucky and not in the least bit prone to worrying about her parents, her job or her weight. She wanted the evening to last for ever. It might have done, had Kate not faced a crack-of-dawn drive back to London in the morning. She couldn't afford to be late when she was still so unproven at her new firm.

"But we'll do this again," said Matt as she was preparing to leave.

"At the weekend," Kate promised. "I'll come down again on Friday night."

There was a West Ham home game on Saturday. Ian would not be coming with her. Matt had stopped asking when they would be introduced.

In her rush to get ready to meet Matt, Kate had left her phone at her parents' house. She got back that night to find several messages from Ian.

"I know I said the wrong thing this afternoon," he told her voicemail. "You don't need to lose any weight. That woman in the bridal shop is a body fascist. I love you just the way you are."

But as she listened to Ian's message, Kate remembered the way Matt had taken hold of one of her wrists that evening, looping his thumb and forefinger round it to see if the wrist still fitted neatly inside. It did.

"You haven't changed at all."

He said he had always admired her fine features and delicate bones. Seeing his hand next to hers sent a shiver through Kate's body as she remembered what it had been like when they made love. They locked eyes for a moment and she knew that he was remembering the same thing.

Kate didn't text Ian back until the following morning.

CHAPTER
THIRTY-NINE

Ian was not unaffected by the rise in Kate's stress levels. It seemed that he could barely open his mouth any more without saying the exact wrong thing. Even apologising for those things he wasn't sure he actually needed to apologise for no longer seemed to appease her. He would never have said it to Kate's face, but it was as though he was suddenly up against 24/7 PMT.

Was this normal? He'd heard from the girls at work that planning a wedding was the ultimate stressful experience in a woman's life, but those other girls weren't like his Kate. They were nowhere near as intelligent and resourceful as she was. He could see how organising a wedding might be beyond their capabilities. Not hers.

Was it still about Kate's mother, perhaps? Ian couldn't understand that. Hadn't the consultant said that Elaine's treatment was going well? It wasn't as though she was in hospital as an inpatient any more. There really was nothing to worry about on that front, surely.

Ian wished he had someone to talk to. He just wanted to know if the way Kate was behaving was normal. Alas, his own father was hardly the role model he craved. He'd left Ian's mother when Ian was just seven. Their fatherson relationship had never been the same after that.

Ian had one friend whom he thought he might be able to confide in. Ian felt he could call him a friend after eight years of sitting side by side at West Ham home games. Keith was the season-ticket holder who had the seat adjacent to Ian's in the West Ham stadium. He was a few years older than Ian. He seemed like a good bloke. Salt-of-the-earth type. Secretly thoughtful. After five years of nodding acquaintanceship, they had started to share information about their lives away from the football. And then they started to share a few beers after the game. The next time West Ham played at home, Ian resolved to ask Keith what he knew about girls.

Ian opened on a jovial tack as they waited to be served at the bar.

"Women — can't live with them, can't live without them."

Keith nodded.

Ian added, "Kate's been like a bear with a sore head since we changed the wedding to April. I can't seem to say anything right. You're married, aren't you? Can't you tell me what to do?"

"Oh, you don't want to take any advice from me," said Keith. "I did everything wrong. I got divorced thirteen years ago."

Ian mumbled an apology. He'd had no idea.

"It's not exactly something I like to talk about in between goals," said Keith. "Even though she said that one of my problems was that I keep everything bottled inside."

"Me too," said Ian, relieved it might be safe to say more after all. "Kate says she just can't read me. I tell her there is nothing to read."

"They're funny, women," said Keith.

Ian agreed.

They ordered drinks and drank in silence.

"I just want to get things right," said Ian. "I'm not used to not knowing what to do. I mean, in the office, I know exactly what's expected of me. I come in, I do my work, and I go home. It's when I get home that everything goes wrong. I don't know what she wants any more."

"And you're expected to guess, right?" Keith observed.

"Exactly."

"I know how that feels. They're just not like us, women. Sometimes you have no idea whatsoever that something's going wrong until they serve you with the divorce papers. Want to know how my marriage ended?"

"If you want to tell me."

"On a mini-break in France of all things. She booked this weekend in Paris for my birthday. Now, I wasn't bothered about going to Paris. It's a girls' place, really. Snooty people and fancy food. If I could have chosen where we went for my birthday, I'd have picked Barcelona or Dublin — somewhere the people know how to have a laugh — but I suppose Mel must have wanted to go to Paris, so that was where we were going to go. Anyway, it was quite exciting to go on the Eurostar, I suppose. And the hotel was nice. Right by the Eiffel Tower."

"Where I proposed," said Ian.

"I reckon we must have seen at least three proposals while we were up there."

"Popular place."

"I can't even see it without feeling ill," said Keith. "That weekend in Paris will haunt me for the rest of my life. I thought it was going well. We hadn't had a row since we got on the train at Southampton to go up to Waterloo. I thought that perhaps this was all that we'd needed — just a couple of days away from the stress of the shop and my work. We could just be ourselves again. Then Mel insisted that we had dinner in this place called La Coupole. It didn't sound like my cup of tea, but Mel said it was a Paris classic."

"We went there," said Ian.

"Massive place. Took us ages to get served. And then, when we got out, we couldn't find a taxi. It was three o'clock in the morning by the time we got back to our hotel. It was a hell of a walk, but Mel didn't seem too bothered. As we walked through the hotel lobby, though, she saw the news on the screen above the front desk."

"What news?"

"Only that Princess Diana had had a car crash. Couldn't have been worse as far as Mel was concerned. You see, she always thought that she and Diana were kindred spirits. They were about the same age. They got married on the same day."

242

"You got married in 1981?"

"I know," said Keith. "Don't look old enough, do I? Anyway, because of that, Diana was really special to her. She took it quite personal when the truth came out about Camilla. There was no chance that car crash wasn't going to affect our weekend. Mel went from being all happy and romantic to weeping like a bloody banshee, right there in the hotel lobby. She wasn't the only one. Some American woman came in and burst into tears like that too. It was bloody crazy. Before you knew it, there were four women weeping in that lobby. Mel refused to come upstairs. She clung on to that American woman like they'd just heard that somebody dropped the bomb on Southampton. I couldn't get near her. It was like she couldn't hear me. And then I made the stupid mistake of telling her that she was making a show of herself.

"Well, Christ, she soon snapped out of it then. She told me I was an unfeeling bastard. She said that as far as she'd been concerned, this weekend in Paris was make or break for her and me, and I'd just shown why we had to get a divorce."

"Bloody hell."

"I tried to talk her out of it. I apologised and apologised, but she told me there was nothing I could do. The following day, she took some flowers to the spot where the crash happened. She wouldn't even let me go with her. She said that there was no point because I would never understand.

"It really shocked me. I mean, I knew that we'd been arguing a lot, but I thought it was just a phase we'd get through. I'd been with Mel since I was thirteen years old. We'd been married for sixteen years. She was my best friend. And now she was saying I didn't understand her. She was coming out with all this stuff that she said she'd been sitting on for years. Everything I did frustrated her. Even the way I blew on my tea."

"I've never seen you do that," said Ian.

"Exactly. I had no idea. I suppose the thing is that when you're talking to a woman, you can't take what they say at face value. All those times I asked Mel if it was all right if I went out with the boys and she said, 'Do whatever you want,' I should have realised she was telling me, 'No.' Communication is the key in all things. Don't be afraid to ask for clarification. Again and again and again."

"Bloody hell," said Ian, taking a thoughtful sip on his pint. "I didn't think it would be so hard."

"When you get it right, it's worth it," said Keith. "I still bloody miss my wife. I wish I'd made more effort. I wish I'd had a clue . . ." He clapped Ian on the back and left him to contemplate the wisdom of his words.

Ian finished his pint. He liked Keith. He was a good bloke and Ian felt much better for having talked to him. That night, he would ask Kate whether it was all right to invite Keith to the wedding. He would definitely be getting him along to the stag night.

CHAPTER
FORTY

26 March 2011

After three weeks of daily hospital visits, Elaine's radiotherapy had finished. It had been a long three weeks that had taken it out of just about everyone in the Williamson family, but though Elaine was tired, she was determined to make good on her promise to throw her all into organising her daughter's wedding.

"You don't need to do anything, Mum," Kate had insisted. "Just rest and get stronger."

Elaine would not be put off. "Organising this wedding is good for me," she said. "I have to focus on the future. Tess will help me, and so will your dad."

It seemed Kate's wedding had become a totem for the entire Williamson clan, as if a successful wedding would represent triumph over the C-word, even though the definitive all-clear was still a long way off.

But as Diana could have told them, with just over a month to go, there was a great deal to be done before victory was assured. The RSVPs were coming in thick and fast. Elaine was as efficient as any professional travel agent as she booked friends and relatives into hotels handy for the wedding venue. A menu had been chosen. A band had been booked, as had a hairdresser and a make-up artist. Elaine was on top of it all. However, much to Kate's chagrin, there was still much that required her opinion.

Choosing flowers, for example, was an urgent item on the wedding agenda. Kate had delegated most of that task to her mother, but Elaine insisted that Kate herself had to have the final choice from the three schemes she had shortlisted out of hundreds. So, on yet another Saturday morning, Kate had to drive to Washam again and accompany her mother to the florist's, where she flicked through a book of bouquets with about as much interest as she perused the coffee menu at Starbucks. They all looked pretty much the same to her. She just picked out the very first bouquet that wasn't as big as a bush.

"That's quite a small bouquet," said the florist. "You want to be certain that it will be in balance with the size of your skirt. What's your dress like?"

"A tent," said Kate.

"It's pretty classical," said her mother. "It has a nipped-in bodice with ribbons down the back and quite a big skirt."

"Do you have a picture?" the florist asked.

Kate shrugged. It hadn't crossed her mind.

"I have one," said Elaine. "I downloaded it from the Internet."

Elaine and the florist pored over the tiny picture of Kate in her dress, while Kate continued to flick through the look book.

"In that case," said the florist, "the Wilhelmina bouquet is going to be nowhere near large enough. You

246

also need something with some trail to it. This posy is really for younger bridesmaids or brides who are going to wear something very simple. You also need some width to balance your hips."

"My bloody hips," Kate exclaimed. "All this focus on my body ... I'm starting to feel like last place in *America's Top Model*."

"I'm sorry." The florist physically backed away from Kate's upset. "I meant the skirt, not you."

Outside the florist's, Elaine took Kate to task.

"You didn't seem very happy in there. Do you want to try another florist? That one comes highly recommended for round here, but I'm sure we can find someone else."

"That florist will be fine," Kate assured her. "I'm just not very excited about flowers, that's all. I've got lots of other things to think about, like how I'm going to be able to leave my office for two weeks after the wedding. This new job is too big to mess with just because I'm getting married. Then I've got to think about selling my flat and looking for a new place so that Ian and I don't start our married life commuting between our two places. Flowers are the least of my concerns. Please, you do it."

"OK," said Elaine. "If you're sure."

"I'm sure," Kate snapped.

Elaine looked as though she had been slapped.

"I'm sure, Mum, really," Kate softened her tone. "Thank you. I'm very grateful for everything you've done."

"Do you want to stay for lunch?" Elaine asked.

"I've got to get back to Ian," Kate lied.

Kate didn't tell Ian that she was going to be back in London that night. She said that she was staying with her parents. Her parents thought she was rushing back to be with him. The truth was, she wanted to spend a night alone in her single-girl flat. She was supposed to have put it on the market, in readiness for merging her finances with Ian and buying their first family home. She hadn't, using the estate agent's suggestion that she give the place a lick of paint first as her excuse.

There was just a month to go before the wedding and Kate didn't feel ready at all. It was everyone else who seemed to be getting excited. Kate tried to console herself with the thought that this was just a taste of what Kate Middleton must be feeling. She could only imagine the vested interests that poor girl was juggling, and of course poor Kate Middleton would never have a night on her own again. From now on security guards would be a regular feature in her life. And paparazzi. And the public.

Kate drew the curtains on her bachelorette bedroom and was grateful for her anonymity. She lay down on her bed and relished having a whole double mattress to herself again. If she could just have twenty-four hours' peace, then maybe she would feel less stressed out about the whole wedding thing. Maybe she would be able to go back to Ian's flat and feel happy to see him, rather than irritated that he wasn't having to spend all his free time choosing cakes, picking flowers and learning how to pee.

For good measure, Kate decided to turn off her phone. But just as she reached for the "off" button, Helen called. Helen wanted to know if Kate was having a hen night.

"You've got to have a hen night," she said. "I've been waiting for you to give me my instructions for weeks."

"I don't really feel like it," said Kate. "I've got a load of work to do if I'm going to be able to take off for a two-week honeymoon without my new firm thinking I'm a waste of space. Plus, apart from you and Anne, I don't think I have a single girlfriend who isn't pregnant, breastfeeding or on some ridiculous diet that means she can only drink slimline tonic water without the gin."

"I can drink," said Helen. "In fact, I'm on a diet that says I can't have any food, but I can have as many G&Ts as I want."

Helen's joke failed to raise a smile at Kate's end of the phone.

"Your mum wants you to have a hen night," she tried instead.

"How do you know?"

"Your sister told me. She wants you to have a hen night too. You can't *not* have a hen night, Kate. It isn't right. At least let us take you for a spa day."

"Oh, Helen, I don't have time."

"Rubbish. Saturday after next. You're not needed at the office every weekend. You deserve some chill-out time. Plus, you have no idea how much I had to go through to get Mark to have the children on his own for a whole day."

"You've already planned it."

"Of course it's already planned."

Kate could hear the smile in her friend's voice. "There's a great place on the A3. Your sister will drive your mum up. I'll bring Anne down from London. We'll get facials. We'll get our nails done. We'll eat macrobiotic food and drink a secret stash of champagne. It will be brilliant."

"OK, OK." Kate agreed to a spa day.

"Attagirl. We can't wait to treat you."

Kate knew she should be grateful, but as she put down the phone, she realised that inside she was resentful of yet another claim on what little free time she had left before she was Ian's wife. Would there ever again be a moment when she didn't have to take someone else into consideration before she made her plans for the day?

CHAPTER
FORTY-ONE

2 April 2011

Ian was of the same opinion as Kate when it came to stag and hen dos. He could take them or leave them. He certainly didn't need to have a weekend in Benidorm to set himself up for marriage.

"I've already done all that," he explained to Kate. "That kind of stag weekend is for a man who's never lived on his own. I've had all the lost evenings I'll ever need."

His best man, Tim, had other ideas, however, and insisted that Ian at least set aside a whole day for the festivities, which would start with an hour of karting, followed by a visit to a brewery, followed by dinner at a restaurant with a steak-heavy menu and some top-heavy staff.

"I'm going to hate every minute of it." Ian winked as he set off.

Down in Southampton, Ben's stag do would be following a similar pattern. Unlike Ian, Ben would have leaped at the chance to spend a weekend in Spain with his closest friends, but Diana vetoed that particular idea very early on. Ben didn't even bother trying to argue his case. Diana only had to say one word to put an end to the discussion: "Lucy."

As far as Diana was concerned, her fiancé was still on probation and would be until the day they said their vows (and possibly beyond). So Ed, the best man, had to put away the Club 18–30 brochures — "You are still just under thirty," he'd pleaded — and make do with a day in Southampton. Just the day. Not even the full twenty-four hours. Diana was of the opinion that Ben should end his stag do at home, where she could make sure he didn't choke on his own vomit in the night. A dead groom did not fit Diana's plans.

Ed agreed to Diana's parameters, but she was still furious when she learned that he had arranged Ben's stag do for the weekend *before* her hen party, meaning that while she was away the following week, Ben would get that precious whole night to himself after all. How could she keep an eye on him when she was off on her own shindig?

"I can't believe Ed's done that!" Diana had raged.

"He didn't know," Ben swore. "He just picked the night that was most convenient for the biggest number of people."

Diana was slightly mollified when it was explained to her that since she and Ben had many friends who were couples, having the hen and stag dos on separate weekends would save those couples from having to find babysitters. They could take it in turns to stay home with the children instead.

So Ben got his stag do on the weekend of Ed's choosing. In order to get some sense of what else the unsavoury Ed was planning, Diana insisted that she drive her fiancé to the converted warehouse on the edge of town where the boys would be blasting each other with paint pellets.

"Make sure you keep your face covered," she reminded Ben. "I don't want anything to ruin the pictures. If you come back with red blotches on your face, I will kill you. And no shooting at his family jewels," she added to Ed, "or I will have yours on a skewer."

Ed promised he would take care of Diana's interests.

"Don't let him drink so much that he has to go to hospital, and it goes without saying that there will be no strippers."

"No strippers," the entire stag party confirmed.

All the boys were on their best behaviour in front of Diana. The moment she left, however . . . To kick-start proceedings, Ed had Ben down half a pint of vodka in one. Ed then made it his mission to aim exclusively at Ben's nuts once they were inside the paintballing range. He started firing before Ben was even strapped into his body armour. And as for the ban on strippers . . . what was Diana thinking? A minibus had been hired to take the boys straight from the paintballing range to Southampton's premier lap-dancing establishment, where the lads feasted on chicken nuggets washed down with champagne, while watching three dancers cavort exclusively for Ben's pleasure.

"You've got to keep hold of the reins," said Ed. "The minute you let her tell you what to do, mate, it's game over."

Ben agreed, as a girl ground her naked buttocks against his lap. "You're right. I've got to tell her the score, starting right now. I'm not going home tonight. I'm going to spend my last night of freedom with whoever the hell I want. Like you, Ed. You're my very best friend."

"Now is not the time to tell me you're going gay, mate," said Ed.

"Me? Never. Let's have another dance," Ben said to the blondest of the three half-naked girls.

All that day Ben talked the talk in front of his mates. With every pint he sank, he became more vehement. He was going to wear the trousers in his marriage, make no mistake. So long as he was firm with Diana, everything would work out fine. The advantages of marriage were manifold: someone to cook for you, sex on tap . . . well, sometimes . . . Ben convinced himself that it was going to be great. Yes, he would be the boss. Marriage would calm Diana's more neurotic tendencies and give Ben gravitas and respectability. They'd certainly be useful at work. But at half past eleven, the stag party at the lap-dancing club was joined by a surprise guest. The guys were so drunk that one of them asked her to dance. He got a slap round the head for his trouble.

"You arsehole." Diana grabbed Ed by the collar and pulled him to his feet with frightening strength. "You told me there would be no bloody strippers."

The lads were at a loss as to how on earth Diana had found out where they were. They had been sworn to secrecy, instructed to mutter vaguely about a pub even

254

under torture. Not even Jerry's wife knew where he really was and she was about to go into labour. Who was the weakest link?

Diana, who was flanked by Nicole and Nicole's sister, Gemma, brandished her mobile phone in Ben's face.

"I don't think you meant to send this to me, you moron," Diana spat at her fiancé.

Ben certainly hadn't meant to send Diana anything. He had meant to send the photograph of himself straddled by three strippers to Dirk, a former workmate who now lived in Tenerife.

"It's his stag night," Ed pleaded mitigation.

"I don't care." Diana turned back to Ben. "You're bloody well coming home with me now or the wedding is off," she said.

In front of his disbelieving friends, Ben found his last official night of freedom being cut brutally short.

Ben was still in the doghouse almost a week later. Meanwhile, Ed was very nearly banned from the wedding.

"He's my best man."

"He betrayed me. I told him no strippers. You had three naked women on your lap."

Diana was so horrified by the thought of those bare bottoms on her fiance's thighs that she had refused even to let Ben put the jeans he had been wearing in the washing machine, insisting instead that he had them dry-cleaned.

"I don't want Ed to come within twenty feet of my house again. Not ever."

"It was a stag party."

"I don't care. You know my feelings about it. How would you like it if I had a naked man at my hen do?"

"I would trust you."

"Well, we've already established that I can't even trust you when you're supposed to be at work!"

"Lucy has gone," Ben reminded her. "She left last month. I didn't even go to her leaving do."

"I can't believe you would even have considered it!" Diana shrieked.

Four weeks from the wedding, the image of the ball and chain loomed larger than ever in Ben's mind.

CHAPTER
FORTY-TWO

9 April 2011

Of course, Diana's hen do had to be as extravagant as her wedding. Not for Diana a simple night out with her friends. Nicole and her sister, Gemma, had put together the ultimate send-off for their dear friend: a whole weekend of activities centred round a luxury spa hotel near Petersfield.

Diana was delighted when she saw the itinerary (though not entirely surprised. She had given Nicole enough hints about what she wanted). There were to be facials, manicures, pedicures, not to mention a last-minute session on a Power Plate. Nicole knew exactly what a bride-to-be needed. Together with the rest of the girls, she had filled Diana's suite with flowers and well-chosen gifts. She had even gone to the trouble of sourcing a bottle of Chanel's hottest new colour for Diana's nails. Diana loved it. Never mind that she had seen the same colour on Ben's big toe when he got a fungal infection. The grey-green shade of bruise was the very latest thing. The other girls would understand how chic the colour was when it was applied to Diana's beautifully shaped nails.

The hen party arrived at the hotel at eleven o'clock, where they were treated to morning coffee with hen-party-themed cupcakes decorated with iced pictures of Louboutins. After that, they were shown to their rooms and went their separate ways for their first treatments. Diana was having the time of her life. The hen party was one of the best bits about being the bride.

But there was a surprise on the list of activities. On the Saturday afternoon, before the girls sat down to a delicious low-cal vegetarian spa dinner, they were going to have a dance lesson.

"It was my idea," said Nicole over lunch. "You could choose paint-your-own-pottery or a dance class. I thought that dancing would be more fun."

"Ben and I already had dance lessons for the reception," said Diana.

"I know, but this is a dance lesson you'll use again and again after you're married, starting on the honeymoon."

Nicole handed Diana a leaflet, which was illustrated with a cartoon of a Betty Boop-style character wearing a basque over stockings and suspenders.

"Juicy Lucy's Bridal Burlesque" was the name of the class the hens would be taking.

"It sounds brilliant, don't you think? One of the girls from work did a class for her sister's hen do last month. Juicy Lucy brings along a whole load of accessories that you get to take away to use at home. My friend's sister said her husband practically had a heart attack when he saw her routine. He was stunned. In a good way," Nicole added.

Diana didn't need to be sold on the idea. She was already picturing herself in a tightly laced corset and a bowler hat like the showgirls in *Cabaret*. She had often pored over pictures of Dita Von Teese and wondered whether she could achieve the same kind of glamour. Now she would find out for sure.

"I can't wait," she told Nicole, "and I especially can't wait to see Mum having a go."

Susie ordered champagne with her lunch as a precaution.

Self-proclaimed burlesque mistress Juicy Lucy certainly knew how to set the scene. While the girls ate lunch, the small aerobics studio where some of the hens had done a stretch session had been transformed into a theatre. Juicy Lucy's assistant, who was dressed like a saucy circus ringmaster and called herself Curvy Clare, welcomed the hen party to the class and settled them down into seats facing the low stage, on which were a single velvet-upholstered chair and a Japanese-style screen. Clare explained that the best way to get an idea of what burlesque really meant was to watch some.

"You mean we've got to watch a girl stripping?" asked Susie.

"It's not like stripping," said Clare. "It's much more complicated than that. For burlesque, you don't have to take all your clothes off. You just give a hint of what's to come. Drives men wild. Far more wild than simply getting naked. Anyway, ladies, for your delectation and delight . . . here is Juicy Lucy!"

Clare threw the light switch so that the only light in the room was a spotlight on the makeshift stage. The music began. From behind the screen, Juicy Lucy stretched out a leg clad in a fishnet stocking. Diana's eye was immediately drawn to Juicy Lucy's shoes, a pair of fabulous sequinned courts in bright green with that giveaway red sole.

"She's wearing eight-hundred-pound Louboutins," Diana whispered to Nicole.

"I'm not surprised, given how much she charges," said Susie.

"I'm worth it, aren't I?" said Diana.

"Every penny, love."

Juicy Lucy was out from behind the screen now. She was dressed in a slinky green satin sheath dress that matched her shoes. She wore matching long gloves that climbed to her elbows. Her red hair (not naturally red, Diana observed) was piled up and secured with a diamanté-embellished clip. Hiding her face was a feathered mask in the shape of a pair of cat's eyes. The only part of her face that could be seen was her perfect pout.

Juicy Lucy paced the stage to the sound of Shirley Bassey singing "Diamonds Are For Ever". Her own sparklers may have been fake, but her confidence made them look expensive. She threw pose after pose that displayed her figure to its best advantage. The girls were mesmerised.

"She's got a backside on her, but she knows how to use it," Susie commented.

Slowly and sensually, Juicy Lucy began to remove one of her gloves. She whirled it twice round her head before tossing it lightly in the direction of her assistant. The second glove followed. Juicy Lucy removed the glove finger by finger, teasing each tight sheath away from its corresponding digit with her teeth. Diana noticed that there was glitter in the dancer's lipstick too.

"I'd worry about that getting on my teeth," she said to Nicole.

Juicy Lucy danced on, used to a female audience being more interested in the detail of her outfit than the creamy bosom that was barely contained by her dress. The dress slid to the floor with a swish, revealing a corset beneath. Juicy Lucy had a handspan waist, Diana noticed with some envy. Shirley Bassey reached a crescendo. Juicy Lucy threw up her arms in triumph and posed like a goddess in just a corset, those shoes and her mask.

The hen party gave a polite round of applause. Juicy Lucy's assistant handed her a satin dressing gown. With her mask still in place, Juicy Lucy addressed that afternoon's students.

"Thank you, ladies. So as you see," she said, "sensuality is as much about what you *conceal* as what you reveal. You've seen a bit of what I do in my stage act. Now let's set free the inner burlesque dancer in each of you. I'm glad to see you've all brought suitable shoes."

Diana admired her own Louboutins. They may have been a plain, nude patent, but to her mind they had every bit as much va-va-voom as Juicy Lucy's shoes. They'd have much more once Diana was up and dancing. She was feeling supremely confident after her champagne lunch that she was going to nail this burlesque thing. She couldn't wait for Ben to see her dance on their wedding night. She'd need help to get out of her wedding dress, of course, but later, she'd slip a simple satin robe over her special wedding underwear and give him the show of his life. All thoughts of the stag-night strippers and that stupid girl in his office would be banished for ever. From that moment forward Ben would only have eyes for his wife.

"Who's the bride-to-be?" Juicy Lucy asked.

"I am." Diana got to her feet. She shook out her hair to give Juicy Lucy an idea of the calibre of raw material she would be working with.

"Great," said Juicy Lucy. "We're starting with you. Put these on." She handed Diana some gloves. "I'm going to show you how to take a pair of gloves off so that the only thing your husband-to-be can think about is the feel of your hands roaming all over him."

Diana pulled on the gloves. They were made of something synthetic and felt cheap, but she grinned at her hen party and gave them a wave. She was going to show everyone how this should be done.

"Move into the spotlight, darling," said Juicy Lucy. "You're going to be there for the rest of the afternoon. It's good practice for your wedding day. Don't be shy. You absolutely need to own the stage."

Diana performed a bunny dip for her friends' amusement.

"Now," said Juicy Lucy, "I'm just going to take this itchy mask off. Can't see anything through these feathers. When I've got this thing on, I'm practically blind, which is a good thing when your audience is a drooling stag party." She took off the mask and handed it to her assistant. "So, this afternoon," she chatted smoothly as she pulled on her own gloves, "we are going to make you the kind of woman no man would ever want to leave. I'm going to show you the moves that have helped me get any man I've ever wanted."

At last, Juicy Lucy turned to face Diana. The two women recognised each other in exactly the same moment.

"Oh shit," said Lucy, Ben's former workmate.

"You fucking slag," said Diana.

And so the burlesque lesson turned out to be rather more entertaining for the other girls in the hen party than it was for the poor, betrayed bride-to-be herself. As soon as she realised Juicy Lucy's real identity as "that fucking slag from the office", Diana flew at the wannabe Dita Von Teese with her teeth bared. She grabbed a handful of Lucy's hair and yanked it hard. Half of it — a hairpiece — came away in Diana's fist. Lucy tried to save her lucky diamanté hair clip — a vintage piece that had belonged to her grandmother — but it fell to the ground. Diana grabbed for her hair again and would not let go. She dragged the poor girl around the stage until Susie and Nicole finally got over their shock and intervened, pulling the fighting women apart.

"She's not worth it!" Susie cried.

"You fucking bitch," Diana spat in Lucy's face. "I'll show you the fucking moves that turned the man you want into my fiancé. If you know what's good for you," she hissed, "you'll stay away from him. You'll stay away from this town. You'll go back to Australia, you fucking dingo slut."

With that, Diana ground Lucy's diamanté clip beneath her foot as a final gesture.

"Let's go for a massage," suggested Susie as she pulled Diana away from her rival. Diana swept from the room, followed by her terrified bridesmaids.

"I'm so sorry," said Nicole over and over. "I had no idea. I swear I had absolutely no idea."

As the last of Diana's party left the studio, Lucy gathered up what remained of her costume. Clare hurried to help her.

"Is that?"

"The witch that Ben is marrying? Yeah. You can see who's got the balls in that relationship."

Clare reached to touch a bloodied patch above Lucy's eye.

"You could call the police and get her done for assault. You've got plenty of witnesses."

"I hardly think any one of those women is going to be queuing up to support me, do you? Besides, I just want an end to it. I had no intention of sleeping with another woman's man. I'm mortified that it happened and I just want to put it behind me."

"You should at least tell him what happened."

"What's the point? It isn't as though he doesn't know what he's marrying."

"You've got to feel sorry for him really," said Clare, "spending the rest of his life with that."

"He made his bed," said Lucy.

CHAPTER
FORTY-THREE

Meeting her rival face to face had really rattled Diana. The photograph on the company website — of course, Diana had looked when she first found out about the fling — had really not done Lucy much justice. In real life, she was far prettier and slimmer than Diana had imagined. Diana was not at all happy to find that out. Suddenly, Ben's transgression seemed much more understandable. Lucy was a far more formidable rival than Diana would ever have believed.

"I can't trust him," she said to her mother and Nicole. "He said that he wouldn't have any strippers on his stag night — that was bad enough — but he told me that woman had gone to Australia. He swore on his life."

"I thought he said she had just gone back for Christmas," said Nicole.

"I'm sure that's not what he said," Diana retorted angrily. "I thought she was gone for ever. She's still here, Mum. She's in Southampton. I could bump into her at any time. I don't think I can guarantee that next time I'll react so calmly. Perhaps I shouldn't go through with the wedding."

"If you don't marry Ben, then that burlesque tart will have won," said Susie. "You've got to go through with the wedding."

"But how can I make sure he won't cheat on me again?"

"You make him aware of the consequences. Like Catherine Zeta-Jones and Michael Douglas. She got a clause in their pre-nup that said he had to pay her millions for every time he slept with another woman. Seems to have worked for them."

"Only because he's nearly seventy, Mum. He was ready to settle down. What if Ben isn't?"

"He is, my love. Of course he is. He wouldn't have asked you to marry him otherwise."

But how could you ensure that a man wouldn't stray? There was no point asking Nicole. She'd never had a steady boyfriend. And as they had a calming cup of coffee in the hotel bar, Diana studied her mother critically. Susie hadn't managed to hang on to her man.

Diana's mother had taught her that even someone with her looks should not take a man's attention for granted. It wasn't enough to say yes to a date. You had to make sure a man was properly reeled in before you let him "get fresh" with you, as Susie put it.

"Men don't respect a woman who lets them have what they want without a struggle. I didn't make your father struggle and look what happened to me."

"Mum," said Diana supportively, "Dad would never have left you if she hadn't trapped him."

The "trap", as Diana called it, was her half-brother, Charlie. Charlie's mother was Chelsea. Dave met

Chelsea when he was fitting kitchens on the new-build estate where Chelsea worked as a sales rep in the show house. Charlie was conceived in the master bedroom, on a bed that looked like a double but was actually only three-quarter-size. Chelsea explained that scaled-down furniture was a trick building companies often used to make the houses they were selling look more spacious.

Anyway, Charlie was conceived the year Diana turned eighteen. In actual fact, the news of his impending birth broke on Diana's birthday. Dave had tried to put things right. He promised Chelsea he would pay for her to go to a spa in St Lucia for a fortnight if she would terminate the pregnancy. Chelsea accepted his kind offer of a holiday but refused to get rid of the baby. She announced as much by breezing into Diana's birthday party in a midriff-baring top that showed her new bump to best effect. Susie filed for divorce a few weeks later.

Dave had tried to explain to his daughter that the marriage had been moribund for a long time. Why else would he have been attracted to Chelsea in the first place? But as far as Diana was concerned, it was clear the blame lay with her father. She forgave him to the extent that she allowed him to buy her a car and pay for driving lessons, but she vowed she would never speak to Chelsea, even when the bitch became her father's second wife. Diana had never met Charlie. She wasn't even interested in seeing the photograph of him on Dave's mobile phone.

It was her dad's betrayal of her mother that made Diana so determined that Ben would not do the same to her. She needed to be certain of his love. For a start, she wanted to cut the hen party short and go home at once. There was no way she was going to leave Ben alone in the house overnight now that she knew Juicy Lucy was still in town. She called Ben up to let him know what had happened.

"She threw the first punch," Diana lied, "just in case she calls you up and says otherwise."

By the time she got back to the house, Diana was feeling a little calmer. Her mother and Nicole had talked her down from the peak of her fury. Her recovery had been helped by an assurance from the spa hotel's manager that they would not be using Juicy Lucy again. The last thing the hotel needed was for Diana to make a formal complaint.

When she got home, Diana found Ben sitting in front of the television, with a round of sandwiches on his lap. Clearly, news of Diana's unfortunate encounter with the slag from his office had not ruined his appetite. Not yet, anyway. When he saw Diana's face, Ben put his half-eaten sandwich back on the plate. Suddenly, he wasn't hungry any more.

"I have forgiven you," Diana announced. "I accept that you didn't know that Ed had booked that lap-dancing club for your stag do. I even accept that Ed didn't really know what he was doing. I've decided he can still be your best man. I also accept that you weren't to know that Lucy had been booked as the entertainment for my hen night. But I'm upset, Ben, and I want us to do something in the service that represents the way things are going to be from now on."

"What?"

"I've been talking to Mum and Nicole on the drive back here about what would reassure me and they have suggested that we write our own vows. I think they're right. We should write something more personal to us than the religious ones."

"Diana, we're getting married in a cathedral. I don't think we can write our own vows."

"I'm going to tell Dad to ask tomorrow morning. I don't see any reason why we shouldn't. It's a free country. They let you say your own vows everywhere else, and Dad's paid a lot of money for our service. Anyway, I have already started writing mine, and I've also done a draft of what I would like you to say."

"Hang on."

Diana handed him a piece of paper.

"I don't think it's unreasonable of me to expect you to say these things in front of our friends and family."

Ben read the densely typed lines. "You really want me to say this?"

"I do. We can have a practice now, if you like." Diana took the paper back and began to read aloud what she had written.

"'My darling Ben, you have been the centre of my life for the past seven years and now we are promising to be the centre of each other's lives for ever. You know that you are my best friend, and I am yours. You are the only other person I will ever need in my life, and I am the same for you. Once we are married, we will need nothing but each other. Our pasts will be as a slate wiped clean.'"

Ben winced.

"'To make sure that slate is wiped clean, we are going to promise today, in front of our families and our friends, that there will be no more secrets between us from this moment forward. You will always tell me where you are going and who you will be with, and I will do the same in return. When I call you, you will always pick up the phone. When I want you to come home, you will be there within half an hour. I will never have to wonder what you're up to again.'"

"Diana, these aren't wedding vows. These are rules. This is you ticking me off in front of everyone we know. I can't say these things."

"Don't you want to?"

"Well, frankly, no, I don't want to."

"But you want me to be happy, yes?"

"Of course I want you to be happy. But this is not about making you happy. This is unreasonable. These vows will make us both look like idiots. Why can't we have the ordinary service? I'm going to promise to love and honour you for the rest of my life. Isn't that enough?"

"What about obey?"

"No one says obey any more. In any case, that was what the woman had to say. The groom never had to say that."

"I want us to have our own vows. It won't be our personal wedding without them."

"I'm not going to say that shit about always picking up the phone when you call. If I don't pick up the phone, it's because I'm busy."

"Busy with some slut!"

"Or working. How about that for a novel idea?"

"Ben, you don't know how traumatic the past six months have been for me. I was completely happy in my life before I found that text from Lucy on your phone. You shattered my trust in you. No one else is to blame. You shattered it, Ben. Everything we built together was shaken because you couldn't keep your dick in your pants. Well, you're not going to do that to me again. It's my way or the highway. If you don't want to promise me the things that I'm asking for, then let's just call off the wedding and you can pay my father back every single penny he's spent on it."

There was the rub. Ben had already calculated that Dave had spent at least £50,000.

"Are you ready to do that?" Diana challenged him.

"Of course not," said Ben. "We're going to get married."

While Diana was on the phone to her mother again, no doubt telling her what a loser Ben was, he picked up the sheet of vows and read them through again. It would be funny, he thought, if he didn't know that Diana meant to make him say every humiliating word. His only hope was that the bishop would veto such craziness, or that he would grow a pair of balls overnight and finally tell Diana what he really thought. But £50,000? He would need to win the lottery at the same time. Ben put his head in his hands.

CHAPTER
FORTY-FOUR

Kate said goodbye to her two best friends and her mother and sister in the lobby of the spa hotel. They'd had a wonderful day together, just the five of them. Elaine said that she felt a thousand times better after an aromatherapy facial than after three weeks of radiotherapy. She said she was pleased too, to see Kate looking so relaxed.

Kate assured her that was only the result of an eyebrow shape.

Much as she had resented another demand on her time, Kate had to admit to herself that it was nice to spend the day with the most important women in her life. Back when they were at college, Kate, Helen and Anne had lived in each other's pockets. Girly moments like that spa day were so rare now. The conversation had moved on too. They no longer talked about the boys they fancied. Instead, Kate nodded sagely as Helen and Anne talked schools with Tess and Elaine.

"You've got all this ahead of you," said Helen. Later, as they walked from the spa dining room to the treatment area, Helen linked her arm through Kate's and asked her if she'd thought about booking an appointment with her GP for a fertility check-up.

"What?" said Kate. "Ian and I haven't even talked about kids yet."

Helen pulled a face. "Chop, chop."

"I beg your pardon."

"Sorry," said Helen. "None of my business."

It was the only bum note of the day. Kate tried hard to keep her annoyance from her face, but later, Tess asked if she was OK and seemed unconvinced when Kate insisted she was fine.

"Thank you." Kate kissed Elaine and Tess goodbye for the twentieth time. Helen and Anne were already on the road.

"Drive safely," they said. As far as they were concerned, she was going straight back to London, but Kate had other ideas. They thought she was going back to Ian. Ian thought she was staying at the spa hotel overnight. Kate texted Matt. It wasn't entirely premeditated.

What are you doing?

Just dropped the children back with their mother.

Got time for a drink? Kate asked him.

He did have time.

So Kate drove down to Southampton and met Matt. They didn't meet in their usual pub this time. Kate went to his house, a small, modern semi on the outskirts of town. It was the first time Kate had been in Matt's personal space since 1997. His taste had changed quite considerably. Or perhaps it was more accurate to say that he had acquired some taste at last. Matt accepted Kate's compliments on his furnishings but admitted that he'd simply ordered straight from two pages of a John Lewis catalogue. "Interior design by numbers." Rosie had kept everything else.

Matt poured two glasses of wine.

"How was your hen night?" he asked.

"Quiet, calm, relaxing. Except when a fight kicked off in one of the aerobics studios. Apparently, another bride ended up scrapping with a burlesque dance teacher."

"Now that I would have liked to see," Matt told her.

"Well, God knows what it was about, but you could hear the shouting from miles away. It made it rather difficult to concentrate on the whale music in the massage rooms. I hate whale music," Kate added. "Makes me think of the dentist."

"Don't mention dentists," said Matt. "Are you nearly ready for the wedding?"

Kate looked down into her glass.

"Not really. I mean, there are all sorts of silly little things to be done."

"I know. I think the week running up to my wedding was one of the worst of my life. You'd think we were planning to invade another country."

"Do you mind if we don't talk about it?" Kate asked.

Kate had come to Matt because she didn't want to think about the wedding at all. She wanted to have an evening without wedding talk and without thinking about the marriage ahead of her. For just one night she didn't want to sink into a sofa next to Ian and bite her tongue while he flicked between channels like a child. She didn't want to look at his bald patch and wonder if the next forty years would all be downhill. Her mother's illness, her father's fear in the face of it and Ian's seeming inability to understand why such things had affected Kate so badly had left her feeling tired and pessimistic. Her new job was more stressful than she had imagined. She wondered if she had bitten off more than she could chew.

Matt was a link to a better, more optimistic Kate. He was a link to a Kate who didn't snap at the juniors in the office because they happened to walk in right after another frustrating conversation about radiotherapy or RSVPs. She wanted him to make her laugh again. Until Rosie came along, they'd had such an easy rapport. They'd always had such ... chemistry.

"Are you OK?" Matt asked. He put his hand on her hand again. Kate felt heat flood her body. She looked up into his eyes and saw her own thoughts reflected back at her. She knew that if she closed her eyes now, he would take it as acquiescence. He would take it as a sign that he should kiss her. His eyes flicked from her eyes to her mouth. She licked her lips, subconsciously making them glossier and more inviting.

"Kate." Matt pronounced her name urgently. "Kate ... we ..." He squeezed her fingers tighter. It was as though that pressure on her fingers broke the spell.

276

She looked at her watch. "My God, is that the time?" she said, all false jollity. "I ought to go. I'm keeping you up."

"You don't have to go on my account," said Matt.

It was precisely because of Matt that Kate had to go.

Ian was already in bed when Kate got back. He barely stirred as she tiptoed into the bedroom. She crept under the duvet and pressed herself against his back. She breathed in the smell of his freshly washed hair and the aftershave balm that she liked so much. She prayed that when she woke up next to him the following morning, those happy feelings of love she'd felt in Paris would be back again.

But the next day, Ian admitted that he had been unable to find the time to organise their honeymoon. It was the one and only significant job on the groom's side of the to-do list.

"It's fine," said Kate, full of guilt from her late night at Matt's house. "I'll do it."

That Sunday afternoon, she Googled hotels in Barcelona. They had left it much too late to find a bargain. It seemed that half the nation was going to be taking advantage of the extra bank holiday for the royal wedding to go on a spring holiday. Kate lost patience as she checked hotel after hotel in the city and found all of them booked or only having their most expensive rooms available. If Ian had only admitted that he didn't have time to sort out a honeymoon, Kate could have been doing this search months ago. Now she was just getting more and more angry as she realised that there was little chance of the five-star start to her honeymoon she had hoped for. Kate tried four more hotels.

Ten minutes later, she was Googling "quickie divorce".

CHAPTER
FORTY-FIVE

28 April 2011

Two days before her wedding, Kate travelled down to the south coast to stay with her parents and make the final preparations for the day itself. Kate's mother had a long list of items that still needed to be checked off.

"Does the florist know that two of these buttonholes need to be smaller than the rest for Ian's little nephews? Have you spoken to the cake lady? Does the hotel have the music you want for your processional, or will we have to take a CD?"

Kate answered the enquiries distractedly. The whole time her mother was firing questions at her, Kate was simultaneously dealing with a barrage of emails from the office, all of them seemingly urgent. Her new colleagues were desperate to get her attention before she disappeared for her two-week honeymoon. (Kate had found a self-catering flat for that.) She had to try hard not to snap as so many things competed for her time. Her mother had insisted on taking all the little details on and yet there didn't seem to be a single thing on her list that she could achieve without Kate's input.

"Dress fitting at five o'clock," was the last thing on the list. There was definitely no one but Kate who could deal with that.

So at five o'clock, Kate was back on the upside-down crate for the last time. Heidi, thank God, was having a day off, so it fell to the proprietor, Melanie, to lift the three-stone dress over Kate's head.

"Working here does wonders for your bingo wings," said Melanie, as the deceptively heavy skirt fluttered down to the ground. "Perfect." She gave the fabric another flounce. "Absolutely perfect. You look gorgeous, sweetheart."

Kate looked at her reflection in the mirror. Melanie's pronouncement was fair comment from the neck down, perhaps. Heidi may have been a cow, but the evil-tongued seamstress had worked wonders with the dress, adding extra boning along the seams that smoothed the line from Kate's waist to her hip. The saddlebags were hidden as if by magic. The bodice fitted so snugly that Kate began to believe Heidi's assurance that she wouldn't have to spend all day hoicking it up. The skirt had been trimmed to the perfect length so that it showed just the toe of Kate's wedding shoes, some blue brocade Blahniks her sister had found on eBay.

"Those are the most fabulous shoes," Melanie cooed.

"Thank you," said Kate.

Now Kate was taking in her reflection from the neck up. Not so perfect at all. Where had that line between her eyes come from? Though she tried to smile, her eyes simply wouldn't stop frowning. Had her jawline always been so square? Two muscular points stood out so far she could have done a reasonable impression of blockhead Formula One racing driver David Coulthard. She realised that she was clamping her jaw. She gave an embarrassed start as her back teeth actually slipped and squeaked across each other in a muscle spasm. Melanie didn't seem to have noticed.

"You're all set," said Melanie, as she picked a tiny piece of fluff from the bodice. "There's nothing left for us to do except give the dress a final pressing. Your sister is coming to collect the dress on the morning — am I right? Remind her she needs to bring a duvet cover. Doesn't need to be an old one, because we're not going to cut any holes in it, but it's really much better than any of the covers that come with the dresses. They're never big enough, so the dress always creases. We want you to look as perfect as possible."

Kate nodded.

"Do you want me to go through the loops on the back of the skirt one more time?"

"No," said Kate, "I think I've got it."

Melanie demonstrated the loops one more time regardless. It was quite a tricky process. The loops were made of fishing wire and were all but completely invisible, as was the white silk-covered button onto which the loops had to be hooked.

"There you are," said Melanie. "Now you can dance the night away. Happy?"

Kate's face crumpled.

"What's wrong?" asked Melanie. "Are you not happy with the dress? Do you think it still needs taking in or something?"

"I think I don't want to get married."

Balling up the skirt of the ridiculous £2,000 dress as carelessly as though it were a dustbin liner, Kate sat down on the sofa where her mother and sister had sat months before. Outside, life carried on as normal. A post van pulled up opposite the postbox. Half past five. Last collection. A harassed young mum tried to persuade her toddler to keep up. The toddler was poking a stick into some dogshit. An old man tied his dog to the special ring outside the Co-op and informed the cross-eyed Jack Russell that he really wouldn't be long. The dog whined as though they were to be parted for ever. Kate felt like whining too.

"It's natural," Melanie began. "Everybody gets wedding jitters."

How many times had Kate heard that now?

"It's a big step you're about to take. You wouldn't be normal if you weren't a bit scared. You want the day to be perfect. The thing is, your guests won't know if it isn't perfect, because they won't know exactly what you planned. So if a few things go wrong — if the flowers aren't quite the right shade — no one will notice. Or the ceremony. If you fluff your lines or something like that, nobody is going to care. Prince Charles fluffed his lines. So did Diana. She even got his name wrong."

"And look how that turned out," said Kate. "I'm not worried about the wedding. Organising a wedding is no sweat for me. I've put together much bigger events for work. And I'm not worried about fluffing my lines when I get to the altar either. It's nothing like that."

Tears appeared at the corners of Kate's eyes. Melanie handed her a tissue.

"If you're going to cry, you should probably take the dress off."

Kate was ready to flee as soon as she had her old jeans back on, but Melanie insisted she sat down again.

"I can't let you get into your car in this state. You'll drive into a lamppost. Do you want to tell me all about it?"

Kate looked at Melanie. She seemed nice enough, but Kate barely knew the woman. Perhaps that was what made it easier in the end.

"I'm not worried about the wedding at all," she reiterated. "I'm worried about *being* married. When Ian and I met, everything seemed right in the way everyone always said it would when I met the One. We didn't go through any of the game-playing. I was so, so happy. I felt comfortable and content. But since we got engaged, I've never felt quite comfortable again. I don't know where my life's gone. It started the minute he popped the question. Suddenly, I was public property. Random strangers started taking photographs. Though I suppose, since we got engaged at the top of the Eiffel Tower, I shouldn't have hoped for any privacy.

"But it started in earnest when we got back from Paris. Immediately the questions began. Everyone at work wanted to know if we were going to have children. It was as though my getting engaged gave everyone the right to ask the most outrageous things. Do you think anyone ever asks Ian whether he's going to give up his job? Do you think anyone ever suggests to him that it doesn't matter if he gets made redundant because obviously I'll keep him? It was as though everyone had been humouring me for all those years when I worked my arse off to become a partner at my law firm. Now that I had a ring on my finger, they didn't have to pretend to take me seriously any more.

"And then my mum was diagnosed with a breast tumour. That really pulled the rug out. I know I'm nearly forty, but the thought of losing Mum is terrifying. Everyone kept telling me how lucky I was to have got engaged before Mum's diagnosis — firstly, because it would cheer her up, and secondly, because obviously now that Ian had asked to marry me, I had someone to lean on through the worst. Except he was far from being the rock that everyone imagined. He was just useless. He froze whenever he saw me crying, like he didn't want to get involved with such messy emotions. He buried himself in work.

"It's like my entire life has been turned upside down. I'm worried about Mum. I'm pissed off about the assumptions people make just because I'm getting married. Even the wedding itself has become one enormous pain in the arse. As soon as Mum got ill, it wasn't even my wedding any more, anyway. It was all about celebrating the end of Mum's treatment. I feel like my feelings are incidental."

Melanie handed Kate another tissue.

"Part of me tries to be reasonable and keeps saying, 'This is just the way it is. This is the way it is for everyone. Getting married is about stepping into a different role and promising to care for another person.' And maybe I have to get used to the idea that caring for

Ian means matching his socks and making sure there's always loo roll in the bathroom cupboard. But what am I getting in return? Ian doesn't pay my bills, he doesn't cook my dinner, and yet he gets to determine what happens for the rest of my life. What if I want to up sticks and move to Italy? I could do that, you know. I was thinking about it before I met Ian. I've got enough put by. But I can't do it if Ian doesn't want to, not if I actually marry him.

"I hate the way that people always ask *him* what our plans are for the future. On the one hand, I feel as though I've been pushed into the role of his mother. On the other hand, I feel . . . I feel infantilised," said Kate. "I feel like I've lost myself."

Melanie provided more tissues.

"Do I sound like I'm going mad?"

"Not at all. When I got married, I felt like I lost myself too," Melanie admitted. She took a tissue for herself. Just in case.

"Oh, Melanie," said Kate, "I'm sorry. Here I am banging on about why marriage is such a bad deal for a woman. Heidi told me that you were widowed. I probably sound like a spoiled cow to you."

"Kate, I spend all day every day acting like getting married is the best thing in the world, but I'm going to let you in on a secret: I'm not even widowed. I got divorced in 1998."

CHAPTER
FORTY-SIX

Upon hearing Melanie's revelation, Kate looked up from her paper tissue in confusion.

"Really? But . . .?"

"I know. The official line is that my husband passed away. I never actually offer the information unless I'm asked, and if I am asked, I decline to go into it."

"Why?"

"Because how do you think it would be for business? A bridal-wear salon run by a woman who came to believe that marriage is just about the biggest con ever known to womankind."

"Then why did you do it? Get married, I mean."

"I was twenty-one. I was in love."

"And why did you divorce?"

"For pretty much the same reasons you're talking about. I just got tired of having to do it all on my own. Running the shop all day, then going home and doing all the housework, the cooking. Making all the plans for our social life. Keeping my family happy. Keeping his family happy. And getting in return? Well, I didn't think I was getting a fair deal, let's put it that way. I didn't even have the baby I'd always wanted. I made the decision the weekend Princess Diana died. I think her death made a lot of people realise that life's too bloody short. Do you remember what you were doing the weekend Diana died?"

Kate found a smile at last. "I'd rather not."

"My husband and I were in Paris, on a make-or-break weekend. Funny, eh? Thing was, it had been going OK up until the moment we got the news about Diana. Having married on the same day as Diana and Charles, I'd followed her progress, even idolised her, I suppose. So hearing that she died felt like losing a personal friend. Keith didn't seem to understand that and so I decided that he would never understand me."

"And so you divorced him."

"Yes, and it was great. For the first time in my life I got to do exactly what I wanted. I had my bedroom painted pink. I went on holiday to all the places Keith never wanted to go. I started dancing again. I dated quite a few men. I'd never slept with anyone except my husband. Going to bed with a different man, that was quite an eye-opener, let me tell you."

"And now?"

Melanie dabbed at her eyes and didn't answer the question. Instead, she said, "Marriage is not for everyone. You've got this far without needing to be anyone's missus. Maybe you could go through your whole life like that. Some of the girls that come in here, I know that marriage will be the making of them. They *want* to nurture someone. They get their sense of worth from taking care of other people. They are quite happy to have a husband who'll end up being like an extra child, which is lucky because so many of them do, but you . . . If you're going to do this at all, you need it to be a proper partnership. That's obvious to me. You need to decide if you can have that with your fiancé."

"It's too late to find out whether I'm in a proper partnership or not. I've got to do it now. The venue is booked for two days' time."

"You know Princess Diana didn't want to get married, not after she found out about Camilla. She told her sisters she wanted out, but they said to her, 'It's too late, Duch. Your face is on the tea towels.' Your face is not on any tea towels, but even if it were, you can say, 'I don't,' right up until you say, 'I do.' I bloody wish Diana's sisters had told her that."

"Can you imagine the fallout?"

"Would probably have seemed like a storm in a teacup compared with the furore surrounding her death . . . Would you like a cup of tea?"

"I didn't think cups of tea were allowed in Bride on Time. All that white material."

"I trust you not to spill it," said Melanie. "You are a grown woman, after all."

Over tea, Melanie told Kate more about her marriage.

Melanie met her darling Keith at a youth club. She had seen him around plenty of times when they were growing up, though he went to the rougher school on the other side of town. She had never spoken to him until the summer of her thirteenth birthday, when her parents decreed that she was allowed to stay out until nine at night so long as she stuck to organised activities.

Keith was sitting on his bicycle outside the youth club when Melanie arrived with her friends from school. They swept past him as haughtily as three supermodels sashaying past the red rope at a nightclub, but Bernice couldn't keep her composure for long. She burst into giggles, and when Melanie reprimanded her for ruining their illusion of cool, Bernice made things a hundred times worse by saying, "Well, you fancy him," with reference to Keith, who was now chewing on a matchstick like a very young Marlon Brando.

Their courtship progressed in typical teenage fashion with both of them denying that they liked each other at all. They protested that they hated each other, in fact. Keith drew an unflattering picture of Melanie in Magic Marker on the whitewashed wall of the boys' toilets. She found out from Bernice's brother. Melanie retaliated by writing, "Keith likes boys," on a cubicle wall in the ladies'. She was caught in the act and had to spend a Saturday afternoon repainting. When she protested that she would never have stooped to graffiti had Keith Harris not drawn that picture of her first, Keith was also roped in to make amends. It was while they were painting that they finally got talking. While they were cleaning paintbrushes, Keith chanced a kiss and the rest was history. When the new school term began, Melanie was proud to be able to tell her friends that she had a real boyfriend.

Melanie lost her virginity to Keith when she was sixteen. He promised her that day that they would be together until they were old. He was going to marry her the moment he could get her father's permission. He kept his promise. He asked Melanie's father for her hand on her eighteenth birthday. He proposed to her at her birthday party in front of all of their friends. They married in 1981 and stayed married for sixteen years. No children, Melanie sighed.

Not a day went by when Melanie didn't think of Keith in some context or another. All in all, they were together for almost twenty-five years. When someone is part of your life for that long, then it's inevitable that you're reminded of them at every turn.

Melanie hadn't seen Keith since 1999, when he turned up at her father's funeral. Melanie hadn't invited him. He said his mother had read the death notice in the local paper and told him when the cremation was being held. At the time, Melanie had told him that he wasn't welcome, that her father wouldn't have wanted Keith there after he let her down so badly, but that wasn't true. Melanie's father had been on Keith's side to the end. He'd told Melanie that he couldn't understand what was wrong with her, casting off Keith's love for some feminist ideal.

"Why didn't you just ask him to do the washing-up more often?"

Now, nearly twelve years later, Melanie saw Keith's gesture — turning up at the funeral like that — for what it really was. It was kind and thoughtful. It was his attempt to let her know that if she needed support, she still had his.

But Melanie didn't even know where Keith was any more. She had seen in the paper that his father had died too. She hadn't gone along to the funeral. Keith's

290

mother definitely wouldn't have been pleased to see her. Now she wasn't sure Keith was still in Southampton. None of her friends had seen him in years. At least, they hadn't mentioned it to Melanie if they had.

"Looking back, I wonder if we could have made it work. Was it just the idea of marriage, rather than our marriage, that was driving me insane? It's possible that it's not Ian who's making you feel like this, Kate. It's centuries and centuries of conditioning. It's the way his mother and father were around each other and the way their parents were around them. It's everything you see on television. It's every novel you read. It's every celebrity who announces that giving up her film career to cook his dinner was the best move she ever made. There's so much pressure on us to do it all, have it all, then don the white dress and give it all up."

"That's exactly how I feel."

"I blamed Keith for so many things that were completely beyond his power to change. It was easier to get rid of him than to try to make him understand. I wouldn't make that mistake again. But it's a big decision you've got to make, my love. I don't envy you in the slightest, but you mustn't think that it's impossible. I believe that you can have a marriage and still hold on to what matters to you, so long as you really want it."

"How will I know if I really want it?"

"You've got all the information you need inside. Right here." Melanie thumped her fist against her chest. "You'll make the right decision."

Kate drove to Matt's house. The curtains were drawn and the place looked empty. She got out her phone and was about to send him a text when she saw a car pull up across the road. In the driver's seat was a small, dark-haired woman. She jumped out of the car and went round to the back to unbuckle two child seats.

Matt came to the door. He looked nervous as the woman ushered the children up the driveway. The children wrapped themselves round their father, but he barely seemed to notice them. He was watching their mother get back into her car. Kate could see in his expression that Rosie still held his heart in her hands. Matt was not going to be her future. He never had been. Kate decided not to let him know she was ever there. She had to go home and think very carefully about her next move. She looked at her phone, hoping for some kind of message from Ian that would convince her the happiness she'd felt on the day they got engaged could come back again. There were still more than thirty-six hours. All she needed was a sign.

CHAPTER
FORTY-SEVEN

29 April 2011

At last the day of the royal wedding arrived.

"Can you imagine what it's like at the palace this morning?" Kate's mother observed as her daughter finally emerged to have her breakfast. "I don't suppose Mrs Middleton has had a proper night's sleep in a month thinking of this morning. At least she doesn't have to worry about the flowers and the catering. But she's giving her daughter up to that family! She must be wondering if she'll ever really see her again."

"I don't think Prince William will ban the Middletons from Buckingham Palace," said Kate.

"His grandmother might. It's one thing her grandson getting married to a commoner . . . Poor Mrs Middleton must be feeling sick. She's got to walk into that abbey with the eyes of the world upon her. They're going to be pulling her outfit apart. I found it hard enough to decide what to wear for tomorrow and I don't have to think about how it'll look in the *Daily Mail*."

"What about Mr Middleton?" asked Kate as her father shuffled into the room.

"I imagine he's just happy somebody's taking his Kate off his hands," said John. "I know I am."

"Thanks, Dad. I'm not quite off your hands yet."

John gave her a squeeze to confirm that he was joking.

"Well, I never thought I'd get to see this day — Diana's little boy getting married and my own little girl going to do the same tomorrow morning."

Kate called Ian.

"What are you doing?" she asked.

"Watching the wedding. Mum is looking for tips on how to behave when she meets your posh family en masse."

"Tell her that Auntie Jean must be addressed as 'HRH'."

"Aren't you watching the wedding?"

"No, I'm going for a walk. I feel like I'm completely wedding-ed out after the past six months."

"Just one more day to go, Miss Williamson."

One more day. Just over twenty-four hours, in fact.

"Your face is on the tea towels, Duch," echoed in Kate's mind. It was too late to do anything but go through with it now, right?

Over at the Ashcroft household, Diana and her mother were watching the royal wedding in an altogether more critical frame of mind. It was as though the royal wedding was a dry run for their big day. Diana wanted to see whether Kate had her hair up or down. She was still undecided about her own do. Susie wanted to see

294

Mrs Middleton's outfit, of course. As it happened, she approved.

"Good colour. I like it. Very elegant and restrained," was Susie's verdict.

"Not at all like a stewardess's outfit," Diana said.

"I'm still convinced I worked alongside her on a flight to Bahrain," Susie commented as the mother of the bride walked into Westminster Abbey. Susie had enjoyed a very brief career as an air hostess before she met Dave and her plan to marry a pilot and move to the Home Counties was scuppered.

Diana perused the faces of the guests.

"It must be really tedious, having to have all those politicians as your guests. Who do you think that is?" Diana pointed at a woman who was veritably waddling down the aisle.

"That might be the queen of Tonga," said Susie. "The king of Tonga had to have a specially made seat when Diana married Charles. It took eight men to lift it or something like that. I remember thinking that I would need eight men to lift me too if you didn't finally make an appearance. You were two weeks over your due date, you were. Nothing made any difference. You just weren't going to come out until you were good and ready."

"I was listening for Kiri Te Kanawa. I was waiting to make my grand entrance," said Diana.

"You certainly were."

While the live television cameras waited for the bride and her father to arrive in their limousine, the television footage flipped back to 1981.

"Ugh. I can never see those bridesmaids without thinking about the excruciating pain of childbirth," said Susie. "I can almost feel the tearing pain . . ."

"Mum, please. I'm trying to eat a sandwich."

"Sorry, love."

The television showed the guests in the abbey again.

"I think it was a mistake, don't you, inviting ordinary people?" said Diana. "I mean, what is that woman wearing? She must be a charity worker."

"I think she's a duchess, actually," Susie pointed out.

"Well, she doesn't know how to dress . . . Oh, if only Ben had a military uniform," sighed Diana as a man in naval uniform found his way to his seat. "He'd look great in a jacket like that. Do you think you can hire them?"

"I expect so," said Susie. "But not modern ones. Isn't wearing a soldier's uniform like impersonating a policeman?"

"Oh, Mum, of course it isn't. You know what? I'm going to have a look online and find out where I can get one."

"It's a bit late, isn't it? For tomorrow, I mean."

"Not if Ben gets up really early. Look" — Diana showed her mother the screen of her iPhone. "I knew there was a fancy-dress store in Southampton. It says here that they specialise in naval uniforms throughout history. How about this, Mum? Ben would look amazing in that."

"I don't know, sweetheart. He's already hired a morning suit, hasn't he?"

"So? He can hire this instead. I like this one. It's a replica of the uniform worn by the senior officers on the *Titanic*. I'm going to ask Ben to have a look."

Ben was home alone. He had told Diana that he would be spending the day with his parents, enjoying his last day as a single man in the bosom of his family. Instead, he was spending it alone in a darkened room with nothing but a few cans of beer and a porn movie for company. The porn movie had been a gift from the boys for his stag night. It was carefully disguised in the box from a Southampton FC DVD. Ben felt pretty sure it was safe like that.

While Diana contemplated sending Ben up the aisle looking like Captain Birdseye, Ben watched two girls dressed in football kit getting it on with one another. Ben's fantasies could not have been more different from his future wife's.

When his phone rang, he let the caller go straight to voicemail. When the phone rang again three times in quick succession, Ben knew it could only be Diana.

"Have you got the wedding on?" she asked.

"Yes," Ben lied. He turned the volume down so that Diana couldn't hear the girls in their football kit scoring with each other.

"OK. BBC?"

"Of course."

"Now, you see that man in the third row from the front on the right-hand side? The one in the white jacket? Now, don't you think that's the best uniform you ever saw?"

"Yes," said Ben automatically. He assumed that was the right answer.

"Then how do you feel about wearing something like that yourself? For our wedding."

"What? I'm wearing a morning suit."

"I know that's what you were supposed to be wearing, but watching the royal wedding and seeing how wonderful all those men look in their uniforms has got me thinking. There's a place in Southampton that hires out costumes. They've got something that would be just right. You could go there first thing in the morning and if it doesn't fit, then fair enough, but if it does . . ."

"Those people have uniforms because they work in the armed forces. I work in IT."

"Ben, it would make my dream complete."

Diana's dream. Diana's dream had long since become Ben's nightmare.

Everyone thought Ben was lucky to be marrying Diana. When they walked down the street together, she turned heads and Ben saw envy in the eyes of his fellow men. But this whole business with the uniform only served to remind Ben that Diana didn't even really see him as a person. Diana was approaching the wedding like a small girl playing with her dolls, and Ben was the biggest plaything of them all. What on earth was she thinking? Having him dress up like he was going to a fancy-dress party? There were less than twenty-four hours to go. Ben looked at his watch and his eyes widened as though he saw a death's head staring back at him. Less than a day.

Diana twittered on. "I'm going to call and leave a message right now. If they've got it in, you could pick it up as soon as the shop opens. Tell Ed to call me with his measurements so I can see if they have something to fit him as well."

Ed would think that Ben had gone mad. There was no way he was going to ask him. Any minute now Diana would tell him that the whole wedding was going to have a *Titanic* theme. It would be appropriate in some ways. Southampton was where the *Titanic* set off on her doomed voyage. Would the next day at the cathedral see the launch of another ill-fated journey for Ben and Diana? Ben was suddenly so disturbed that he couldn't even bring himself to finish watching the porn film.

CHAPTER
FORTY-EIGHT

Of course, the staff of Bride on Time had a day off for the royal wedding, but Heidi and Sarah had arranged to meet at Sarah's house to watch the wedding together. They had asked Melanie to join them. Both Heidi and Sarah were single now, Heidi having finally dumped the man she'd clung on to for Valentine's Day, Sarah's romance having never really got off the ground. They assumed that Melanie, being a childless widow so far as they knew, would be equally keen to meet up. Indeed, Melanie did go along to Heidi's house for a cup of tea in the morning, telling herself that it was the right thing to do for the sake of staff bonding.

Sarah had made some special royal-wedding cupcakes in red, white and blue. Heidi had spent a king's ransom on commemorative china on which to serve it.

"This will be worth a fortune in twenty years," Heidi was convinced.

Of course, that day's coverage of the wedding contained plenty of flashbacks to 1981. Melanie felt her chest tighten as she saw footage of Diana arriving at St Paul's again and she was transported back to her childhood bedroom at her parents' house with her grandmother, long gone now, helping her into her dress. She remembered her mother, now so doolally she thought Melanie was not her daughter but her sister, trying to iron out the creases in her skirt. None of them were happy memories any more, tinged as they were by the sadness that followed.

This day could be the start of something different, though, couldn't it? As Catherine Middleton arrived at the abbey, her beautiful smile was bigger than ever. The nation rejoiced in a true love match.

"I think I'll go back to my house," said Melanie, as the new princess and her husband began to exchange their vows.

"You can't go now," said Sarah. "Don't you want to see them riding back to the palace? And the kiss? And the flyover?"

"I'm not feeling too good," Melanie lied. "If I go home now, there won't be any traffic."

"Oh, all right," said Sarah.

"I'll see you both at work tomorrow morning. Bright and early! I imagine we're going to get lots of orders for that dress!"

Melanie saw herself out. Heidi and Sarah didn't wait until she was safely out of earshot before they started speculating on the real reason for Melanie's departure.

"Do you think she's OK? She hasn't seemed very happy all morning."

"It must bring back terrible memories of her dead husband," said Heidi. "All that stuff about Charles and Di in 1981. I expect she's going home to have a cry."

That much was entirely right, but not for the reasons Heidi and Sarah imagined.

Melanie had known for some months that her feelings were reaching a crescendo. She could either continue to be miserable or she could do something about it. That evening, for the first time, she typed Keith's name into Facebook. The networking site immediately came back with more than six hundred possible matches. Melanie sighed at the enormity of her task. Was that him? She peered closely at a photograph of a man wearing nothing but Speedos and a snorkelling mask. No. Too young. Keith might have had a six-pack twenty years ago, but the chances of him having one now were pretty slim. There were a frustrating number of profiles that had no picture whatsoever. All Melanie had to go on were the friends in those profiles' friends lists. But she didn't recognise anyone. There were so many people in the world. Even typing in "Keith Harris Southampton" only narrowed the options down to a couple of hundred. Melanie typed in her own name and was greeted by similar hordes. That brought a wry smile to her face. We all go through life thinking we're so different from everyone else. Facebook puts the lie to that. How many people even used their own names?

After two hours, Melanie must have checked the details of at least forty Keiths. Some were easy to dismiss. Too young. Wrong nationality. Messages on their wall about the kind of things that would never have interested her ex-husband.

Some were more difficult. One profile didn't have a profile picture, but when Melanie clicked through, she found she was able to access a whole host of family photographs, mostly of a woman in her late thirties or forties with two brown-haired children in school uniform and football kit. Obviously, this Keith Harris was a doting father. Melanie enlarged the photos of those children as far as she could and studied their faces for signs of her own Keith. His children would have had brown hair, she thought. And perhaps the little one had similar blue eyes.

Melanie felt her stomach lurch. Had Keith found a new wife and started the family he claimed he didn't want to put her mind at rest when they couldn't get pregnant together? If so, then that evening's fantasy would have to remain just that. She couldn't possibly get in touch with him if he was a fully paid-up family man. She felt a wave of unhappiness such as she hadn't felt in years. She clicked to open another page of photographs.

Torturing myself, she told herself off.

But at last she found a photograph of the two small children with a man, and in yet another, older, photograph, the man and the woman from the other photos stood side by side on the steps of a church. This Keith Harris was not Melanie's own. Melanie clicked the profile shut.

She opened another.

"Keith Harris is excited about an evening at GAY."

It wasn't impossible, but . . .

Another profile. This Keith Harris wrote all his wall posts in French.

It was like searching for the proverbial needle in a haystack. And even if she did find the Keith she had been married to and there was no evidence of a new wife or girlfriend, really, where would she begin?

Just three more, she promised herself. Then she would have to go to bed. She had an early start in the morning. That Saturday was going to be the busiest April Saturday the staff at Bride on Time had ever seen. Fifteen brides would be stopping by in the morning to pick up their dresses. There was always at least one that would need emergency work, a rescuing stitch.

It seemed that Keith Harris number one only befriended Russian glamour models.

Keith Harris number two gave his date of birth as 1929.

Keith Harris number three was friends with Alison Abbott, a girl from Melanie's class at school, and Richard Jones, who had been in the year above them. And there was the final piece of evidence: this Keith Harris had included "West Ham" among his "likes". Melanie was sure at last that she had found her man.

Melanie felt as hot about the face as she had done when she'd walked past Keith on her way to the youth club all those years before. She clicked frantically on every tab in his profile, trying to glean as much as possible from what little was written there. Frustratingly, he had left his personal information blank. Nothing about his whereabouts or his marital status, though he had written "West Ham for ever" under "religious views". That was very Keith. His wall posts, too, seemed largely useless when it came to enlightening Melanie on how the years had treated her ex. She read them carefully and clicked to see exactly who had "liked" what. She was gratified to see there was no flirtation. But no real information either. Until she came to the very first post on Keith's wall, which was at this point almost three years old. It was from Richard Jones, the old school friend.

"Are you still in London?" Richard asked. "I get up there from time to time on business. Would be great to meet up and have a pint."

Beneath it, Keith had replied, "Absolutely, mate. Let me know. I'm still at Cowells."

Cowells. That one word was the key that Melanie needed. Minutes later, she knew that her ex-husband was now a partner in a London accountancy firm. The website even carried his picture. He had a lot less hair than Melanie remembered, but other than that, he seemed hardly to have changed. He had stayed as skinny as always. And that smile. How could Melanie forget that smile? Keith's grin inspired everyone who saw it to grin back at him, as Melanie was doing now, just looking at the screen. But then she found herself wondering who Keith had been smiling at when that photograph was taken. Was he feeling as happy as he looked? Though thirteen years had passed since the divorce, Melanie was surprised to find herself jealous of the people who had seen that smile in the flesh.

She looked closely at the clothes he was wearing. His suit looked well cut. Had he chosen that himself? And that tie? Hadn't he always said that he thought ties with those tiny cartoons on them were for toffs? He would never get more adventurous than a stripe. He had certainly said that when Melanie splashed out and bought him a tie from Ferragamo. Seventy quid it had cost her and he wouldn't wear it.

But hang on. Melanie did her best to enlarge the photograph. She turned the screen to its maximum brightness. Wasn't the tie Keith was wearing in that picture the very one he had turned his nose up at all those years before?

It can't be, thought Melanie.

It was.

This had all sorts of implications. If Keith was still wearing a gift that she had bought for him, then he must still think about her. Perhaps he had hoped that one day she would see the photograph on his corporate website and understand it as a secret signal.

Melanie Harris, you are daft, she told herself. Totally daft.

Men weren't sentimental in the same way as women. Keith hadn't thought anything when he reached for that tie. It must have been the nearest one to hand.

Still, Melanie couldn't stop thinking about it when she finally went to bed. It was a strange coincidence if nothing else. Something to mention when she sent her first email. No, she couldn't email him. What was the point?

Melanie turned her pillow over and laid her face against the cooler side, but it was no use. She couldn't sleep. She wouldn't be able to sleep until she had done something. That stupid tie was a sign. Keith was reaching out across the years to her. There was no evidence of a new woman in his life on his Facebook page. What did Melanie have to lose except her dignity? And really, she didn't even have to lose that if she didn't let anyone know what she was about to do.

Melanie turned her laptop on again. She clicked through to the website of Cowells Accountancy ACA. She could email him directly through that website. But then a secretary might read it. Melanie went back to Facebook and trawled through seven more wrong Keith Harrises before she found her man again. She opened a message window and started to write.

On the other side of town, someone else was writing a very important letter indeed.

CHAPTER
FORTY-NINE

Midnight, 29 April 2011

This is the hardest letter I have ever had to write. I don't know how to begin. I suppose I should start by saying I want you to know that I love you, whatever happens. I always have done. You have brought so many good things into my life and I have so many happy memories from our life together. I can't thank you enough for all the good times. They will be with me for the rest of my days, but the fact is that I'm not happy and I just can't be with you any more.

I have to come right out with it. I haven't really been happy since the day we got engaged. You know that it came as a shock to me, our getting engaged. It's not that it hadn't crossed my mind, but it definitely happened quite a bit earlier than I expected it to. I felt in many ways that it was forced upon me, given the circumstances. There was no way I could have said "no" to your request to get married when it was clear how important marriage was in your view of our future together.

The truth is, I felt I had no choice but to get engaged back in October. So many people would have been disappointed if I'd decided to do anything else. At the time, I told myself that it was what I wanted too.

I did think that perhaps it was the wedding-planning that was getting me down. When I talked to other people, they all told me that they hated their wedding day and only got through it by thinking of the marriage beyond. They also told me that it was natural to feel like a door was closing.

The thing is, I can't see the marriage beyond the big day. You might say that it won't be that different from what we already have. Perhaps that suits you, but it doesn't suit me. I think that what we already have isn't enough for me any more. I think I thought that before we got engaged, but the wedding day itself has thrown my feelings into focus. I'm not happy. A wedding ring won't change that, no matter how much I wish it could.

I cannot tell you how sorry I am to do this to you right now, the night before our wedding. Believe me, my heart is breaking as I write. I comfort myself with the knowledge that your family is already with you and they will hopefully help you get through the worst of it. They'll probably tell you that I'm an idiot. Perhaps they're right, but perhaps I'm right and calling off the wedding now will save us both more heartbreak in the long run. Neither of us wants a divorce.

Maybe if I'm making a mistake, I'll realise the day after we should have got married. I hope that you'll give me a chance to explain myself in person one day. I am so sorry, my darling, that I won't be there tomorrow, but right now, I know it's for the best that we're apart.

I love you.

CHAPTER
FIFTY

30 April 2011

The day after the royal wedding dawned like a midsummer day. By the time Diana Ashcroft awoke, the sun was already streaming in through the curtains of her childhood bedroom to stripe the duvet cover she had chosen for her eighteenth birthday (along with a car). Anyway, it seemed right that Diana should sleep beneath the brightly striped covers. They looked deeply unsophisticated to her now, but they were symbolic of Diana's childhood. That night, her last night as an unmarried woman, had officially signalled the end of it, and just before she turned thirty. Praise the Lord.

Diana jumped up from bed and slipped into her pristine white dressing gown with the pink-princess coronet on the back. When she got to the top of the stairs, she saw her mother at the bottom by the front door, gathering up a pile of junk mail.

"They don't take any notice whatsoever of my 'No junk mail' sign," Susie complained as she stuffed the pile of pizza menus and unsolicited estate-agent offers straight into a recycling bag. "Look at this — all of it's rubbish."

"I don't care about junk mail," said Diana. "It's my wedding day! What time is Gran getting here?"

"She said she'd be here by nine."

"Good. Nicole's already texted to say she's on her way."

"Are you sure she's going to be able to manage on her own at Bride on Time?"

"Melanie said that one of her assistants will lay the dress out in the back of Nicole's car. You know, I still can't believe that Melanie turned down the invitation to my reception."

"She must get invited to a lot of weddings," said Susie. "She probably gets a bit bored of them."

"I know, but my wedding is going to be seriously amazing. There are plenty of people who would kill to be invited. If she wants to be a miserable bag about it . . . I just hope you can remember how to loop up the skirt."

"Have you spoken to Ben this morning?" Susie asked.

"No," said Diana. "I called him to say goodnight when I went to bed and then I told him that I didn't want to speak to him again until we're standing at the altar. It's bad luck otherwise."

Susie nodded.

"I've made you your favourite breakfast," she told her daughter. "Do you want to have it now, just you and your old mum, before all the bridesmaids arrive?"

"Oh, Mum," said Diana, "you're not that old, and you'd look amazing if you'd just have some Botox between your brows. I'm going to have it regularly from now on."

Diana examined her face in the hall mirror. "I think I was right to get it done for the wedding, don't you?" She attempted to frown but only succeeded in producing "bunny lines" radiating out from the sides of her nose instead. "I mean, it's not as though I need to frown in my wedding photographs."

Susie led the way into the kitchen where Diana's favourite breakfast was all ready to go. She'd cooked Belgian waffles and smothered them with fresh strawberries and thick whipped cream. There was orange juice and a bottle of champagne on the table.

"Your father sent the champagne over," Susie explained.

"It's not vintage," Diana complained. "Still, we're having vintage at the reception, I suppose. What time is he coming over? I'm glad he's not bringing that slag with him. I mean, I know they're married now and everything, but I told him that today is my day and she still isn't related to me."

"Quite right," said Susie.

Nicole's red Mini, a present from her father on her thirtieth birthday, pulled onto the driveway. Susie dashed out to help her bring the dress inside. Even though Nicole had taken a king-size duvet cover to the bridal salon, the dress could barely be contained. Susie tucked the escaping frills back in before she and Nicole carried it to the front door between them as reverently as if it were the ancient relic of a saint.

"Careful!" Diana yelled as Nicole tripped over the front step and dropped her end of the precious cargo. "For heaven's sake, is it all right?"

"I think I might have broken my toe," said Nicole.

"Put some ice on it," said Diana as she checked the dress for any damage.

The hairdresser arrived at the same time and unloaded enough hair products to dress the entire cast of *Glee*. The make-up artist was ten minutes late, having got stuck in traffic. Fortunately, Diana had built quite a margin of error into the proceedings.

"Have you spoken to the groom this morning?" the make-up artist asked as she mixed up a light tangerine foundation that would match Diana's face to the rest of her body.

"No. I told him last night I wouldn't speak to him again until we got to the cathedral. Everybody knows it's bad luck to talk to the groom before the ceremony."

"Oh, I thought it was just bad luck for him to see you in the dress. I didn't know it extended to talking before the ceremony too. I couldn't stop ringing my husband on the day of our wedding. I drove him mad. I think I just couldn't believe that he was actually going to turn up."

"I'm not worried about that," said Diana. "Ben knows what's good for him. If he doesn't turn up, I'll have his balls on a barbecue."

"Ben will be there," Nicole concurred. "He totally loves her. You've never seen a man so in love."

Diana smiled at her reflection in the mirror as if to say, "And why wouldn't he be?"

"Nicole, will you tell Mum to make me a cup of tea?"

Nicole scuttled away.

"My mum is so excited," Diana told the make-up artist. "She's been driving me crazy all morning. All this is for her, really. All this fuss. I would have had something simple, but through me I wanted Mum to be able to have the wedding she never had."

"That's very kind of you." The make-up artist brushed blue powder onto Diana's eyelids.

"Isn't it?"

The doorbell rang again.

"Photographer's arrived."

CHAPTER
FIFTY-ONE

Kate's father went to wake her with a cup of tea, made exactly how she'd always liked it: weak as water with a splash of milk. Alongside the tea was a boiled egg with five Marmite soldiers and a handful of "Congratulations" cards that had arrived in the post that morning. John knocked quietly on the spare bedroom door.

No answer.

He knocked again.

Still nothing.

Elaine was eager to see her daughter at the start of this momentous day.

"We'll have to wake her up. The hairdresser's going to be here in forty-five minutes."

This time, Elaine knocked and pushed the door open simultaneously. What she saw surprised her. The bed was made. Kate was nowhere to be seen.

"Is she already up?" John asked.

"I haven't seen her."

There was nowhere for Kate to hide in the bijou retirement house they'd downsized to.

"She can't be in the house," said John. "She must have gone out."

"But where's she gone? She's getting married at lunchtime."

"Maybe she went for a walk."

"Wake up, John. She's done a runner," said Elaine. "That's what's happened. She must have climbed through the window. The blind's all wonky — look."

"But why would she do that?"

"Tess said she was acting strangely when we went on that spa day, and she didn't seem right when she came back from the dress fitting on Thursday afternoon. She looked like she'd been crying. I should have said something. I didn't dare. I didn't want to start her off. Oh, I thought it was just wedding jitters." Elaine started to tear up. "Everybody gets wedding jitters."

"Did you get wedding jitters?" John asked his wife.

"Of course I did."

"Then maybe there's no need to panic just yet. It's only nine in the morning. The wedding is three hours away. There's plenty of time for Kate to come home and put her dress on."

"But she could be on a plane out of Southampton Airport by now! Oh, John, what are we supposed to do?"

Tess was ringing the doorbell. Lily sprang into the hallway ahead of her.

"Where's Auntie Kate? I want to put my dress on."

Elaine's expression said it all. Tess cottoned on at once.

"She's gone, hasn't she? I knew it! Didn't I tell you the other night?"

"I should have asked her! Oh, I don't believe it. She must have been in such a state. You don't think she's done something stupid?"

John invited his granddaughter to share a boiled egg and Marmite soldiers in the kitchen before his wife and younger daughter could reach hysteria pitch in the hall. Too late. They were already there.

"I'm going to call the police," said Elaine.

"Not yet," said John. "Let me go and look for her first. I'm sure she won't have gone far."

"But she might have done something stupid."

"I don't think there's anything stupid about deciding not to marry if you don't want to," said John.

"Oh, you idiot!" Elaine swatted him with a tea towel. "You know I'm not talking about that. Go out and bloody well look for her, and the minute you find her, you tell her that whatever she wants to do is perfectly OK with me. I just want her to know that we love her no matter what, and I want her to come home."

"I'll tell her," said John, shrugging on his coat.

Tess had been listening from behind the half-open kitchen door, desperate to keep track of the drama unfolding while at the same time making sure Lily was kept in the dark about her aunt's disappearance until the last possible moment. Now she had to speak up.

"Tell her the same from me, Dad. Tell her that if she's not going to go through with it, I am a hundred per cent behind her. Tell her that Mike, Lily and I love her too, whatever she does."

John nodded.

"Oh, sod this," said Tess. "I'll tell her myself. Mum, you keep an eye on Lily. I'm going out with Dad."

"I should come too," said Elaine, her voice close to cracking.

John and Tess shared a look that they had shared many times before. It was shorthand for "We have to keep her out of this."

"No, Mum. You stay here with Lily. We've got to make sure that there's someone in the house in case Kate decides to come back here before we find her."

"OK," Elaine conceded. "Should I call Ian?"

"Don't call Ian," John and Tess said at once.

"Grandma!" Lily called from the kitchen. "I want to make a cake."

Elaine squeezed her husband and her younger daughter. "Coming, Lily. I'll see what we've got in the cupboard."

Outside the house, Tess called Mike to ask him to get down to her parents' place as quickly as possible. Then she and John divided up the terrain. At the top of the road, Tess would turn to the left, while John and Snowy, Tess's dog, turned to the right. The plentiful walking that had made it such a pleasure for Tess's parents to move down to the coast was now presenting a real problem. Would Kate have chosen to go towards the common, or would she have gone down to the sea?

"I'll take the seafront," said John. His grim expression spoke of the potential agonies of that path.

"Dad," said Tess, linking her arm through his momentarily, "she won't have done anything like that. Kate may have been confused, but she wasn't suicidal.

I'm sure that before you know it, one of us will be walking her home."

"I hope so."

"Come on, Dad. We *know* so."

They came to the main road and took their different directions.

Tess's plan was to cut through the housing estate to the alleyway that led to the common. Since she and Mike had moved down to the south coast for his work, Kate had visited them often. Kate would often accompany Tess when she walked the family dog around the scrubby land towards which Tess was now headed. They'd shared some happy afternoons there, sitting on the dry grass while the dog made friends with its fellow canines and Lily gathered posies of wild flowers. It had been the scene of many deep and meaningful conversations. Away from the possibility of being overheard by Mike, and while Lily was still too young to be interested, Kate and Tess had talked about everything. Tess knew Kate's darkest secrets and vice versa. In any case, the common seemed an obvious place for Kate to aim for on her own.

Tess thought about some of the conversations she and Kate had shared recently. As young children, they had been inseparable. The teenage years had them at each other's throats, and there was a tricky period when Tess first got married, but they had grown to appreciate one another more and more as each year passed. They shared the unique bond of siblings whose joint experiences are impossible to replicate in any ordinary friendship. Who else but a sibling really knows what your family life was like?

Had their family life doomed Kate to make the decision not to marry after all? Kate had always idolised their father. Their parents' marriage was a textbook example of getting it right. Was every relationship Kate had doomed to fail because it couldn't live up to the idyll of their childhood?

Tess had certainly discovered marriage to be rather less than she had hoped for. It did get boring, being with the same person for years without end. Motherhood, too, was dull and grinding more often than it was a joy. Tess wondered if it was in fact the way she had groaned and moaned about her own married life that had made Kate decide she would be better off with the constant round of spa breaks and shopping trips of single life.

They had all so hoped that she would marry Ian. It was obvious from the first time the family met him that Ian adored their precious Kate as much as they did. Had they put too much pressure on her to say "yes"? It was just that he was such a breath of fresh air after the Dan years. How strange it had seemed that Kate could have been in a four-year relationship with a man they'd never met. Before that, the only boyfriend of any real significance was Matt. Tess had never really liked Matt. She found him smug and cocky. It was hard to imagine he had much of a bedside manner even now. Tess knew, of course, that her sister had been seeing something of him.

If Kate really had decided to do a runner, then the rest of the day was going to be a nightmare. Tess knew that her parents would get over a cancelled wedding eventually. The important thing was that Kate understood that she had the right to choose in favour of her own happiness, because once the ring was on her finger, it would be a whole lot harder. As she stepped onto the common where she had often contemplated her own great escape, Tess could vouch for that.

CHAPTER
FIFTY-TWO

Melanie had stayed up half the night trying to put together a suitable message to send to Keith via his Facebook account. It wasn't easy. How on earth do you start an email to the ex-husband you haven't seen in over a decade? Do you have to authenticate yourself first? Melanie had set up a Facebook account for the purpose of trying to track Keith down. It bore her name, but there was little else to prove that she was who she said she was. No photograph. Why shouldn't Keith just delete her message right away?

What was her motivation for doing this? Did she really think that any letter she sent would be gratefully received? Over the years that they had been apart, the righteous anger Melanie had once felt that she "wasn't getting her needs met" had mellowed so that at last she could see how unreasonable she had been. Keith had hardly been getting his needs met either. However, it was possible that Keith, who had so generously shouldered all the blame back then, had come to see things quite differently.

Melanie decided in the end that she would not send the message. Not yet. Besides, despite the royal wedding, that Saturday was to be no different from any other Saturday at Bride on Time. The last thing Melanie needed was to be preoccupied and waiting for an answer. There were brides to be dressed. Melanie prided herself in never having let a bride down, and she wasn't about to start.

Heidi and Sarah were both in the salon early.

"The royal wedding just sort of fizzled out after you went home," said Sarah. "We went to the pub in the afternoon, but it was just like any ordinary Friday only with free sausage rolls."

"Not even good sausage rolls," Heidi chipped in.

"Are you all right?" Sarah asked then. "We know it must be hard for you, thinking back to 1981."

"It is hard," said Melanie brusquely, "but life goes on."

"You are brave, Mel."

Maybe, not right then, but soon, she would have to tell Heidi and Sarah that life was very much going on in Keith's case. She wondered how they would react when she told them she was not in fact a widow but a divorcee and she had spent the previous evening looking for her ex-husband on Facebook.

"We've got fifteen girls today," said Heidi. "I feel like collapsing already."

"Oh, here's to their happy ever afters," said Sarah, raising her coffee mug, "and here's to my early night."

"I'm beginning to understand why you have that rule about not going to any of the weddings you're invited to," Heidi said to Melanie. "Come Saturday lunchtime, I don't honestly care if no one ever marries again in the history of the whole bloody world."

"Do you want to come over to my house for dinner tonight?" Sarah asked. "I've got loads of leftovers from the buffet I did for Princess Kate."

"That's kind, Sarah, but I've already got plans."

Sarah and Heidi looked disbelieving. They knew that Phil the widower had been off the scene since February and Melanie hadn't mentioned anybody else.

"Where are you going?" Heidi asked, because she knew that Sarah wouldn't dare.

"Just out," said Melanie.

"Come on, you can tell us."

"All right," said Melanie. "I'm going to a wedding."

CHAPTER
FIFTY-THREE

Preparations for Diana's wedding were almost complete. Diana was resplendent in her dress, sipping from a flute of pink champagne while her seven bridesmaids buzzed around her skirts. Pete, the photographer, was recording every moment. Outside, her father, Dave, had just arrived. He'd tricked out his old silver Jaguar with white ribbons so that Susie, Diana's grandmother and two of the bridesmaids could be driven to the cathedral in style. He'd even persuaded one of his fitters to don a chauffeur's cap and play driver for the occasion.

"I had it valeted," Dave told Susie as she admired the shine on the bonnet.

Susie smiled at her ex-husband for the first time since they swapped expletives outside a supermarket on the day Susie heard he was getting remarried, ten years before.

"Thank you, Dave," she said now. "That means a lot to me."

"It's all for our little girl," said Dave. "Would you look at her?"

They could see Diana through the living room window. Nicole was helping her step into her Louboutins.

"She's beautiful, isn't she? Every bit the princess she was named after."

"At least one good thing came of our marriage," Susie agreed.

As they stood on the front doorstep exchanging pleasantries, Susie and Dave heard the sound of horses' hooves at the top of the street. They turned to see the bridal carriage pulling into the cul de sac. It was a white, open-topped carriage straight out of a Disney cartoon. A liveried driver held the reins. A matching footman balanced on the running board. The carriage was pulled by not one but two perfectly white horses. But these were no ordinary horses. They were unicorns.

"Oh my God," said Susie. "Are they for real?"

Each horse wore a very convincing prosthetic horn on its forehead.

"Don't you remember that first wedding drawing Diana did when she was six years old?" said Dave. "She told me she wanted to be taken to her wedding by unicorns. Unicorns is what Diana wants and so unicorns is what Diana gets."

The bride and her attendants gawped from the window. Diana leaned out.

"Your carriage awaits," Dave said with a chivalrous bow.

"Oh my God, Dad! Unicorns! You remembered!" Diana raced out of the house as fast as her huge dress would allow her and soon she was on the verge of happy tears.

"Don't cry. Don't cry!" The make-up artist bobbed around her. "Your false eyelashes will come off."

Diana was wearing a pair of falsies that put the long lashes of her "unicorns" to shame. Susie handed her a handkerchief so that she might dab her tears and protect them.

"Oh, Dad," said Diana, "this is the best bridal carriage ever."

"Because you're the best girl in the world."

"Aaaaah," chorused the bridesmaids, led by Nicole. The bridesmaids were all dressed in pink. It didn't suit all of them, but it did match Diana's flowers.

"Dad" — Diana gave him a hug that left a big foundation-coloured smear on his collar — "I know you haven't always been the best father in the world, but I want you to know that I forgive you. I forgive you for leaving Mum and marrying Chelsea. I even forgive you for having Charlie."

"He would have loved to have seen his big sister getting married," said Dave.

"I didn't say I would ever think of him as my brother, Dad."

"We're going to head on to the cathedral in the Jag," said Susie before an argument could start. "Have you got everything you need, Diana love?"

"I think so."

"Something old?"

"My baby charm bracelet." She waggled her wrist to jangle the bracelet that Dave had bought the day he discovered she was a girl and not the automatic Southampton FC season ticket he'd hoped for.

"Something new?"

"My dress, obviously."

"Something borrowed?"

"Nicole's belly-button ring."

"Nice touch," said Pete, giving Nicole a saucy wink. "Something blue."

Diana hitched up her skirt to show a garter with a bow of blue ribbon. The older bridesmaids whooped.

"All present and correct," Diana confirmed.

"Hang on. She still needs a silver sixpence for her shoe," said Diana's grandmother.

Diana looked panicked.

"I haven't got one!"

"I've got one for you," said her grandmother, pulling a little velvet pouch out of her handbag. "Well, it's not a sixpence, but it is a silver coin. Your grandfather bought it for you on the day you were born. They were minting them especially for the royal wedding. He said I should hang on to it until you got married. He would have loved to see this day."

Diana took the velvet pouch and tipped the commemorative coin out into her palm. On one side was the familiar image of the queen, on the other side Charles and Diana in profile.

"Oh, Gran, that's brilliant," said Diana.

"You've got to put it in your shoe," her dad reminded her.

Diana had Nicole help her take one of her shoes off again, so that she could slip the coin inside, but it was thicker than the silver sixpence of the rhyme and it was far too uncomfortable for Diana to be able to walk around with it in place. She took the coin out and handed it back to her gran.

"You'll have to carry it."

"At least you know that your grandfather is with you in spirit today."

"Yes, Gran. I can feel it. Now, shouldn't you all be on your way to the cathedral?"

Diana's grandmother, her mother and two of the bridesmaids squeezed into the back of the Jaguar. The other five bridesmaids would be following in a people carrier, but not before they had helped Diana up into her fairy-princess carriage with its unicorns. Up and down the street, Susie's neighbours had turned out to watch the bride set off on her journey to the cathedral. They had always known that Diana Ashcroft would get a spectacular send-off, but no one had expected unicorns. At least, no one in their right mind had expected unicorns.

"Daddy" — Diana cuddled close to her father in the back of the carriage, as Pete fired off another fifty photographs — "this is the best day of my life."

The horses took off at a far statelier pace than they had arrived at, thanks to the weight of two new passengers and a wedding dress that weighed the same as a child. Diana made the most of the slow exit from the cul de sac. She gave her mother's neighbours a regal wave. Two young girls were open-mouthed with awe at the spectacle of this cross between Kate Middleton and Katie Price.

"I bet that one day they'll ask their fathers for a carriage just like this," Diana observed as she blew the girls kisses.

"I bet they will," her father agreed.

At the top of the road, Diana's carriage passed the recycling truck. The bin men waved and whistled at the bride before they carried on into the cul de sac, where they would be picking up one particularly important bag of rubbish.

CHAPTER
FIFTY-FOUR

All the time her sister and father searched for her, Kate was not far away. She was sitting on the seafront in Warsham. She'd been sitting there for ages, since seven that morning. She had, as her mother suspected, climbed out of the bedroom window. It was a groundfloor window. It was easy. Far easier than leaving through the front door and having to answer questions about where she was going at such an early hour and why.

Where to begin? Somehow, Kate thought to herself, I never really believed I would get to this day. Even when the wedding was just twenty-four hours away and the dress was ready and the flowers being arranged, Kate had not been able to imagine herself into place at the top of the aisle. And she realised then that when she had managed to think herself into a wedding scene, she had not been able to picture Ian standing beside her. The idea had never really taken shape in her mind. That frightened her.

Now the moment when she should be standing by Ian's side was just a few hours away. Out on the Solent, an ordinary Saturday morning was in progress. A flotilla of small sailboats containing eager children was pulled out to sea by a tug, like a family of ducklings following the mother duck. In the middle distance, the Isle of Wight ferry took holidaymakers, enjoying the long weekend, to visit Osborne House or browse for dinosaur bones on the beach. Behind the ferry, a container ship headed into the docks at Southampton. That ship was as big as a block of flats. It dwarfed the refinery as it moved on by, silent as a ghost.

Kate idly wondered what Princess Kate was doing that morning. Did she have a hangover? Was she full of excitement at the start of her married life, or was she wondering what the hell she had just signed up to?

One day, she hoped she would be able to tell Ian what she had been through these past few months and how what should have been one of the happiest moments in her life had become such an almighty source of misery. She hoped that he would understand. He probably wouldn't like what she had to say, but he was a good man and she knew that he had only ever wanted the best for her. Just like her dad.

Kate had always felt a similarity of mind with her father, so she wasn't in the least bit surprised that it was he who tracked her down. Actually, the first family member that morning to get to her was her sister's dog. Snowy, who had never really taken to training, leaped at Kate's back in her excitement and almost pushed her off the sea wall.

"Snowy!"

Snowy had no idea that today should be any different from normal. She was full of her usual exuberance at the idea of a walk. Any walk.

"There you are," said John.

"Dad."

"Do you want me to find you, or shall I go back and tell your mother that you called to say you were on your way to Rio while I was walking the dog?"

"What do you mean?"

"You know we'll still love you whatever you decide to do. It doesn't matter about what anyone else says. It's your life, Kate. It's your decision."

"What are you talking about? I'm just getting a breath of fresh air."

"But it's nearly ten o'clock."

Kate looked at her watch. "What?" She sprang to her feet. "I didn't realise how long I'd been sitting here. Has the hairdresser arrived? Is Tess there? Has she got Lily ready? Oh, Dad, I've just been sitting here thinking, having a moment of calm before the storm."

"But you climbed out of the window."

"I was going to climb back in before anyone woke up. I just wanted to get out of the house without having to answer loads of questions. I just wanted a moment on my own."

"Your mother thinks you've run away."

"Oh my God, I'm sorry. Let's go back."

Kate jumped up and brushed down her jeans.

Snowy jumped with her, excited to be on the move again.

"Are you sure you weren't really running away?" asked John. "Because, you know, if you're not sure, your mother and I and your sister and Mike and Lily, we're all right behind you. Well, perhaps not Lily. She'll raise merry hell if she doesn't get to be a bridesmaid."

Kate laughed.

"I know, Dad. But I am sure. I've never been so sure in my life."

Elaine burst into tears as her elder daughter walked into the kitchen.

Tess threw her arms round her sister's neck. "Am I getting the dress out of the car or what?"

"Get the dress," Kate instructed. "Mum, put the kettle on."

CHAPTER
FIFTY-FIVE

Dave peered closely at the message on his mobile phone.

"What is it?" Diana asked.

"It's from your mother."

"What does she say?"

"She says she thinks we should go round the block another time."

Dave conveyed the instruction to the carriage driver.

"What do we have to go round the block again for?" Diana persisted. The cathedral was within sight.

"Well, I suppose your mother thinks that we should keep everyone waiting a little bit longer. It's tradition for the bride to be late."

"Yeah, but I don't want to be too late. There's a lot to get through at the reception. The string quartet is only booked till half past three. God knows how long this ceremony will take. The bishop has a tendency to go on."

"It'll be fine, my love," Dave assured her. He patted her hand. "We've got all the time in the world."

But by the time they had "been round the block" again, Dave had received another text message from Susie asking him to "just keep going".

"What's going on?" Now Diana was suspicious.

"Nothing." Dave gave his daughter's knee a squeeze. "Nothing at all. The traffic's been bad on the road from Portsmouth and there are just a few people yet to arrive. We don't want to start the ceremony without them."

That kept Diana quiet for another minute.

"Dad," she asked eventually, "who exactly hasn't arrived?"

Dave didn't need to say anything. The look of sheer panic on his face told Diana everything she needed to know.

"You are joking," she said. "Dad, tell me you're bloody well joking!"

Dave could only shake his head.

Diana's mouth dropped open. For a second she was lost for words. Just for a second.

"He wouldn't do that to me. He loves me. He wouldn't do that."

"Let's just wait in this nice layby."

"No! Take us straight to the cathedral!" Diana shouted at the guy who was driving the carriage.

"Sweetheart, I think we should wait here," said Dave. "Your mother has got everything under control. There's no point us rushing in there just yet. If I know Ben, he won't let you down. There will be some perfectly reasonable explanation. Maybe there's traffic."

"There had better be bloody traffic," Diana hissed. She was prevented from phoning Ben because she didn't have her phone with her and Ben's number wasn't on her father's, but she was not going to take her father's advice and hang around in a layby looking like a refugee from a pantomime because nobody could tell her where her fiancé was.

"Drive on," she commanded.

The carriage driver didn't know who to take his orders from. Should he listen to the father, who seemed to be the voice of reason, or the bride, who looked as if she might at any moment lose her head?

"Drive on," said Diana. Her expression was steely. She was not to be messed with.

"We need to wait here," said Dave. He wasn't to be messed with either.

The driver looked from one to the other. Which one would be the less angry? In the end, Diana made the decision for him. While the driver was hesitating, trying to remember if his wife, who arranged the rental, had already cashed the cheque, Diana clambered over the seats and grabbed the reins from his hands. Giving the reins a swift jerk, she scared the horses into motion again and fell back heavily into her father's lap when they took off at a gallop.

"Whoa!" The driver tried in vain to bring his horses back under control, but there was no chance. Somehow Diana had frightened them beyond such reason as one can expect from an animal and now they were hurtling towards the traffic.

"Make them slow down!" Diana yelled.

"Stay calm, stay calm. Just hang on to the carriage," the driver instructed as Diana and her father embarked upon the ride of their lives.

"Stay calm!" the driver shouted again, but soon Dave was cowering on the floor of the carriage with Diana right on top of him. Dave hung on to the side of the carriage. Diana hung on to her father. Her enormous dress billowed around her, but, alas, didn't seem to act as any kind of brake. Her cathedral-length veil was ripped from her head as they passed beneath a low-hanging branch.

"Daaaaaddd!" Diana screamed. "You've got to get us out of here."

At this point, the driver, terrified by the dual carriageway in his near future, hurled himself onto a dogshit-covered grass verge. The footman had fallen off long before. Now Diana and her father were completely alone.

The horses thundered on, as though they were late for the Apocalypse. There was nothing Diana or Dave could do except pray that the other road users would be able to avoid them. Father and daughter clung together as the mad dash continued for long enough for a local news network to pick up the spectacle on the camera on their traffic helicopter.

"Ladies and gentlemen, you're never going to believe this — we have what looks like an out-of-control carriage pulled by a pair of wild unicorns."

CHAPTER
FIFTY-SIX

"Jeez," said Tess as she hauled Kate's dress into the house, "I have put my back out."

"You should try wearing it," said Kate. "I wouldn't be surprised if I'm two inches shorter by the end of the day."

"Thank God I don't have to iron it," said Elaine. "I had to iron my own wedding dress, you know."

"Yes, Mum," Tess and Kate chorused.

"But that was back in the war," Tess teased, "when fabric was still being rationed."

Only Lily, who had never seen the dress before, was properly awed by the acres and acres of silk.

"Auntie Kate is going to be a princess."

"Let's see how impressed she is when she realises she's got to carry the train," Kate laughed.

"All right," said Elaine. "Let's see how you put this thing on. Did you step into it, or does it go over your head?"

"Over my head," said Kate. "The waistband is too tight to get over my enormous arse."

Kate shivered in her underwear while Tess and Elaine tried to work out the logistics. It was difficult to know when the dress was up or down or inside out. If you let go of the bodice for even a second, it would be swallowed into the skirt like a peak sinking back into well-whipped egg white. There was plenty of swearing. Tess and Elaine found the dress was too heavy to lift even as high as Kate's shoulders. At last, she sat down on the edge of the bed and they were able to flip it over her head.

Kate stood up only to discover that she had the dress on back to front. She tried to wrench the dress round, but in the end, it was easier to start again.

"Now I need a drink," Kate announced.

Tess poured more champagne while Elaine attempted to button up the back of the bodice. Now she understood why the women at Bride on Time had given such detailed instructions. Not only did Kate's wedding dress have buttons, it had a zip on the inner bodice and ribbons to cover the buttons once they were done. Elaine found the buttons impossible, even with the recommended crochet hook. Tess, who had already downed two glasses of champagne to calm herself after the excitement of Kate's momentary disappearance, did not have much more luck. It took twenty minutes to get the dress fastened.

"No wonder Miss Havisham never took hers off," said Kate.

Thankfully, Lily's bridesmaid's dress was altogether easier to get into. The little pink number had just a zip at the back. There was a brief moment of panic after Lily was dressed when she disappeared and was found outside jumping over a rainbow in a puddle, but fortunately, Tess had remembered to pack spare white tights. They lasted just half an hour before Lily put a hole in them.

The make-up artist arrived fresh from another wedding. "Thank God you want the natural look," she said. "I've run out of blue eye shadow."

The make-up artist also pinned Kate's hair up into an artfully dishevelled bun, adorned with one of the roses from the bouquet, which had only just arrived. The florist had been right about the bouquet, thought Kate, as she posed in front of the mirror. Anything smaller would have looked silly with the dress's generous skirt. Trudy, the photographer, snapped some frames of the bouquet while Kate submitted to the last few tweaks of her hairdo.

"You look so beautiful." Elaine gave a tearful sniff.

"Mum, please. You'll ruin your make-up."

John appeared in the doorway. "Are you girls nearly ready? I know it's traditional to make the groom wait, but . . ." He tapped his watch. Kate turned from the mirror. "Someone stole my daughter and replaced her with a princess."

"Oh, Dad."

Kate would not be travelling to her wedding in a horse-drawn carriage. For a start, she'd never really trusted horses, having been bitten by a supposedly docile nag on a childhood trip to a petting farm. And then there was the incident at her cousin's wedding: that dead horse really took the fun out of the reception. Plus, it wasn't her style. Kate would be travelling to the ceremony in her first ever car, a Fiat Panda that Tess now used as a runaround.

"Are you positive you don't want a Rolls-Royce?" her father had asked during the planning.

"No," Kate reassured him. "This Panda and I had many adventures together back when I was a single girl. I'd like it to be part of the proceedings."

Of course, Kate had made that particular plan before she bought the enormous frock.

Loading the dress into the Panda was difficult, but not impossible. Photographs of John and Kate in the back of the car turned out to be 90 per cent skirt.

With the rest of the bridal party safely in the back of a proper, hired car, Kate savoured her last moment of singledom.

"Thank you, Dad," she said, "for always being there for me."

John gave his daughter a squeeze.

"This is your last chance to get out of here," he reminded her. "If you say the word, I will turn this car round and we'll go straight home. I'll sort everything out. No questions."

"Dad," said Kate, "stop asking me. I've made my mind up. The only thing worrying me now is whether Ian might have changed his mind instead."

Smiling, John prepared to turn into the hotel driveway, but suddenly a carriage decked out with a hundred white ribbons was thundering towards them.

John braked. Both he and Kate ducked their heads uselessly as the carriage hurtled past.

"My God," said Kate, when she dared to look up again, "did I just see two unicorns?"

CHAPTER
FIFTY-SEVEN

Diana's unicorns showed no sign of tiring as they did a second circuit of the town centre. By this point the police had been alerted by several members of the public, though no one was quite sure what to do. The carriage driver eventually managed to limp to a phonebox and dial 999. His only suggestion was that the police close a few roads and let the horses run themselves into the ground. Would the horses run themselves into the ground before the police were needed at that afternoon's football match? The carriage driver had no idea. This had never happened to him before.

"I think the horns might have made them a bit crazy," he said.

By now, Diana's journey to her wedding was breaking news on BBC 24. Links to the helicopter footage were soon appearing on Twitter. The centre of the city ground to a halt as the police tried to guess which direction the horses would take next and closed roads willy-nilly. On board, Dave suggested that he and Diana should try to jump for it too.

"I don't want to ruin my dress!" Diana shouted.

That was academic. Diana's dress was fast coming to resemble Cinderella's frock after midnight. There were bits of it on branches all over the town.

"Then we're going to have to hang on to the bitter end," said Dave. "I love you, Diana," he told her. "Whatever happens, you must remember that. You'll always be my princess."

Diana was barely aware of her father's sentimental pronouncements.

"I am going to kill Ben Wilson," she said through bared teeth. "When I get hold of him, I am going to tear him limb from limb."

Diana's anger made her strong. It enabled her to cling on to that runaway carriage for a full half-hour while the horses just kept running, eyes rolling and mouths foaming as though they were driven by the Devil himself. Pinned beneath Diana and her enormous skirt, Dave wasn't going anywhere either. He screwed his eyes tightly shut. He had always said he would die for Diana. Dear God, don't let this be the day I have to prove it, he prayed.

On and on the horses galloped. No police cordon would stand in their way. Thundering, thundering, they rampaged through the city while the live footage was beamed around the world and pundits from Pennsylvania to the Punjab offered their sage advice.

"Shoot them," was the general consensus.

"The horses, or the bride?" asked a wag big on animal welfare.

But no guns were sighted and at last Diana's tenacity paid off when, as if guided by a celestial hand, the horses finally came to a halt right outside the cathedral like a pair of homing unicorns.

"God saved us." Dave kissed the carriage floor.

Clinging on to the carriage door for support, Diana slowly pulled herself upright. Outside the cathedral, her mother and her bridesmaids were in a huddled conversation with the bishop and the one member of the groom's party who had shown up. Ben's best man, Ed, was dressed in jeans and a polo shirt. There was no sign of the naval uniform or even the pink cummerbund and cravat that had been the original plan. The bridal party had not yet seen the Twitter coverage of Diana's ride from hell. As far as they were concerned, she was still trotting quietly round the block waiting to get the all-clear.

Susie and the bridesmaids turned to see Diana standing up in the carriage. With her hair in disarray and her dress torn to shreds from her wild journey, she looked less like a bride than Boudicca fresh from a battle.

"Oh my God," said Ed. He slipped to the back of the welcoming party, as though Diana's six-year-old twin-cousin bridesmaids could spare him from her wrath.

"Where is he?" Diana asked, quite quietly at first.

Her audience only gawped in silent awe. What on earth had happened to the bride?

Dave tried to stand up too but fell straight back down again, exhausted from his brush with death.

"Where is he?" Diana's fists were balled at her sides. Her face was grim. Her eyes flashed fury.

Still no one spoke.

"Where is my bloody fiancé?"

When Ed finally admitted that Ben wasn't coming —
"He said he told you. He put a letter through your door
last night" — Diana screamed bloody murder. She
jumped down from the carriage and landed a punch on
Ed's jaw.

"I'll give you a bloody letter!" she screamed as she
pushed him to the ground.

While Ed writhed on the ground, Diana stormed
past her mother and the bridesmaids into the cathedral.

"Where is he?"

She shouted so loud that her voice reverberated
throughout the whole nave, terrifying her wedding
guests as thoroughly as if they had heard the voice of
God.

"Where is heeeeeeeee!!!!??? Aaagh. Aaagh.
Raaaaaaaaaaaaaaaaaaaagggh!"

Standing by the cathedral door, Susie and Dave
regarded each other in slightly stunned silence. Dave
reached for his ex-wife's hand for the first time in over
a decade. The smaller bridesmaids clung to Nicole's
skirt for comfort. Nicole herself felt a curious mixture
of abject fear and sheer ecstatic delight as she watched
the "best friend" who had often treated her so badly
finally get her comeuppance. While everyone else was
absorbed in the spectacle, Nicole took a sneaky pic with
her iPhone.

Inside the cathedral, Diana fell to her knees at the
high altar and sobbed all over the flowers. Her cries
were like the cries of a soul in purgatory, until suddenly
she began to rip the heads off her Princess Diana roses.

Unsure what else to do, her guests began to file out of their pews.

Outside on the cobbles, the horses were still shuddering in the aftermath of their exertions. Diana's unicorns had both lost their horns.

CHAPTER
FIFTY-EIGHT

Ian had not changed his mind. Just as on their first date, when he had arrived fifteen minutes ahead of time to make sure Kate didn't have to walk into the bar on her own, he made damn sure that he was at the hotel well ahead of her. He had been standing in front of the registrar's lectern for twenty minutes when the call went up that Kate and her father had arrived. Later, he would discover that they had hoped to be earlier but were prevented from turning into the driveway by a runaway carriage. Whatever, at last she was there. When the hotel pianist struck up the first chords of "Here Comes the Bride", Ian turned to his future wife with the biggest smile she had ever seen.

Everything fell into place in that second. All the doubts fell away. Kate wondered how she had ever considered not turning up for this, the most important moment in her life. Ian grabbed for her hand as soon as she got close to him. She squeezed his hand hard in return. She knew absolutely that she would love him until the day she died.

When they shared their first kiss as husband and wife, Kate could hardly bear to let him go to turn and receive the applause of their guests. All the people she loved were in that room: her parents, her sister, her niece; her best friends, Helen and Anne, led a standing ovation; Matt gave her a thumbs-up from the back of the room. Kate found herself crying and laughing all at the same time. Ian hung on to her tightly. Kate placed her left hand on his cheek. There was his ring on her finger, representing his promise. They were husband and wife.

"I will love you for ever," she said.

CHAPTER
FIFTY-NINE

"There's a statistic that suggests one in eight people meet their future spouse at a wedding," Matt told the girl sitting next to him.

"Is that so?" she said, leaning back in her chair to give him a better view of her impressive décolletage. Kate had chosen well when she decided to seat her ex-boyfriend at the same table as her office manager. An afternoon in Gina's company could cheer up any unhappily single man.

"What about meeting your ex-spouse at a wedding?" asked Melanie, who was sitting to Matt's left. "What are the statistics for that?"

"I don't know," said Matt, "but you'd have to be pretty bloody unlucky. If I saw my ex-wife at a wedding, I'd be looking for the nearest wooden stake."

"Oh," said Gina, putting two and two together, "you're *that* Matt."

"*That* Matt?" He preened.

"The one Kate went out with at college, the one who's got much f —" She bit her tongue. "Much nicer in his old age."

Matt was happy about that.

Melanie soon found herself edged out of the conversation. Not that she was especially bothered. She had no interest in flirting with a twit like Matt. As far as she was concerned, Kate had lucked out the day that Matt broke up with her. Her groom, Ian, seemed like a much steadier man. Melanie was very glad she had accepted Kate's invitation, even though it had been issued at rather short notice just the day before. Melanie had been so relieved to hear that Kate hadn't decided to bail after their heart-to-heart. This wedding felt right. It had been one of the most romantic ceremonies she'd ever seen.

But something was bothering Melanie about one of the guests on a table she guessed to be made up of Ian's friends. This particular bloke had not been at the service. He had arrived late for the reception itself, coming in as Kate's father was making his speech in her honour. Melanie had caught sight of him as he tried to make an unobtrusive entrance, but he was seated behind her and she didn't want to turn round to look at him while the speeches were going on. She didn't want to make it obvious that she wanted to know who he was. But now the speeches were over and Melanie saw her opportunity in a trip to the ladies'.

"Excuse me," she said to Gina and Matt. They didn't notice as she slipped away from their table.

She wanted to get a good look at that bloke.

It was him. It was definitely him.

Melanie just about made it to the ladies' room. She sat down on a chair upholstered in pink velvet and fanned her face with the order of service from her handbag.

"You all right?" a woman her age asked. "I get them flushes all the time these days. I got myself one of these." The woman fished a small battery-powered fan out of her fake-crocodile clutch. "Best two pounds I ever spent. Want to borrow it?"

Melanie declined. "I'll be all right," she said. "I just had a bit too much champagne."

She stayed on the chair and waited for the ladies' room to empty out; then she stood in front of the mirror and examined her face. Of course, she looked shiny. It was hot in that dining room. The delicious champagne — too delicious to resist — had brought quite a flush to her cheeks. But beyond that, Melanie wondered, how did she look? Did she look good for her age? Did she look like the woman he had fallen in love with? Why hadn't anyone warned her he would be there?

Because they didn't know, of course. How could Kate have had any idea that Melanie had been married to one of their other guests?

Melanie decided that she would have to leave. She was about to walk straight out through the hotel lobby when she remembered that her jacket was on the back of her chair in the dining room. She would have left it behind, but it had her car keys in the pocket. She cursed herself for not having put them in her handbag.

Taking deep breaths in front of the mirror, Melanie considered her options. Perhaps she could ask one of the waiting staff to go into the dining room and fetch her jacket for her. No, that was silly. Why didn't she just walk right up to Keith and ask him how he was? After all, just the previous night she had been thinking about getting back in touch with him for old times' sake. He had moved to London, but now he was just a few feet away from her. How much of a bigger hint did she need Fate to give?

But who was he sitting with? Melanie closed her eyes and tried to remember the other people at Ian's table. He had walked into the dining room alone, but that didn't necessarily mean he was alone. There were women on that table. Young, pretty women. What if Melanie strode up to Keith, only to find herself being introduced to some young girlfriend, someone who would not have been taken for having a menopausal flush?

This is ridiculous, Melanie told herself.

She was a successful businesswoman. She liked to think she was anybody's equal. She could hold her own against some new young girlfriend. If she walked over to the table where Keith was sitting and discovered that he wasn't alone, she would leave the wedding at that point. She would never have to see him again. It would be painful, but it would be done. The big thing to do was reintroduce herself. Only a coward would sit in the same room as her ex-husband and refuse to acknowledge his existence.

I can do this. I can do this.

Melanie practised some of the deep-breathing exercises that she recommended to all her brides. She dabbed a little powder on her shiny nose and reapplied

354

her lipstick. She fluffed up her hair. She smoothed her skirt down over her hips and readjusted her cleavage. She still had it. She prepared to wiggle her way through the dining room and shake hands with the man who had broken her heart.

Melanie didn't have to go into the dining room. She walked out of the ladies' and smack bang into Keith's back. He was on his mobile phone. He turned to see who had bashed into him.

Melanie shook her head and tried to rush on. Keith grabbed her arm.

"No. Wait. Mum, I'll call you back."

He finished his call.

"It is you. I knew it was. I saw you across the room. What are you doing here?"

"I dressed the bride."

"I sit next to the groom at the Boleyn."

"You still support West Ham?"

"To the end."

"I didn't expect to see you."

"Funnily enough, I thought I would see you. I thought I did see you this morning, when I was driving through Southampton. I thought I saw you on every street I turned down. I started hallucinating you in that red coat."

"Can't fit into that any more," said Melanie.

"What are you talking about?" asked Keith. "You look fabulous."

"Middle-age spread," Melanie muttered.

"You look fabulous," Keith repeated. "Always have done. Always will."

They smiled at each other in silence. The silence stretched until it started to become uncomfortable.

This is it, Melanie said to herself. We've got nothing to say to each other beyond hello.

"I was just calling my mum," said Keith. "She's not been well. I've got her up in London with me. I was going to bring her down here today so she could visit some of her old friends, but she wasn't feeling up to it, so I've left her with . . ."

"Your wife?"

Keith laughed at that. "My next-door neighbour. Retired nurse. They'll have spent all day yakking. I'm still a sad old singleton, as my niece calls me."

"You mean Nikki?"

"The very same. She's at university now. She'll be pleased to hear that I saw you. You were always her favourite auntie."

"I should have kept in touch."

"No, you're all right. She understood. It was difficult, I know."

Ian's best man swayed past Melanie and Keith. He paused and slung his arm round Keith's shoulder.

"If you're single," he said to Melanie, "you could do far, far worse than this guy, Keith Harris. You've probably heard of him. You know he used to work with Orville."

"Leave it out," Keith begged.

"I've already had him," Melanie quipped.

"Wahey!" The best man made an obscene gesture and tottered off.

"Sorry about that. I met him on the stag night. He seems like a decent bloke really. Got three kids."

Melanie nodded. "Well," she said, "I suppose we ought to go back in there. They're taking the coffee round. It's been nice to talk to you."

"You too."

Melanie made to return to the dining room.

"Better call my mum back," said Keith.

"Sure. Give her my love," said Melanie, which was the most ridiculous thing she could have said. There was not much love lost between her and her former mother-in-law. It had been a reflex comment. She hoped that Keith wouldn't think she was being rude. Making a point. Her cheeks burning with embarrassment, Melanie decided against going back to her table for now. Instead, she followed a sign that led her out onto the golf course. Walking through the gardens, she sighed at the relief of the cool air on her face. Her encounter with Keith had left her with all sorts of conflicting feelings.

He had been friendly. That was all. He hadn't asked if they might stay in touch. He didn't want to build a friendship with her. Melanie admitted to herself that she didn't want to build a friendship with him. She had hoped, as she tried to work out from his Facebook profile whether he was still single, that there might be something else left. A spark. For all his saying that she looked fabulous, Melanie very much doubted that Keith was telling the truth. He worked in London. He was probably surrounded by beautiful young women all day long. Melanie imagined what might be going on in

Keith's head. Maybe seeing her had finally convinced him that their divorce was a good thing.

Oh, and she still had to go back into that room and possibly see him again.

By the time Melanie got back to her table, the coffee had been served and cleared away, and staff were trying to persuade the guests into the bar so they could set up the dining room for the evening disco. Melanie grabbed her jacket and was making for the exit when Kate caught her arm.

CHAPTER
SIXTY

"Thank God I've found you," said Kate. "Look, I know I promised I wouldn't use you as the hired help today, but apparently we've got to dance soon and I've forgotten how to hitch the back of the dress up. Mum's all fingers and thumbs. Tess has had too much to drink, as have Anne and Helen."

"Of course I'll do it," said Melanie. "Come into the ladies' room."

With her expert eye, Melanie quickly located the invisible loops of fishing wire and matched them to the transparent button. It took her less than a minute to hitch up Kate's skirt so that she was ready to take to the floor.

"Thank you," said Kate. "And thank you for everything."

She gave Melanie a hug.

"I don't know what I would have done without your pep talk the other day. I really didn't know who else to talk to."

"I don't think I said anything useful."

"You said a lot of things I needed to hear, and you made me feel heard in return. That was important."

Melanie sniffed back a tear.

"Oh, don't you start as well!" said Kate. "I've had people crying over me all day."

"It's just lovely to see two people who really deserve it getting together."

Kate hugged her again, and Melanie rode the urge to tell Kate what had really brought tears to her eyes.

"I'm so glad you changed your mind," said Melanie.

"Ian sent me a letter," said Kate. "I've got it here in my little bag. It said everything I needed know. Do you want to read it?"

"I'm sure it's private."

"I'd like you to read it. You're the only person I properly confided in. I want you to see this letter because it gave me a jolt. He stuck it through my parents' door at one o'clock in the morning. I saw him sneaking away. I thought he'd left me a 'Dear John'."

Melanie unfolded the paper and began to read.

Dear Kate,

It's the day before our wedding. I don't know about you, but I'm totally full of nerves. I just managed to burn a third round of toast.

I know that I haven't been the world's best fiancé. I suppose I didn't really think much about what the job meant. I knew that I loved you and I wanted to marry you. I didn't think beyond the engagement and the ring except in some vague happy-ever-after way, where you and I lived in a big house with our beautiful children. I didn't think about how we were going to get there.

I don't think I appreciated how much stress the whole wedding thing would put you under. I went along with the big wedding because I thought that was what I was supposed to do. I realise now that you felt bullied into changing our plans, and if I had been less accommodating and insisted we stuck to what we planned in the first place, you *would* have had less to deal with. On top of your mother being ill. I know I handled that badly. I suppose it was because we hadn't been together very long. I thought that it would be more stressful for your parents to have me around than not. I made the wrong decision. I'm sorry.

Kate, I am a novice at this whole relationship thing, but I want to get it right. I want to grow to understand what you want and need without you having to tell me, but while I'm still learning, please bear with me. Please have the patience to tell me again and again. I can't stand the thought of losing you because you've given up trying to make me understand. To understand and to love you for the rest of my life are my reasons for being here.

I can't wait to see you tomorrow morning. If, after all this waffling, you decide you're still going to turn up at the ceremony, you will make me the happiest man in the world.

Yours for richer, for poorer, in sickness and in health, and promising to make you a cup of tea every morning until I'm too old and tired to lift the kettle. My love for ever,

Ian

"Oh, Kate, that's just beautiful." Now Melanie could not hold back the tears. So much of the tone of that letter was familiar, so much like something Keith might have written.

"Thank goodness I didn't just run away on Thursday. I was so close, Melanie. So close I can't tell you. Now, promise you won't go anywhere until after we've danced. I'm sure I'm going to put a heel through my skirt."

"You will be fine," Melanie promised her. "But I will stay."

The first dance had always been Melanie's favourite part of any wedding day.

CHAPTER
SIXTY-ONE

Kate let Ian lead her onto the dance floor. She stood alone in the middle for a moment, bathed in a spotlight, while Ian gave the DJ his instructions. Kate really didn't know what to expect. She didn't have a great deal of faith in Ian's taste in music. She could only hope that he wasn't going to expect them to take their first dance steps as man and wife to Madness's "One Step Beyond". Ian returned from his conversation with the DJ with a big smile on his face.

Kate put her hands on her hips and gave him a comical pout that made the assembled guests laugh.

"What is our first song, anyway?" she asked.

"I told you, it's a surprise. You have to trust me, and you have to let me lead. Just this once."

Kate would never have guessed the song that Ian chose. She'd told herself that they didn't really have "a song", but this particular song was perfect. With the opening bars, Kate was back at the first moment she heard it. They had been sitting in Ian's flat after their fourth date. They still hadn't kissed at that point. In fact, Kate was beginning to wonder if they ever would, or whether Ian would pluck up the courage to tell her that he didn't think it was worth pursuing their acquaintance any further. In retrospect, remembering that evening in his flat, Kate wondered how she could ever have thought Ian wasn't that into her.

The CD he chose to put on was *The Seldom Seen Kid* by Elbow. He asked Kate if she had ever listened to their stuff before. She had, but the only Elbow song she really knew was the one that talked about having grounds for divorce.

"This track is much better," said Ian.

He played "Mirrorball". And during the second verse, he kissed her.

Kate had almost forgotten how, in the week after their first kiss, she had hummed that song constantly. It was the perfect soundtrack to the way she was feeling right then, speaking as it did of that moment when you realise that someone is going to be important to you, that moment when you realise that one person has the ability to change your life for ever. In a good way.

As Ian took her into his arms on the dance floor, Kate felt tears well up in her eyes. Her throat tightened. How had she ever considered throwing what they had away? He was the love of her life.

"Everything has changed," said the lyrics. And it was true.

Epilogue

Back in 1981, Melanie and Keith had made their first dance as a married couple to Kool & the Gang's "Celebration". It was one of the biggest hits of the previous year and had remained popular ever since, in a cheesy sort of way. So Melanie wasn't surprised when the DJ put "Celebration" on the turntable right after Kate and Ian took their first dance. It was something to liven the party up after the beautiful melancholy of Elbow's "Mirrorball".

What did surprise Melanie was that within seconds of the opening bars of Kool & the Gang's biggest hit, she felt a hand on her waist.

"Come on," said Keith. "I do believe this is our song."

"Oh, no," she said. "Are you serious?"

"Can't a man ask a beautiful lady for a dance?"

"But I haven't danced to this in ages."

"I'm sure the moves will come back to you. I won't take no for an answer."

Dancing with Keith, it was as though the years just fell away. Though they had become virtual strangers to one another, some memory of their relationship persisted in their limbs. Keith twirled Melanie as he had twirled her when they were just twenty-one. Melanie couldn't help but smile. And then she started laughing.

"This feels like Fate," said Keith, "you being here tonight."

"I looked you up on Facebook the other day."

"I've been stalking you via the Bride on Time website for years. Can I have your number?"

Melanie nodded.

"It would be good to get together and talk properly, you know, and then . . ."

"And then what?" Melanie asked.

Keith didn't know. Neither of them knew what the future might hold, but dancing together for the rest of the evening certainly seemed like a good start.

Something else had a good start at Ian and Kate's wedding reception: Kate's old boyfriend Matt found himself spending the night with Gina, the office manager. She was still by his side a year later, when his divorce came through.

Ben was horrified to hear that Diana had gone to the cathedral after all. As far as he was concerned, he had given his fiancée plenty of warning that he would not be waiting for her at the altar. How was he to know that the letter he had silently pushed through her mother's letterbox at two o'clock in the morning would be buried under a pile of junk mail and find its way into the recycling bag without ever having been read? He could only imagine Diana's fury as she barged into the nave to discover that Ben's side of the place really was empty. He knew his family wouldn't be there, of course. He'd told his mother that the wedding was off via text message. Ben's sister had promised him that she would tell the rest of his party to stand down. Ben assumed that, having read the letter, Diana would be doing the same for her guests.

As it turned out, Diana was carried from the cathedral on a stretcher. The wedding might not have happened, but Diana's guests had certainly witnessed a spectacle, as promised. While Susie accompanied her daughter to the hospital for a check-up, Dave corralled the guests onto the buses that had been specially hired to take them to the reception, where they ate the food and drank the champagne that Dave had already paid for. And why not? Dave wasn't going to get any of the money back.

Meanwhile, Diana's mother demanded a summit at her house, where Ben would explain himself in person. That was never going to happen. As soon as Ben let the thick cream envelope, pinched from work, slip through Susie's letterbox, he was outta there. Prior to even delivering the ill-fated letter, he had packed a couple of suitcases and loaded them into the back of the car. He headed straight from Susie's house to Gatwick Airport, from whence he caught the first flight somewhere sunny, which happened to be Majorca. He had two weeks off work and a fistful of credit cards. He was going to stay well out of the way.

At some point, Ben knew, he would have to return to Southampton. Though he had dodged signing on the line of a marriage certificate, having bought a house together, he and Diana had at least as many material possessions to divide as any couple who'd been married for five years. For now though, Ben didn't care. He was starting a new life.

Diana, meanwhile, was plunged into something approaching hell. The television coverage of her runaway unicorns meant that she couldn't possibly hope to get over her embarrassment quietly. The papers wanted to know the identity of the bride in the carriage. They wanted to know whether she had gone ahead with the wedding after all. When they discovered that Diana's hell-ride had been topped by a jilting, they had a field day. Diana was quickly dubbed "the unluckiest bride in Britain". Nuptialsnet was abuzz for months with Diana's humiliation, kept alive by juicy snippets from Nicole, posting as "Anon".

Six months later, Ben left his job and he left Southampton. He accompanied Lucy to see her family in Sydney and never came back. Prior to his departure, Diana and Ben had managed to separate their assets fairly amicably. Diana kept the house, of course, since her father had paid for it. She did, however, have to go back to work to pay the bills. Feeling deeply humbled, she took a job as a personal assistant to a divorce lawyer.

Diana's notoriety as Britain's unluckiest bride began to fade and eventually she was eclipsed by a bride whose cathedral-length train caught fire as she walked up an aisle lined with flickering tea lights. (That bride had to strip to her knickers to avoid going up in flames. She escaped with minor effects of smoke inhalation, but the church burned to the ground and her fiancé took it as a sign from God that they should not be married.)

About a year after her big, fat wedding fiasco, Diana started to count herself lucky for having dodged a bullet. A jilting was infinitely better than a divorce, as her boss kept reminding her. He should know. He'd presided over several hundred and had been through two of his own.

Now that she needed to work for a living, Diana surprised herself by coming to take pride in her job. She was not the clueless airhead she had allowed herself to be. After two years as a PA, she trained to be a paralegal. She volunteered at the Citizens' Advice Bureau and was especially keen to help women who had handed over control of their lives and their finances when they embarked upon doomed relationships. As a result of all this enlightenment, Diana took quite some persuading when her divorce-lawyer boss, with whom she had fallen passionately in love, finally asked her to marry him, three years later.

"Can we get married in a register office?" Diana asked.

As for Kate and Ian? Well, of course they lived happily ever after.

369

Acknowledgements

With thanks to my agent Antony Harwood and everyone at Hodder who worked so hard to bring this book together in double-quick time. Especially Carolyn Mays and Francesca Best, who read the first draft during their Christmas holidays, and Laura Collins for her eagle-eyed copyediting. An author could have no better team.